# Daisies in
# the Canyon

# Daisies in the Canyon

Carolyn Brown

Montlake
Romance

Text copyright © 2014 Carolyn Brown
All rights reserved.

Published by Montlake Romance, Seattle

www.apub.com

Amazon, the Amazon logo, and Montlake are trademarks of Amazon.com, Inc., or its affiliates.

ISBN-13: 9781477826546
ISBN-10: 1477826548

Cover design by Mumtaz Mustafa

Library of Congress Control Number: 2014910623

Printed in the United States of America

*In memory of my precious sister and my best friend,*

*Patti G. Russell*

*1953-2013*

# Chapter One

*D*ry-eyed and silent, Abby Malloy focused on the wooden casket that held the remains of the father she'd never known. The north wind rattled the bare limbs of an old scrub oak tree in the corner of the small cemetery. The preacher read the twenty-third Psalm, but the words were whipped away with the fierce wind.

Dozens of people bunched up under the tent and sang "I'll Fly Away." She looked at the words on the back of the funeral program, but she didn't sing along. On the last verse of the song, someone tapped her on the shoulder, and she looked up into the green eyes of a man with a daisy in his hand. He shoved it toward her and she took it, then he moved on down the row of three folding chairs and gave one to each of two other women. Abby wondered what in the hell she was supposed to do with it. Didn't folks usually put a rose on the casket if they followed that tradition? Could the women next to her be Ezra's other two daughters?

She glanced over at them, covertly studying each of them as they stared straight ahead at the casket. The will said that the sisters all had to live together in Ezra's house, that if any one of them left, they could have a third of his money but not a bit of the ranch. The last one standing got the land, the cattle, the house, and the whole shebang. If more than one was left at the end of one year, then they would share the ranch. Neither of those two looked like they were interested in anything but the cash-out, especially the prissy one right next to her. And the wild-looking hippie on the end would probably get bored real early, no doubt about it.

Abby wasn't totally sure if she wanted anything of Ezra's—not his money or his damned land—but she'd stick around a few days to see what happened. Hell, without the army anymore, she didn't have anything else to do, and she might like ranching once she learned how to do it.

Her stomach twisted into a pretzel, more from stress than hunger. Would it be a sin to eat one of the miniature candy bars she had tucked away in her jacket pocket? She was reminded of how she'd felt in Afghanistan—the same emptiness surrounded by nervous energy—especially that horrible day with the little girl. Today was not her fault, though. Today the burden fell on Ezra, even if he was dead.

The cold January wind didn't feel like the scorching wind that pushed the desert sandstorms. The colors were different. Everything over there was shades of tan; here they were an array of orange, ocher, and mustard. But the lonesome aura surrounding her remained the same. Maybe it was because she had a war to fight here, too.

Her mother, Martha, had died in January twelve years ago, but that day Abby'd cried so hard that her eyes swelled shut and she broke out in hives. Not so today at her father's funeral, but then, she'd never known Ezra Malloy. Never even laid eyes on him, according to her mother. Ezra had wanted a son and he'd had some screwball notion that once a woman had a girl, that's all she'd ever have. So when Abby wasn't a boy, Ezra gave her mother a healthy settlement and sent her back to Galveston, Texas.

She looked around at the small crowd: neighbors and friends bundled up in coats against the winter chill. When they'd sung, she'd heard a few off-key quivers, the hallmark of sucking cold air into your lungs.

A man in a uniform with a sheriff's patch on his arm stood a few feet away from the right end of the casket. Dirty-blond hair, entirely too long for an officer of the law, tickled the collar of his shirt. Instead of regulation uniform pants, he wore jeans that hugged his butt and thighs like a glove and that stacked up just right over his shiny black cowboy boots. His brown eyes were pools that drew her in when she caught him studying her. It was winter and yet he had a deep tan that said he spent as much time outside as indoors. And those little crow's-feet at the sides of his eyes told her that he had a sense of humor. His dark brows knit together as if something had suddenly worried him. Her fingers itched to touch those creases on his forehead and tell him everything would be all right. Then the creases disappeared, and the sexiest mouth she'd ever seen turned up in a slight smile.

She blinked and looked at the casket, but her eyes strayed back to the sheriff. His uniform shirt was starched and ironed and fit across his broad chest. Her eyes dropped lower to his belt buckle and she almost blushed.

*Get a hold of yourself, Abby! Shit fire! You are at a funeral, not in a bar with a bunch of randy soldiers,* she fussed at herself.

The man who'd given them the daisies stood beside the sheriff. He was younger and not nearly as sexy, but he sported the same longish hair, though his was brown. Was longer hair a prerequisite to living in the Palo Duro Canyon? The cowboy's green eyes looked sad behind his wire-rimmed glasses and his square-cut jaw was set in a solemn expression. Creased jeans bunched up over his highly polished cowboy boots. This must be that Rusty the lawyer had mentioned when he'd called.

Two men in suits came forward and opened the casket. Abby had attended funerals with an open casket, but never seen it done at the cemetery. Curiosity made her want to look in the casket, to see Ezra, maybe to figure out what it was about him that had drawn her mother to him. But another part of her wanted to leave right then and never look back.

The people filed past, most of them shaking hands with the guy who'd handed out the daisies, the sheriff, and the preacher. None of them tarried long before they hurried off to their vehicles to get out of the cold wind. Now it was time for Ezra's daughters to stand up, to go forward, to look at the father they never knew lying in his casket.

The lawyer who'd called had said she had two younger sisters, and in fact, they'd all been seated in a way to let her be first to go. So she went, more to get it over with than to exert any authority or seniority. She didn't want to look in the casket, and she damn sure didn't want to press the daisy in the pages of a fat book or put it in a glass of water to remind her of the father who didn't want her because she wasn't a boy.

She wanted to walk right past the casket without a sideways glance, to throw the daisy on the ground and step on it, but her military training surfaced subconsciously. She snapped to attention, hands at her sides, head and back in alignment in front of the casket, proving to Ezra that she was every bit as strong as any son he might have had.

She glanced down and blinked several times. He was just an old man with wispy gray hair and wrinkles. He wore bibbed overalls, a red flannel shirt, and a day's worth of gray stubble. Why had her beautiful mother fallen in love with this man? He should have spent his life kissing her feet, because he was lucky she'd even glanced his way.

Clamping her jaws tightly, Abby looked up at the guy with the glasses, who nodded as if he knew how she felt. He couldn't begin to understand the mixture of emotions jumbled up inside her gut. She couldn't even get them sorted out. In frustration she tossed the daisy in the casket and it landed on Ezra's heart.

"I'm Rusty Dawson," the man said softly. "The lawyer probably told you about me. That's my black truck out there. I'll lead the way back to the house."

The preacher shook her hand and told her he was sorry for her loss. She nodded politely, but how could you lose something that you never had? She headed straight for her silver-colored truck. When she was a little girl, she'd pretended that her father was a superhero off fighting wars, who couldn't come see her because he was saving the world. As a teenager she'd pressed her mother for answers, and her mother had told her the truth; from then on Abby had figured him for a son of a bitch. However, seeing the scrawny old man in the casket brought only disappointment. She reached inside her coat pocket and brought out the bite-size candy bar, unwrapped it as she walked, and popped it into her mouth. The paper went in the left-hand pocket and by the time she swallowed, she had another one ready to eat. She crawled inside the truck, out of the bitter north wind whipping down the canyon, and watched the sheriff interact with the people.

"Damn fine-lookin' man," she mumbled as she reached for another candy bar.

She waited until Rusty got into his truck and pulled out onto the gravel road. The sun was high in the sky and only four vehicles were headed that way, thank God! She didn't want or need a bunch of neighbors and friends telling her what a fine man Ezra had been. Two miniature candy bars later, the black truck came to a stop, and she pulled in beside it.

Cows roamed around in the pasture outside the small yard, roped in with a white three-rail fence in need of paint. Bare rose-bushes and naked crepe myrtles waited patiently for the warmth of spring to bloom. A trio of dogs bounded off the porch of a long, low-slung ranch-style house with a wide front porch. It would have never passed muster in the army, not with that peeling white paint.

Rusty stopped long enough to pet each dog and said something that made their tails wag. What was it Abby's mother said about kids and dogs and people? Oh, yes—a person might fool some folks, but never a kid or a dog. Evidently Rusty had a few good qualities, if the dogs liked him.

For a cowboy, he wasn't showing off his manners too well. But then, why should he? If Abby or either of those two strangers who were her half sisters threw in the towel before a year was up, he'd get the whole thing. That was a pretty good incentive to make their lives miserable so he'd wind up with the ranch.

Once out of the truck, she circled around behind the vehicle, picked up a dark green duffel bag, and hoisted it up on her shoulder. There were no more candy bars in her pocket, but a separate small suitcase was filled with more, along with bags of chips, nuts, and trail mix and the little wooden box holding her mother's ashes. Thank God she had a high metabolism or she'd weigh as much as a baby elephant. Food had always been her stress relief: from doughnuts when she was a little girl and things didn't go her way to chocolate bars in high school to make it through a test to potato chips in the service when she was wound too tight to sleep. When she was nervous, she ate. When she was sad, she ate. When she was happy, she ate. Even at that very moment, she needed food.

The dark-haired prissy sister pulled two suitcases out of an older-model maroon minivan. Matched luggage with her initials engraved on them. Abby could see several boxes with writing on the side also stacked perfectly inside the van.

The blonde hippie sister drove a small truck that had been red at one time but now was faded and rusted in spots. The tires were so bald that it was a wonder they made it down the canyon incline without blowing apart. A crack in the back window ran from the bottom corner halfway across, but duct tape kept the wind and rain from seeping inside. Evidently she didn't have suitcases, because she slid plastic grocery store bags along one arm and picked up two more with the other hand.

Rusty opened the door and stood to one side to let them enter the house. "I've asked the executor of the will to join us, since the lawyer had another appointment today. He and his wife will be along in a couple of minutes. They were talking to some folks when we left. If y'all want to have a seat in the living room, we'll wait for them there."

"What is that?" Abby sniffed the air.

"It's a small community down here in the canyon. Folks brought covered dishes for our dinner. It's a respect thing," he said. "We'll eat after you hear what Jackson Bailey has to say. I asked the sheriff, Cooper Wilson, to join us for lunch."

"Why?"

"Because he was Ezra's friend and I wanted to. You got a problem with that?"

"Not unless he puts a hand toward my piece of fried chicken," she said. That smart-ass remark brought a picture of his hands to her mind. Strong, wide hands that looked as if they'd know how to please a woman. A tingle shot down her spine when she let her mind wander, thinking about just how his hands would feel on her. She quickly blinked away the image and concentrated on her surroundings.

The house faced the east and the living room sported a big window looking out on the porch and over the front of the property. While he drank his morning coffee, Ezra probably sat in the well-worn old leather recliner and watched the Texas sunrises. Abby dropped her duffel bag beside suitcases and plastic bags tied in knots at the top and did her best to ignore the recliner.

The room looked like it had been arranged by a man interested in comfort instead of beauty. The sofa took up most of the space on the back wall, with the recliner and an end table at one end and a floor lamp at the other. The coffee table testified by the scuff marks that lots of boots had been propped on it through the years. Two wooden rockers faced the cold fireplace, but Rusty had turned them around, making a semicircle. Without waiting for the ladies to sit, he'd claimed one chair. The prissy sister sat in the one next to him.

"If we've got folks coming, we'd best bring in some kitchen chairs," the hippie sister said.

Abby noticed the sparkly diamond stuck in the side of her nose when she passed her. No, sir, that girl wouldn't make it past the first week, much less a whole year. The only sound in the house was the scrape of two chairs being dragged across the floor. Hippie sister ignored the recliner and sat down in a wooden chair. Abby took the second one.

"There's only three people coming," Rusty said. "And there's a recliner right there."

"This is fine," Abby said.

Someone rapped on the door, and Rusty yelled, "Come on in."

The sheriff walked in, followed by a tall, dark cowboy and a very pregnant lady with flaming red hair.

Rusty stood up and made introductions. "This is Jackson Bailey and his wife, Loretta, and Cooper Wilson. Jackson owns Lonesome Canyon on one side of Malloy Ranch. Cooper's ranch is on the other side. Y'all come on in and have a seat. We were waiting on Jackson to explain things before we had dinner. Y'all are welcome to stay and eat with us."

"Smells good in here. Ezra would have liked the idea of a dinner for his daughters," Cooper said.

Dammit! Why did he have to have a deep Texas drawl to go with those brown eyes? He could have had a name like Andy or maybe Greg, to cancel things out, but not Cooper. Before Abby could blink, she'd already conjured up a picture of him whispering sweet words in her ear that sent her hormones reeling.

*Get a hold of yourself, woman. At the outside best, you'll be here one year and then you will sell this rotten piece of earth to the highest bidder. Remember your rules for life: number one is that you don't start things you can't finish.*

Abby inhaled deeply. She didn't give a damn what Ezra had liked in life or after death. He hadn't even cared enough to take a look at her when she was born and he hadn't been around to see one single solitary accomplishment in her life, so he didn't deserve the right to call her daughter after he was dead.

Loretta sat between the two men and smiled brightly. "We know that you didn't know Ezra, but we are sorry for your loss all the same. I can see y'all three got his blue eyes. He and I were friends of a sort, even though he was quite a character. Welcome to the canyon. It's kind of bare right now, but in a few weeks when the wildflowers pop up, it's lovely. Bluebonnets, wild daisies, coreopsis, and flowering cactus sure give it a different look. And trust me when I say it grows on you. The sunsets are beautiful and pretty soon you'll wonder why you ever wanted to live anywhere else."

It would take six bags of chips and at least a dozen of those little chocolate bars to wipe out the anger in Abby's heart. Ezra could have a relationship with Loretta but not with his own daughters. That was just plain wrong.

Jackson combed back his dark hair with his fingers, laid a hand on Loretta's knee, and said, "Ezra asked me to be the executor of his will and I brought a copy with me to leave here for you three to go over. But to cut past the legal jargon, the deal is like this. Rusty will pay each of you on Friday evening for forty hours of work at minimum wage. Room and board is provided. Rusty will bring in staples once a week. If you want anything he hasn't bought, then it's up to you to buy it yourself."

"I wasn't expecting a salary," Abby said.

"The money is yours if you sit on the porch and do nothing or if you learn the business of ranching. Rusty will teach you if you have a mind to learn. Next item. Ezra died on New Year's Day. Whoever is still here on that day one year from now inherits this ranch. If anyone of you wants to buy out the other two, there will be enough money to do that in the money he has left to you. If you leave before the year is up, you get your share of the money but relinquish any rights to the ranch. So if any of you want to go today, you can leave here a fairly wealthy woman. That's your choice. Just call me or tell Rusty when you are ready to go and we'll take care of the rest."

"Is that all?" Abby asked when he paused.

"That is pretty much the whole thing," Jackson answered.

"Y'all sure you don't want to stay and eat with us?" Rusty asked.

"Thank you, but we've got family over on Lonesome Canyon," Loretta said to the group at large. "Y'all are welcome to come visit anytime. Nona, that's my daughter, and I would just love to get to know you better."

"Thank you, ma'am," Abby said.

The other two nodded.

Jackson stood up and held out a hand to his wife. "So I take it that for now you are all planning to stay." His eyes wandered to the array of bags setting right inside the door.

Three heads bobbed.

"Okay, then. Good luck," he said. "Rusty, give me a call if you need anything."

"Will do and thanks, Jackson, for everything."

"See y'all in church on Sunday," Cooper said.

"I'll be the one who's waddling." Loretta laughed.

The door shut behind them and five complete strangers were left in the room together. Abby knew the cowboy's name was Rusty Dawson and the sheriff's was Cooper, but the two that she shared a father with—that was a different story.

"Okay, I'll go first. I'm Abby," she said.

The prissy one with dark hair nodded. "I'm Shiloh. Full name Shiloh Rose Malloy, born twenty-seven years ago in November."

The wild hippie with the nose stud and stringy blonde hair said, "I'm Bonnie Scarlett Malloy, born twenty-five years ago in November. Mama had a thing for *Gone With the Wind*. And just so we're straight, I'm not leaving. You can't run me off. Money is only paper. Land is something solid. Are you military or what?" She pointed at Abby.

"I was in the army for twelve years." Abby didn't tell them that she, too, was born in November, thirty years ago. Maybe old Ezra didn't have any luck getting the son he so desperately wanted because he was getting his wives pregnant at the wrong time of the year.

Rusty and Cooper both stood up. "The food is in the kitchen," said Rusty. "Coop and I are going to start. Y'all can come on in when you want."

Abby didn't hesitate for a minute. Her stomach had been growling since she had been rudely awakened that morning in a rest stop. Half a dozen little candy bars couldn't begin to satisfy her hunger.

To get there for an eleven o'clock funeral, she'd left Galveston at midnight with no sleep at all. She'd made good time so she'd pulled off the road on the west side of Wichita Falls at a welcome center to rest her eyes for an hour. She might still be dozing in the front seat of her pickup if it hadn't been for some little yappy dog that saw a squirrel chasing up a tree and pitched an unholy fit. As it was, she'd had to really floor the gas pedal to get to the funeral on time.

Sheriff Wilson wore starched jeans and his uniform shirt bore all the right patches to look downright official. Abby had always been a sucker for uniforms, which made military service tricky, but not as much as she was a sucker for tight-fitting jeans and boots. Yet it was the way his brown eyes kept catching hers when Jackson told them about the will that really caught her attention. Lord, it would be so easy to let those eyes lead her straight to a bed, but it wasn't going to happen.

Granted, it had been a long time since she'd had a relationship, but she had to get a grip on herself. She hadn't come to the canyon for a one-night stand with a cop; she'd come to lay claim to her birthright, and nothing was standing in her way.

As luck would have it, when they lined up around the cabinet, subtle whiffs of Cooper's cologne drifted back to her—something woodsy and musky that heated her hormones up to the boiling stage in spite of her resolve not to let any more pictures pop into her head. Add that to the fact that he looked like a young version of Travis Tritt, one of her favorite country music artists, with that cute little close-cropped goatee and mustache, hair kissing his collar, wide shoulders and twinkling eyes, and she had trouble keeping her eyes off him. To top it all off, he had a swagger that would put Timothy Olyphant to absolute shame. Dammit! Dammit! She had to switch her mind to something else.

# Chapter Two

Cooper's breath tightened in his chest when Abby removed her jacket and hung it on the back of a kitchen chair. The camouflage pants belted in a small waist and the black turtleneck hugged a well-toned body that would turn any man's head a second time. She pulled the ponytail holder out of her hair and tucked it away in her pocket. When she shook her long blonde hair loose, it fell to her shoulders in soft waves. Cooper tucked his thumbs in his back pockets to keep from reaching out and touching it, just to see if it was as soft as it looked.

Rusty picked up one of those Styrofoam plates with sections and said, "The church ladies put the food on the cabinet and I set up the folding card table for the desserts. We'll be eating leftovers until the middle of next week."

Shiloh shucked out of her duster and tossed it back into the living room onto the sofa. She pulled her shirttail out from tight-fitting jeans and picked up a plate. She sure wasn't bashful.

Bonnie unzipped her leather jacket, revealing a snug red knit shirt with rhinestones scattered across the chest. The jacket went on the back of a kitchen chair on the opposite side of the table from Abby's.

Cooper picked up two plates by mistake and handed one to Abby, who was right behind him in the lineup. His fingertips brushed against hers and static popped all around them. Dammit! He'd always been attracted to redheads, especially tall ones, like Loretta Bailey, but not blondes, and definitely not those with an attitude. And for damn sure not one who was likely to grab the dollar bills and be gone in an instant.

"The cook over on Lonesome Canyon made the fried chicken and the potato salad. She's awesome," Rusty said. "The corn salad, baked beans, and chicken salad are all good, but unless you really like pickled beets, leave that purple stuff alone. Paper towels are over there by the stove—the chicken is pretty greasy."

The small kitchen table was made to seat four, but Rusty brought out an extra chair from the living room. Abby sat down where she'd hung her coat and Cooper eased into the chair right beside her. Bonnie was straight across the table from Cooper and Shiloh claimed the spot at the other end.

Cooper picked up a chicken leg and bit into it. "Mmm. This is some fine food."

He wanted to ask Abby where she'd lived and how far she'd driven, but he couldn't figure out a way to do it without sounding nosy, so he ate in silence. He'd seen her get into the fairly new truck after the funeral, but he hadn't thought to check the license plates. He'd do that on his way out after dinner. Nothing could possibly come of the attraction he felt for her, seeing as how those cold blue eyes didn't show a bit of the heat he'd felt when their hands touched.

Not a single one of Ezra's daughters looked like she wanted to be there, but then, they had their reasons—and they were damn fine ones.

Abby really took his eye, even though she didn't show much respect, showing up at a funeral in military camouflage and combat boots. But then, neither did the other two women. Shiloh wore an outfit that looked like she was about to go out dancing at a honky-tonk, and Bonnie reminded him of a punk rocker, with eyes a darker blue than her two sisters' and rimmed with lots of black eye makeup. There was a cool determination in those blue eyes that said she might be the one who actually inherited Ezra's place. It was the same look that Ezra had had in his eyes when he'd set his mind to do something. Everyone in the canyon knew that when he did, there was no talking him out of it.

Abby was still the prettiest one of the three, with a mouth made for kissing and porcelain skin that begged to be caressed.

"Okay, Abby? What's your full name?" Cooper asked.

"On the birth certificate it's Abigail Joyce Malloy. Mama called me Abby Joy when she wanted to make me feel special, and she used all my names when I was in trouble," she answered.

"My mama refused to call me Coop. She said it sounded like a place where chickens live," Cooper said.

Seeing the joy in her face when she mentioned her mother, Cooper could not disagree one bit. He'd be willing to bet all three of the women were unique in their own way and their mothers had made them that way because they didn't have a father. His grandparents had done the same for him after his parents were killed. They hadn't spoiled him, but they'd sure made him feel special.

*Oh, Ezra, you sure missed a lot,* he thought, *especially your oldest one. She's a fighter just like you were.* Cooper reached for the saltshaker sitting in the middle of the table. His leg brushed against Abby's and sparks danced around the room. If a mere touch through clothing could create that much heat, what would happen if his bare skin touched hers?

"The lawyer said y'all were all in different states, but he didn't tell me where," Rusty said.

Cooper owed Rusty a beer the next time they wound up at the local watering hole, the Sugar Shack, for asking the question he so desperately wanted to know the answer to.

"I was raised in Galveston, Texas, right on the beach, but I haven't lived there in twelve years. I got out of the army two weeks ago and I'm ready to start over right here on . . . what's this ranch called anyway?" Abby answered.

"It's the Malloy Ranch. I thought I could hear some Texas in your accent," Cooper said. "My place is next door on the south."

She turned her head to look at him, those blue eyes boring into his. "I thought you were a cop."

"Sheriff is an elected position. I've always been a rancher, always will be," he said.

"I'm changing the name next January," Bonnie said.

"What are you changing it to?" Cooper asked.

Bonnie shrugged. "I've got a whole year to think about that."

"What if I like it just the way it is?" Shiloh asked.

"If you're still here, we'll talk about it," Bonnie answered.

Cooper slid a sidelong glance toward Abby. She kept eating and didn't argue or comment, which made him wonder if she'd even unpack her bags. By Monday morning she could easily be headed back south to Galveston.

"How about you, Shiloh? Where'd you come from?" Rusty asked.

"Lewisville, Arkansas, since I graduated from high school. Before Mama went into business with her sister in a truck stop, we lived in Jefferson, Texas."

Bonnie didn't wait to be asked. "We got our mail out of Chappell, Kentucky, but we lived between Harlan and Chappell, back in one of the hollers. I was six when we moved there from Texas."

Rusty nodded. "I can hear the Texas accent in all your voices. Ezra only spoke of having three daughters that last year of his life, and I wondered where you were located. Now let's talk about bedrooms. I've moved my stuff out of the room I'd been using since Ezra got sick and back out to the bunkhouse. There are three bedrooms down the hallway off the living room and one bathroom."

Abby cocked her head to one side. Another gesture like Ezra's.

"Tub or shower?" she asked.

"Claw-foot tub and a small walk-in shower we had installed when Ezra couldn't get in and out of the tub anymore," Rusty answered. "One room was Ezra's. I've cleaned out the closet and the drawers. Packed it all up and put it in storage out in the barn. Who wants that room? It does have the added benefit that it has a small half bath to go with it."

Bonnie blanched and shivered like someone had shoved an icicle down her backbone. Shiloh's nose practically curled.

"I'll take it," Abby said.

"Did he die in there?" Bonnie asked.

Rusty nodded. "But he did not die in the bed. He got so weak that we rented a hospital bed. I sent it back yesterday. I was hoping Abby would take that room. Bonnie, you can have the room across the hall from her and Shiloh gets the last one."

"Why?" Abby asked.

"That's the way Ezra said it was to be done. I didn't ask questions, but I would have changed it if no one wanted to stay in his old room," Rusty said.

Abby shrugged and went back to eating. Someone dying in a room didn't appear to bother her one bit. She polished off her first plate of food, trashed it, and filled another, taking two chicken wings and a thigh, another helping of potato salad, and a big scoop of sweet potato casserole.

She sat back down beside him and their knees bumped against each other as she got settled. The heat in his leg took a while to cool even after she moved hers.

"Hungry?" Cooper asked to take his mind off the electricity bouncing around under the table.

"In my business, you eat when you can and especially when the food is good like this is," she answered. "So, Rusty, what's the plan? I know nothing about ranching. Do lessons begin tomorrow or Monday?"

"Work is every day. If you want to learn, you get up at five, have breakfast, and be ready to go by six," he said. "Quittin' time is dark or when the job is done."

"Then I'll get up at four to get my PT—that's army lingo for exercise or physical therapy—done before five. I started in the army as a recruit. I'm willin' to start on the ranch in the same capacity."

*But for how long? A day, a week, a whole month?* Cooper wondered.

# Chapter Three

*A* few snowflakes drifted down from the gray skies and came to rest on Abby's jacket when she left the house right after lunch. Her duffel bags and the rest of the things from her truck were stacked neatly in the corner of the bedroom. She had taken time to unpack her snack suitcase, and now the top drawer in the dresser was filled to capacity. A bulging pocket gave testimony that she couldn't get another piece of candy or bag of chips tucked in that drawer.

The small wooden box holding her mother's ashes sat on the dresser. They'd never traveled with her before, but she couldn't leave them behind this time. The rest of her things she could unpack and arrange after dark, but right then she wanted to see exactly what this ranch looked like. If it didn't feel right, she would reload her things into the truck and go back to Galveston and be a beach bum. As sleep deprived as she was, she might not make it far that night, but she didn't have to hurry. She had money in the bank, a good truck, and a destination. That was enough to keep her for a few months until she decided what she wanted to do with her life.

According to Rusty, she should walk down the lane to the cattle guard with the ranch sign above it. That's where the Malloy Ranch stopped. From there on to the road, the land belonged to Lonesome Canyon. She was to pick a direction at that point and keep following the fence line until she reached the canyon wall, then circle back around.

The crisp winter air cooled her lungs as well as her cheeks. She shivered when the north wind picked up and the snow invited sleet into the winter mix that Saturday afternoon. It was a foolhardy mission on a day like this, but she'd done PT in far worse, from snow that was knee-deep in Michigan one winter to the blistering heat on the base in Afghanistan. Besides, another minute in that house would have her climbing the walls. A big argument on the first day would make the other women dig their boots in to show her that she couldn't run them off. She took a butterscotch hard candy from her pocket, removed the wrapper, and popped it into her mouth.

She smiled when the ringtone on her phone said her best friend, Haley, was calling. She had trouble fishing it out of the cargo pocket on her pants without removing her gloves, but she managed to answer on the fourth ring.

"Hey," she said.

"Is it over? I'm dying to know about your sisters. Tell me about the funeral. Did you see your father?" Haley, her friend since they were in the nursery together in the little church on the outskirts of Galveston, finally stopped to catch a breath.

"Yes, it's over and yes, I saw him. It was like looking at a stranger. I can't tell you much about Ezra's other two daughters other than the youngest one seems bound and determined to stick out the whole year. The place is even more desolate than the pictures we saw on the Internet and I'm not sure I can handle it for a year, Haley. It's colder than a witch's tit in this place. I'm out for a walk around the property to see if I even want to unpack. I did bring Mama's ashes, though."

Haley gasped. "You didn't tell me you were going to do that. Your mama would feel strange about being back."

"I didn't know I was going to until I went to the bank and opened up the safe-deposit box. There they were and something told me to bring them with me."

"There's a reason for everything, and maybe Martha wanted to go back to that canyon. Maybe it was to remind you that she's with you in spirit. What in the hell is that noise in the background?"

"Bitter cold north wind rattling the tree limbs and sleet hitting the phone."

"Holy shit! Pack up your stuff and get out of that place. Galveston is your home. Give your portion to those other two. You don't need the money or the aggravation in your life," Haley said.

"Not until I see what is here."

"Well, then, go have a look and then come home where you belong. Call me from the first hotel you stop at and we'll talk then. Hugs," Haley said.

"Hugs back," Abby said.

*Good-bye* was something they didn't say anymore. The last time Abby told someone good-bye, she'd finished basic training and had a week at home before going to Georgia for training school. Tears hung on her eyelashes as she remembered that last moment with her mother. Martha wore a tan-colored knit shirt with the Martha's Donut logo on the back. Khaki shorts peeked out from the bottom of a white-bibbed apron that the wind whipped to one side.

" 'Bye, Mama," she'd yelled as she pulled away from the curb. She watched through the rearview mirror as her mother waved until the road made a curve and she couldn't see her anymore.

She'd planned another trip home at the end of her training in Georgia, but it was only a week later that she got the call that Martha had been killed in a robbery. She'd vowed she'd never tell anyone good-bye again.

She slid the phone back into her pocket and pulled a ski mask from a pocket on her cargo pants. After she tugged it over her head and tucked it under her collar, she stuck her gloved hands into her pockets and trudged on down the gravel lane toward the Malloy Ranch sign. On the positive side, she was sweating so much inside her clothing that her whole body was damp. On the negative side, she hadn't seen a damn thing to keep her from unpacking.

Black cattle, with a brand that looked like a capital *M* with an *R* sharing the last leg of the *M*, huddled up under the trees to her left. If she stayed on, that brand would be redone even if she had to get rid of every cow on the place and start with fresh stock. Everything that had Ezra's name, brand, or idea behind it would be erased. It would have a strong name like its neighbor, Lonesome Canyon, but warm and inviting.

"Malloy Ranch sounds as bitter cold as this weather. I don't blame Bonnie a bit for wanting to change it," she mumbled from behind the ski mask.

She knew nothing about ranching. She was aware that the black ones were Angus. She made a mental note to ask Rusty if there was another breed that would grow as well in the canyon. Maybe she'd replace them with those brown ones with white faces she'd noticed in the pastures when she drove up through Texas.

"Or maybe even Texas longhorns. I'll have to do some research on them," she said.

How in the hell did this place produce enough grass to feed cattle anyway? All around her were crazy-looking formations shooting up from the ground, some a hundred feet or more, in varying colors of orange, burnt umber, and brown. One looked like a chimney; another like a giant sand castle kids might build on a beach.

The bits of snow collecting on the fence posts reminded her of daisies, which happened to be her favorite flower. They were wild, hearty enough to grow in rock, and were some of the first flowers to bloom in the spring. Were they Ezra's favorite flowers, too? Was that why they'd been given them to put in his casket at the service?

"I hope not," she murmured. "If they are, I may change my mind about them."

A movement in her peripheral vision caught her attention and she followed it until she focused on an eagle with something in its claws. It soared toward the sky and finally lit on one of the formations that shot up from the ground. The majestic sight took her breath for an instant. Was it an omen for her to stay and get above the problems of the past before she made a decision to kiss Texas good-bye? Abby didn't believe in omens, fate, or any of that superstitious mumbo-jumbo shit. She always said that folks made their own decisions and lived with the consequences of them.

"You best enjoy your last year," she told the sign above the cattle guard. "If I'm here next year on this day, you are coming down and that's a promise. And if I'm not here, Bonnie is going to change your name."

The bumpy gravel road went on east, but she couldn't see the highway from where she stood. Why in the hell hadn't Ezra extended the ranch to the road? If she stayed, she intended to use the money she'd gotten when she sold the doughnut shop in Galveston to buy that land and haul in gravel to fix the potholes in the road.

She turned north and followed the barbed-wire fence. The wind whistled through bare mesquite limbs, and the winter mix, as the weatherman called it, turned into more sleet than snow. Refusing to let the strong blasts hitting her right side keep her from her mission, she hunched her shoulders and kept walking.

Over there on the other side of the fence was Lonesome Canyon. She liked that name for a ranch and she'd liked Jackson and Loretta in the short time she'd met them. They looked a little old to be having another child, but if Abby decided to have kids, she could possibly be as old as Loretta when she started a family.

Thinking of that sent her back to Cooper sitting beside her at the dinner table. When his strong thigh touched hers, fire had shot through her veins. Then when her knee bumped his, it happened all over again. He'd sat there as cool as an icy-cold beer, but her pulse had raced and her gut had twisted up into a knot. What would he be like in bed? She shivered at the mental pictures that popped up in her head.

"Shut up!" she mumbled. "Stop it. There's a hard year ahead of you, Abby. And this is going to be your home if you decide to stay on for the long haul. Don't shit where you eat." She cracked a smile against the yarn of her ski mask. "Talk about awkward."

A dog barked and she looked to her left. It wagged its tail and took a couple of steps toward her, then ran back to the cemetery gate. She recognized it as one of the three dogs that had met them when they arrived at the house. Surrounded with an old iron fence with lots of ornate scrollwork, the gate groaned when she pushed it open. Another thing on her list was to give the whole fence a fresh coat of paint and to oil the gate hinges.

The dog ambled on toward the back of the cemetery and stopped at the tombstone in front of the fresh mound of dirt. Abby propped a hip on the cold gray granite and pulled another candy from her pocket to dispel the thoughts of the little girl in Afghanistan that came to mind whenever she thought about parenthood. "I'd share, but all I've got is hard candy, and I don't suppose you should be eating that."

The mutt put its paws on her leg and wagged its tail.

She squatted down and scratched the dog's ears. "You and I could be friends. What's your name? I always wanted a pet, but we lived above the doughnut shop, and Mama said that the health department would pitch a fit over anything that had hair and wasn't human."

Abby had never been to a private family cemetery before that day. It must be a rural custom or maybe it was just a Malloy custom to bury their dead right there on the ranch. Whatever it was, she did not intend to bury her mother's ashes in that place. She'd take them back to Galveston and throw them out into the ocean before she put them anywhere near Ezra.

She stood back up and started to leave, when she glanced back over her shoulder at the tombstone. Ezra Malloy, born November 5, 1933. The death date had yet to be added, but it would say January 1.

*Start off the New Year with a death, end with a birth.* She remembered the old wives' tale Granny Spencer had related. She hadn't really been her granny, but she'd always been thankful that Haley had shared her family with Abby. They'd spent so much time either at the doughnut shop, in the apartment above it, on the beach, or out at the farm where Haley lived that most folks thought they were sisters or cousins at least. It had been Haley who'd insisted that she go to Ezra's funeral and that she make the trip to the canyon even if it was just to meet her siblings.

She cocked her head to one side and frowned, studying the dates until finally it hit her. "Holy shit, Mama! He was more than fifty years old when I was born. You were only thirty-two that year. What in the hell were you thinking? Was he good-looking back then or did he have some kind of charisma when he was young? All I saw was an old, withered-up guy wearing overalls."

"You think you'll get any answers by staring at that chunk of rock?" The deep Texas drawl startled her so bad that she automatically reached for the pistol strapped to her leg, but it wasn't there. Heart thumping in her chest and pulse racing, she spun around to come face-to-face with Cooper. Only he wasn't a sheriff anymore. He was a full-fledged cowboy, in a mustard-colored work coat, a black cowboy hat shading his brown eyes, scuffed-up work boots, and a plaid shirt showing beneath his coat.

Her eyes met his and the same feeling she'd gotten at the dinner table came rushing back. If all the sparks flittering around inside her were set loose, the bare trees surrounding the cemetery would go up in flames.

"I'm not so sure I'm even interested in answers. What are you doing here?" she asked.

"Hiram, the guy who owns the funeral home, left one of the tent poles. I told him I'd pick it up and bring it into town tomorrow. What are *you* doing here? Is that butterscotch I smell?" He took a couple of steps closer to her.

She crammed her hands deeper into her pockets to keep from reaching across the short distance separating them and brushing away that little bit of white sleet sticking to his facial hair.

"I'm making a mental list of everything I want to fix or change if this place is mine and yes, it's butterscotch. Do you want one?" She held out her hand with one in it.

"No, thank you. I'm plenty full from dinner. Where are your two sisters?"

"I wouldn't know where they are. Probably unpacking or filing their fingernails," she answered.

"Sounds like you don't like them too much."

She removed her ski mask and with her fingertips combed blonde hair full of static back away from her face. "Don't know if I like them or not. We are all strangers who will share quarters until one by one we get tired of this shit and leave. I don't see either of them lasting a month."

"That youngest one seems pretty determined."

Her right shoulder popped up slightly. "Right now, she does. But I hear that ranchin' is hard business."

He bent from the waist and petted the dog. "I see you've made one friend."

"Maybe," she said. "Could be that she'd follow anyone around the ranch, not just me. Maybe she's lonely since Ezra died."

He rose and nodded. "I imagine so. He did love his dogs. You said that ranchin' isn't easy. How do you know that? Weren't you in the army for the last decade? How would you know anything about how hard ranchin' is? Or about life on the outside anyway?"

"Yes, I was in the army. The rest is need to know."

Cooper chuckled. "Well, maybe someday I'll get upgraded to that level of classification, Sergeant Malloy. Looks like you've got a bodyguard there whether you want one or not."

"She wanted inside the cemetery, so I opened the gate. I expect she'll go on back home now," Abby said.

His arm grazed hers as he headed toward the tent pole, and there it was again. Sparks. Sizzle. Steam. It was a wonder that it didn't create a warm fog right there beside Ezra's grave.

He retracted the pole until it was only about four feet long and headed out of the cemetery. She looked for a truck, berating herself for letting anyone sneak up on her like that. In the war zone, it could have meant instant death. His whistling grew fainter as he disappeared behind a herd of cattle. So he liked to walk, too, did he? But wait, how did he know she was a sergeant? She looked at the patches on the sleeve of her jacket, smiled, and put the ski mask back on. If he knew that much about the army, maybe someday he would get his classification moved up a notch.

When she finished her walk, with the dog right beside her the whole way, she sat down on the porch for a few minutes but the cold began to seep in so she went on inside the house. Shiloh was in the living room, curled up on the sofa with a thick romance book in her hands. The cover picture was a half-naked cowboy, and although Abby shared her taste in books, her half sister was crazy as bat shit if she thought she could learn about ranching by reading about hunky cowboys.

Abby made a trip through the kitchen, opened the refrigerator door, and took out the chicken and potato salad. It wasn't really suppertime but she'd worked up an appetite with her long walk around the ranch. She rolled off two paper towels and tucked them into her jacket pocket, picked up a paper plate, and loaded it with cold fried chicken, coleslaw, and potato salad, leaving one section empty for a piece of the chocolate cake. She stuck a plastic fork in her jacket pocket and carried all of it to her room, where she set it on the nightstand beside the bed, then pulled off her jacket and hung it in the closet.

Then she sat down in the worn harvest-gold recliner facing the window and unlaced her boots. When her toes were freed from socks and boots alike, she padded barefoot to the bathroom right next door to her room. The female soldiers she'd shared a bathroom with in her last duty post in Kuwait would have fought the war with nothing more than their bare hands to get a chance to soak in a deep, claw-footed tub like that. The shower was basic, with a white plastic curtain keeping the water off the linoleum floor. The toilet had crazed marks on the water tank, but it was clean. What had started off as a wall-hung sink now had a crude cabinet built around it: no doors, just shelving holding towels and extra rolls of toilet paper. It might not be five-star-hotel quality, but it sure as hell beat the showers in the army barracks. And the towels under the counter were big, thick, and fluffy. Evidently, Ezra had liked a few luxuries.

Abby could make do with sharing with the other two. On her way back to her room, she caught the strains of country music coming from the bedroom across the hallway. So Bonnie liked country music, did she?

She leaned against the doorjamb into her room for a minute and recognized Miranda Lambert's voice as she and the Pistol Annies sang "Hell on Heels." That particular CD had kept Abby awake on the long trip from South Texas. The next song, "Lemon Drop," was one of Abby's favorites. The lyrics said that her life was like a lemon drop and that she was sucking on the bitter to get to the sweet.

That's the way she felt as she went into her room and realized in that moment she *was* going to unpack everything and wait until spring, when the daisies bloomed, to make a definite decision about leaving. She'd take a few months of the bitter to find out if there was a sweet middle in the lemon drop.

"Well, shit!" she exclaimed when she shut the door and remembered that she had a half bath all of her own. She went to the door and opened it to be sure she hadn't imagined Rusty telling her that Ezra's room came with her own private bathroom.

One of those old metal medicine cabinets with a mirror door had been hung above the sink to the left. The toilet sat right beside it with only enough room for a toilet paper hanger between it and the wall. A tall man's knees would have hit the other wall, but she wasn't tall, so it was fine. And it was hers and she didn't have to share it with the other two.

She settled into the recliner and took a deep breath. The faint scent of cigarettes still lingered in the velvet, reminding her of her mother. Martha was a pack-a-day smoker right up until she died, although she never smoked in the house or the doughnut shop. But hugs with a little smoke smell in them always reminded her of her mother's love and care.

She'd learned to eat fast, often on the run, and sometimes not even finishing what she did have before her, but that evening she forced herself to eat slowly as she looked out the window toward the south. If the gray clouds hadn't covered the sun, she could have seen it setting.

Something her mother said one time when they were sitting on the beach at the end of the day, watching the brilliant yellows and oranges of the sunset over the water, came to her mind. It was one of the very few times that Martha Malloy had mentioned the past, and all she'd said was that as beautiful as it was, that sunset couldn't compare to the ones in the Palo Duro Canyon. Her eyes had misted, but she'd quickly smiled and the moment had passed, though her eyes had held a haunted look the rest of that evening.

There would be lots of sunsets in the next year and Abby vowed to remember her mother every time she saw one, but right now she couldn't focus on that or she'd start crying. It had only been two days since she'd cleared out the bank box in Galveston and tucked her important papers and her mother's ashes in the suitcase with all her candy and snack food.

"I should have tossed them out in the Gulf. That's where we had such good times," she said. "But I couldn't, not after I found that letter tucked away in the bank box when I went to store your ashes there. I'll pick an evening when the sun is setting and the daisies are blooming to scatter the ashes. Maybe in the spring. Not on a cold day like this, and definitely not the day that Ezra was buried. I want to remember it with a smile."

Bonnie was the only one in the kitchen when Abby carried her empty plate out to throw it away. Her youngest sister looked less hippieish in faded blue-and-black plaid pajama bottoms and a lime-green knit shirt under a shirt of red-and-yellow flannel with sleeves that had been rolled up to her elbows. Their blue eyes locked across the bar and neither of them blinked for several seconds.

Finally, Bonnie moved toward the refrigerator and said, "My eyes are like my mama's. Yours and Shiloh's can be like Ezra's."

"Abby can have that honor. I got my eyes and my dark hair from my maternal grandmother," Shiloh said from the doorway.

Abby jumped like a little girl with her hand in the cookie jar. Twice now someone had managed to sneak up on her blind side—in the cemetery when Cooper had appeared out of nowhere, and now in the kitchen when Shiloh had done the same thing. That aggravated her more than any genetic traits from Ezra Malloy.

She gritted her teeth so hard that her jaws ached. "What difference does it make? He's dead and we'll never know him."

"Did your mama ever talk about him?" Shiloh asked.

Abby removed a can of beer from the refrigerator and pulled the tab off the top. "Once, when I was a teenager and pressed her for the story."

"My mama talked about him. She cussed him every time she got drunk and every time she got a divorce or threw a boyfriend out of the trailer. Everything from a bad hair day to a flat tire was Ezra Malloy's fault." Bonnie brought out ham, cheese, and mayonnaise for a sandwich as she spoke. She set a pitcher of sweet tea on the counter and frowned at Abby's beer.

"What?" Abby raised an eyebrow.

"I don't like the smell of beer."

"Well, I don't like mayonnaise, so we're even."

Shiloh poured a glass of milk and went straight for the dessert table. "My mama said it was best to let sleeping dogs alone. She told me that he didn't want a daughter and gave her enough money so she could buy a small bed-and-breakfast place in Jefferson, Texas. After I graduated she sold it and went into partnership with her sister, Audrey, on a convenience store outside of Lewisville, Arkansas. I tried a few more questions, but she told me to forget the past and move on to the future."

"So what the hell did three different women see in that man who was in the casket and why in the hell did we put daisies in there with him? I've never seen that done before," Bonnie asked.

"Good questions. I have been to a couple of funerals where they laid roses on the top of the casket, but I've never seen daisies put inside." Abby carried her beer back to her room, leaving the other two to bond over conversation. She felt like she had the first time she was deployed to Afghanistan. Everything was so unexplainably different there, with everyone a stranger even though they all served the same country. She dug her phone from the cargo pocket on the side of her pants and hit the speed dial for Haley. She almost wept when her friend answered on the second ring.

"Hey, what did you decide about the ranch? Are you coming home? Tell me about the foreman." Haley asked questions until she had to stop for breath again. That was Haley to a tee. Hearing her voice put a smile on Abby's face.

"I'm staying. Did I tell you about the daisies at the funeral?" Abby went on to tell her about it, leaving out nothing.

"Did I just hear you right? You put them in the casket with him like roses?" Haley asked.

"That's right. Only his daughters had them. No casket piece or potted plants or wreaths around the casket. The place where they buried him is bare—it was strange. But hell, my sisters are strangers, Haley. I don't feel any kind of love, hate, or even indifference for them. It's like they are people I saw one time in a shopping mall."

"Tell me your first impression of them."

"Shiloh is kind of prissy and Bonnie is tough as nails. That much I've figured out so far," Abby said.

"The foreman?" Haley asked.

"Isn't my type, but the sheriff could be if I was going to stay here forever. Which I won't. I have decided not to leave until spring, but after that is a day-to-day decision. I'm so confused and rattled. I don't know what I'll do."

"The sheriff? When did you meet him? Did you get stopped for speeding?"

"No, I did not. The sheriff was at the funeral and he came to dinner. Rusty, that's the foreman, invited him."

"And what does this sheriff look like and what is his name?" Haley asked.

"Looks like Travis Tritt and name is Cooper Wilson," Abby answered.

"Oh. My. Sweet. Jesus. You are doomed. Lookin' like your favorite singer and with a cowboy name like Cooper. You are going to grow roots right there in that canyon. I can feel it in my bones." Haley laughed.

"Your bones have been wrong lots of times before," Abby said.

"You've run from settling a long time, Abby. A year in a remote place outside of the army is just what you need to get your head on straight. And my bones are not wrong this time. Got to go. The kids are fighting over a stupid board game. Keep me posted. Open up your laptop and send pictures. I want to see what these other two women look like. And pictures of the sheriff, too. I want to see them all. Big hugs," Haley said.

"Big hugs back to you." Abby hit the "End" button.

Haley had married right out of high school and had two kids by the time she was twenty-five. That was her whole family—a boy and a girl—and she'd declared she was finished until two years ago, when she and her husband had been surprised with a set of twin girls. Tonight was one of those times that Abby envied her friend the family, even when the older two fought over board games.

"I'm not ready to grow roots," she argued out loud with herself as she pushed out of the chair. "And Cooper Wilson probably has every available woman in the canyon out after him. It's the stress of all this that had me fantasizing about him. It's either sneak candy or let my mind wander into the gutter when I'm worried."

A set of sheets and pillowcases had been placed on the antique four-poster bed. Had she been conceived in that bed?

She pushed the unanswered questions out of her mind and quickly stretched the sheets over the mattress, tucking in the corners and leaving no wrinkles. Then she started on the unpacking business—duffel bags first and then the suitcases.

The first thing she pulled up out of the biggest duffel bag was her CD player. Music took her to another place when she was

worried or mulling over something. She set it on the chest of drawers beside her mother's ashes, but there was no place to plug the
cord in. She went looking and found that the room only had one
outlet with two receptacles, and that was behind the recliner. She
moved the player to the table beside the recliner and the cord was
too short. She moved the recliner over six inches, then did the same
with the table and it worked.

The next thing that came out of the duffel bag was an oversized
case of CDs. She flipped through them until she found the ones by
Travis Tritt and started to take one out. She stopped and stared at
the picture that reminded her so much of Cooper.

"No! Not these. Not today," she said. Instead she chose Blake
Shelton. She wiggled her shoulders to the music when it started
and wondered if Cooper Wilson liked country music. What kind
of dancer would he be? She imagined herself with those big strong
arms around her. One around her waist, maybe dipping down lower
until it rested on her butt; the other with his fingers laced with hers
as they swayed to the music. She inhaled deeply and imagined looking deeply into his eyes.

"Dammit!" She stomped her foot and swore. She didn't need to
be thinking of anyone. Especially not the sheriff, who was also the
neighbor, and she damn sure didn't care what kind of music he liked.
A vision of his swagger as he walked away from her in the cemetery
appeared in spite of her determination to forget all about him.

"Stop it right now. He's too damned sexy not to have a girlfriend or maybe . . ." She stopped unpacking and blinked several
times to get rid of the image.

*Wife?* The voice in her head asked.

She shook her head. "There's no ring, so there is no wife. Dammit again! What am I doing? Get a hold of yourself, Malloy! Put a
bullet in that biological clock that starts ticking every time you talk
to Haley."

She hit the "Forward" button on the CD player again and sang along with several songs while she hung her meager supply of clothing in the closet. Two pairs of camo pants and three pairs of jeans occupied one end. A couple of sweaters and a long skirt on the other. Two or three shirts and a little black dress with a jacket, just in case she had to go somewhere important. Her combat boots would have to be cleaned up and polished before she set them on the floor beside her cowboy boots and one pair of high-heeled shoes.

She picked up a long, hard plastic case and very gently put it on the bed. She didn't need to open it to see what was inside, but she did anyway. There was her history right there in the gun case. Her mother's pump shotgun, all cleaned and ready for use, not that it had done a damn bit of good when those three drug addicts came into the doughnut shop and killed her when there was only $110 and change in the cash register.

The .22 rifle was a perfect match to Haley's. The two girls had gotten the smart idea that they wanted to be hunters in their early teenage tomboy days. They'd asked for .22 rifles and for Haley's dad and brothers to take them squirrel hunting with them. Haley was a natural just like her brothers and her father. She could aim, shoot, and a squirrel fell out of the tree every time. Not Abby. She could aim, but she couldn't pull the trigger any more than she could eat the squirrels that Haley's dad fixed on the grill.

The Glock was hers and she fully intended to find a site at the back of the ranch, maybe up against the canyon wall, for target practice at least once a week when spring came. She'd finally learned to shoot in the army and had scored so high on target they'd thought about sending her to sniper training. But that had fallen through when she took the psych exam. She had found out early on that it was easy to shoot someone coming toward her with a pistol in one hand and a grenade in the other, but she had never been able to shake the nightmares when that had happened.

When Blake started the last song on the CD, she sat down in the rocking chair and stared out the window. He sang about his granddaddy's gun. She'd never known any of her grandparents. Her maternal ones had been gone before she was born. Cancer took them and her mother had always feared she'd contract it early and not live to see Abby raised.

Tears rolled down her cheeks and left wet spots on her shirt. Did Ezra have guns or had he given them to Rusty? He'd probably loved his foreman more than any of his own blood daughters. She didn't weep for Ezra or for his guns, but for what could have been, for the father she'd never known.

※ ※ ※

Cooper stretched out on the brown leather sofa and rested his head on a throw pillow when he got home that afternoon. His dog did a low belly crawl from in front of the fireplace to lie on the floor beside him. Instinctively, he dropped his hand and scratched her ears.

"It's been a long day, Delores."

Her tail thumped against the leg of the heavy wood coffee table.

Cooper continued to pet the dog as he replayed the day, scene after scene. It had all started when they brought Ezra's body to the cemetery. He and Rusty were the only ones there at that time and it had reminded him of the sad day they'd buried his grandfather. That day he'd said good-bye to his last living family member. But his grandfather had been more than just family. The old guy had been his best friend, his confidant, his mentor on the ranch, and his support when he ran for sheriff. His parents had died when he was just a little boy and his grandfather and grandmother had raised him from that point on. She'd died several years before his grandfather and for those next few years it had just been him and Grandpa on the ranch. Funerals reminded him of the fact that he was totally alone in the world except for friends and neighbors.

His mind shifted back to today when the neighbors and friends had begun to arrive. They'd gathered round close together, making a semicircle around the three empty chairs. A lump had formed in Cooper's throat as he'd looked at those chairs. What if not a single one of Ezra's daughters showed up? He couldn't blame them if they didn't, not after Ezra sending them away at birth, but still, to have that final moment on earth with no family?

"But they did, even if Abby was almost too late," Cooper told Delores. "I wonder what Grandpa would make of Ezra's daughters? He'd have something to say about each of them, for sure. Bonnie with her nose ring. Abby in her camouflage and Shiloh with her better-than-thou attitude. I'm surprised Ezra didn't raise up out of that casket when they filed past it. Especially Abby, decked out in that army stuff. In Ezra's world, women stayed in the house where they belonged. They damn sure didn't join the army."

It must have been the funeral, but Cooper really missed his grandfather that night. Or maybe it was because he wanted to talk to him about the sparks that flew when he was around Abby. Ezra's other two daughters didn't affect him like that, not one bit, but that oldest daughter? Dammit, but she got under his skin from the time she'd sat down in the last chair. He'd thought his reaction to her touch might be a fluke, but then the same thing had happened at the cemetery. The feeling had been so damned strong that he'd wanted to take her in his arms, kiss those full lips, and hold her forever.

He'd have to kick the physical attraction out in the cold, because there was no way she'd stay in the canyon. And to Cooper's way of thinking, there was no use starting something he couldn't finish. Folks said that more babies were born nine months after a funeral than any other time because people needed to feel alive.

Maybe that's what he'd experienced with Abby . . . the desire to feel a woman in his arms as proof he was alive.

"What do you think, Delores? Is it time for me to start getting serious about finding someone to share this big old ranch and my life? It just can't be that particular woman, even if she did throw a couple of extra beats into this old heart of mine. There's no way she'll stick around for the long haul. She'll take her third of the money and be gone by spring."

Delores didn't answer.

## Chapter Four

*U*npacking was done, boxes cut up and put into the trash, duffel bags inside the suitcases and stored on the closet shelf. Boots were brushed off and set beside the rocking chair so she could put them on first thing in the morning. No fancy purple running shoes for Abby. She ran in combat boots. All she needed before she fell into bed was a quick shower, but first she wanted a breath of fresh air. The house wasn't too warm, but the walls were closing in on her. She felt Rusty's presence on the porch before he spoke, which gave her back the confidence that she hadn't completely lost her skills.

"Good evening. I was just feeding the dogs," Rusty said.

One nosed her hand and she sat down in one of the three rocking chairs and scratched the animal's ears. "What kind are they and what are their names?"

"Mongrels mostly. Some Catahoula with some bluetick hound thrown in. Ezra said that their mama was a bluetick over on Lonesome Canyon. That one that you're petting is Martha. The one with floppy ears beside the food pan is Vivien and that lazy old gal scratching her ribs is Polly," Rusty said.

Abby quickly put her hand in her lap. "Are you shittin' me? Tell me the other two aren't named after Shiloh and Bonnie's mamas."

"He told me that he named them after his ex-wives and had them spayed before they had any puppies, because he figured all they'd throw would be more bitches. No offense meant. I'm just repeatin' what he said."

"How old are they?"

"Five or six years old, near as he could remember. Jackson offered to give away the mixed-breed pups and all that was left was females when Ezra got around to making a trip over to Lonesome Canyon to look at them. He took them all and he trained them himself. They're fine cattle dogs and fair huntin' critters."

"Does Martha take up with everyone?"

"Pretty much. She's the friendliest one of the lot, but she's also the best cow dog of the three. I save her for the last if the other two can't run a rangy old bull out of the mesquite," Rusty said.

"Why?"

"She goes for the lip and she don't let go. They know her, and when I turn her loose, believe me, they don't want what she's about to bring to the fight. If you've a mind to learn ranchin', then you can start tomorrow. It's Sunday, so all we'll do is chores. Other than that Ezra always said it was a day that God made for restin', so that's what we do. I'll be takin' care of feedin' chores and I'll be leaving right after six from that barn out there." He pointed to the south. "Good night, Abby."

He was gone before she could say another word. Martha slipped her big head into Abby's lap and whined. Abby rubbed the dog's ears and said, "Next January, your name is changing to Spot or Jane or Fluff Butt, anything but my mother's name. Ezra might have thought it was funny to name you dogs after his ex-wives, but I don't see a damn thing amusing in it."

Vivien and Polly ignored her, but Martha wagged her tail and whined for more petting. The door opened and Shiloh came out, sat down in a rocking chair, and propped her feet on the porch railing. Her slippers were those oversized things with Tweety Bird's head on the toes. Martha eyed them for a few seconds before she decided that they weren't dangerous, then she went straight to Shiloh. Fickle bitch. She didn't deserve her name and it *would* be changed. Fluff Butt was looking better by the moment.

"Wonder what their names are." Shiloh rubbed the dog from head to tail several times.

"Martha, Vivien, and Polly. Which one was your mother?" Abby gripped the arms of the rocker so hard that her knuckles ached. Shit fire! She hadn't meant to ask questions. She didn't want to get to know either of them.

"Polly is my mother. She's still livin' and you are shittin' me, right?"

Abby shook her head. "Rusty just now told me and I don't think he'd make that up. So your mama's namesake is the one over there scratching her ears."

"What about ears?" Bonnie stepped out on the porch. She wore a stained work coat over her mismatched pajama pants and flannel shirt and cowboy boots on her feet.

"Your mama is the bitch over there eating the last of the dog food," Shiloh said.

"My mama might not be a saint, but you ain't got no right to be callin' her a bitch," Bonnie said stiffly.

"I'm not. Ezra named his three dogs after our mothers. Mine is Polly. That would be the lazy old gal who's now curling up on the rug in front of the door. Vivien is eating and this one who wants to be petted is Martha, Abby's mama."

"The old bastard." Bonnie sucked in a lungful of air and went back into the house.

Abby followed her without saying another word and Martha tagged along behind her all the way into the bedroom, where she curled up in the recliner and went to sleep. Abby grabbed her bathroom gear with the intention of taking a shower, but the tub looked so good that she turned on the water and adjusted the temperature.

She shucked her clothing, leaving them hanging on the nail beside the door, and slid into the warm, steamy water.

"Oh. My. God!" she muttered, leaning on the sloped back and sinking down until nothing but her head was sticking up. The only thing better would be a Jacuzzi in a hotel suite with a cowboy like Cooper.

She opened her eyes wide and focused on the water faucets. She was not going to think about Cooper anymore. She'd gone for a whole hour without letting him into her mind so it wouldn't be that difficult.

She closed her eyes again, and as if on cue, a picture of him at the cemetery with that black hat pulled down over his eyes popped into her mind. She let her eyes drop to the way his butt filled out the jeans as he walked away from her in that sexy swagger. Mentally she brought him into the bathroom with her and watched him undress slowly, then slide into the bathtub with her.

She blinked several times and then swore when the visual refused to leave. "Dammit to hell on a rusty poker. I can control this. I can and I will."

She banished every thought or picture from her mind and dozed, dreaming of a little girl peeking out of an upstairs window of a building. The child waved shyly a split second before the whole building went up in smoke and crumbled to the ground. Abby had given the command for the soldiers in her company to paint the building. The planes flying away had bombed it on her command and now that sweet little girl was dead. If she'd had a drop of parental instinct in her body, she would have sent someone inside to check for civilians, especially kids, before she gave the signal to light it up.

She awoke with a start. The water had gone lukewarm, so she pulled the plug and crawled out, goose bumps dancing down her back as she tucked a towel around her body. Shiloh stepped out into the hallway and closed her door softly, nodded at Abby, and carried her own supplies into the bathroom. In seconds, the shower was running. More country music came from Bonnie's room; this time it was Conway singing, "Goodbye Time." No wait a minute—that was Blake Shelton's voice, not Conway's.

Abby had watched the video of that song so many times it was burned in her memories. Be damned if Bonnie didn't look like the girl in the video. Kind of rough and yet innocent at the same time when she looked up with those blue eyes. When the song ended, it started all over again. Had Bonnie said good-bye to some old boy back in Harlan, Kentucky, to come to Texas? Would he follow her?

She shut the door to her room as the song started over for the third time. Maybe it wasn't going to be as easy as she thought. If Bonnie had given up a man for this dream of having her own ranch, she wouldn't budge as quickly as Abby had figured. One thing for sure—it was past time for her to say that it was good-bye time to those crazy feelings that Cooper had stirred up, so maybe the song was as much to her as it was to Bonnie.

Sleep was slow to come to Abby and then it was fitful, the nightmares returning to haunt her. At midnight she sat straight up in bed, eyes wide-open, pulse and heartbeat in competition to see which one could pound the loudest in her ears. She couldn't remember what she was dreaming about, only that it was terrifying. She envied the soldiers who went home to a spouse who could comfort them in times like this.

She flopped back down on her pillow and shut her eyes. Martha whined from the recliner, crossed the floor, and jumped up on the bed with Abby. She licked her face and then curled up on the foot of the bed, her head lying on Abby's feet. That time Abby slept until five minutes before her alarm sounded; she hit the button and swung her legs out of the bed. Time for a morning run to clear her head and get her ready for the day. Run, eat, and then it would be day one of chores with Rusty.

The house was still quiet as she eased out the door. Martha dashed out the moment she opened the door and barely made it off the porch before she squatted. Abby bit back the laughter and said, "At least you were polite enough not to do that on my bed or on the carpet."

She did a few stretches using the porch rail as a bar, and then started a slow jog down the lane. She'd run to the main road, which by her calculations was about two miles, and back. It would be a short run, but she didn't want to miss Rusty and she didn't think he'd wait for her. Why should he? If they all left, he inherited the ranch.

She'd barely left the yard fence behind when she realized that she had a running companion. Martha was right beside her, step for step, not getting ahead, not lagging behind, but keeping up without even letting her tongue hang out.

"At least she has manners, Mama." Abby grinned.

They made it to the road and Abby ran in place for a minute before turning around and starting back. She didn't plan on turning left and running down the fence line separating Malloy Ranch from Cooper's place, but Martha herded her that way. She'd only gone fifty yards at most when suddenly Cooper was on the other side of the barbed-wire fence, jogging along with her.

"Early riser, are you?" he asked.

"Always have been. Mama had a doughnut shop that opened at five. She rousted me out of bed at three to go to work with her." Dammit! Why did she feel compelled to tell him anything?

She focused on his shoulder nearest to her as they ran. Surely to God there wasn't anything sexy about a shoulder, was there? Then she imagined cuddling with him on one of the porch rocking chairs, his arms around her, his lips on that tender part of her neck as her head rested on that strong shoulder.

"Me, too, only it wasn't a doughnut shop, it was plain old ranchin'. My grandfather left this little spread to me when he passed on. He was about Ezra's age and I grew up right here working beside him my whole life," Cooper said.

Not many men could run and talk at the same time. She had to give him kudos for being in shape.

"Where were your parents?" Hopefully if he talked about something like his parents she'd lose this crazy infatuation.

"Right here until I was four. I don't remember much about them. The smell of Mama's perfume brings back a comforting feeling and sometimes it's like I know my dad is proud of me for bein' sheriff and keepin' the Lucky Seven runnin' at the same time, but other than what I see in pictures, I can't bring them up in my mind. They were killed when the brakes on their truck gave way as they came down into the canyon from Claude," he said.

She stopped when she could see the house against the canyon wall. He went on, but then turned and came back, running in place.

"You quittin'?" he asked.

"Time's up. Lights are on in the house and I want to help with feeding this morning. Have a good run. Martha and I are going home now," she said.

He nodded and took off again. Martha flopped down close to her feet to rest while she watched Cooper's backside keep going. Lord have mercy! That cowboy even strutted when he was jogging. She might as well quit trying to erase every thought she had of him and simply realize, even though they kept returning, she wasn't going to do anything about them.

"Okay, girl, let's go home and get some breakfast. I'm having another helping of cold fried chicken and some more cake. You've been a good runnin' buddy. You want me to save you the bones?"

Martha wagged her tail and stood up as if she understood every word. They walked back to the house, woman and black-and-brown brindled dog with one blue eye and one brown one. When they got there, Martha flopped down on the porch under a rocking chair and shut her eyes.

"Had enough of that, have you? Well, I'll bring you some bones anyway." Abby went inside with a lighter heart than she'd had since she'd left Galveston.

Bonnie was sitting at the kitchen table with a bowl full of peach cobbler topped with a double scoop of ice cream in front of her. Shiloh had something that looked green and horrible in a tall glass, sipping on it while she watched the Weather Channel on television. They were both dressed in faded jeans and work shirts. Shiloh's dark hair was braided and Bonnie's was pulled up in a ratty-looking ponytail.

One of Bonnie's shoulders raised slightly. "Guess you intend to go with Rusty to feed, too. I thought you were still in your room."

"I've already had a four-mile run like I do every morning," Abby said. "Where's the rest of the chicken?"

"Rusty ate it for breakfast. There's plenty of other things in there, including bacon if you want to cook," Bonnie told her.

"Well, shit! I told Martha I'd give her the chicken bones for running with me."

Bonnie rolled her eyes toward the ceiling. "You ain't never had a dog, have you?"

"What's that got to do with anything?"

"You don't give chicken bones to a dog. They ain't good for them. They splinter," Bonnie said.

"And what makes you so smart when it comes to dogs?"

"Mama gathers up strays like cats gather fleas. Ain't never been a time there wasn't half a dozen sleepin' up under the trailer porch and there has always been enough cats in the house to clog up the vacuum brushes every time I cleaned," Bonnie said.

"Does she work as a vet's helper or something?" Abby asked.

"Hell, no! She's a bartender. She owned the bar at one time, but she lost it when she mortgaged it to get one of her boyfriends out of jail. He skipped bail and the bank foreclosed, but the man who bought it kept her on as the bartender. Better get something to eat. Rusty said he ain't waitin' on none of us," Bonnie said. "And he showed me where the dog food is. I'll take on the job of feeding them a can in the morning and one at night and keeping their automatic feeder full out in their pens."

It aggravated Abby to have Bonnie tell her what to do and to know more about dogs than she did. Truth was, the youngest Malloy daughter had probably had a much rougher life than Abby or Shiloh. That meant she had more reason to work hard and try to stick out the year.

Shiloh finished her ugly smoothie, put on her coat, and headed out the kitchen door toward the barn, setting off toward the fence line separating the Lucky Seven and the Malloy Ranch. Bonnie scraped every single bite of the cobbler and ice cream up out of the bowl and rinsed it before she grabbed her coat and followed behind Shiloh. That left Abby, who still hadn't eaten. She grabbed two pieces of ham and cheese, rolled them up together like a pencil and ate them on the way, taking time to pinch off a bite for Martha when she cleared the porch.

"Okay, ladies, there's room for one person in the front seat of the truck. The other two have to sit in the back," Rusty said. "You want to draw straws?"

"Who was here first?" Abby asked.

Shiloh held up her hand.

"Then she should go first today. Are we ready?" Abby asked.

"Not hardly. We'll need about twenty bales of hay stacked on the back of the truck. You and Bonnie can ride on top of it or leave a little legroom between a couple of bales and sit on the side," Rusty said. "If you didn't bring work gloves, there's extra in the tack room.

Ezra bought a dozen pair at a time. But you do not get a new pair every day. A pair should last six months at the very least. If you lose them, the price of new ones comes out of your weekly paycheck."

The cowboy had leadership qualities. She could have whipped him up into a good soldier in no time. He pointed toward a room toward the back of the barn with a window in the door. It was the only one that had light shining, so she figured that was the tack room.

"Ezra was partial to these small traditional bales. I wanted to go to the big round ones so we would only have to feed two or three times a week, but he wouldn't have any part of it. Stubborn as a mule, he was. Guess he passed it on to y'all," Rusty said.

Abby bit back a sarcastic remark. If this was ever her ranch, she'd have big round bales like she saw scattered over the pastures on her way from South Texas. Especially if it meant only feeding cows three times a week.

Rusty sat down on a bale of hay and motioned toward the left where the hay was stacked from dirt floor to the rafters of the barn. "To make it fair, we'll take twenty-one bales. That's seven for each of you. We had a damn fine hay season last year, which means if it's scant this year, we won't be hurting next winter. Ezra believed in keeping the barns full. Never knew him to buy hay, but he said back in 1990 he ran plumb out and had to get fifty bales from Lonesome Canyon. It aggravated him so bad that he cleared off another forty acres that next spring and put in more alfalfa.

"After you get the feeding done, there's eggs to be gathered, a cow to milk, and the pigs to feed. In a few weeks, we'll plow up the garden behind the house and put in the potatoes and onions. Ezra said if we don't produce it here, we don't eat it."

"Cannin'?" Bonnie asked.

"Every day in the summer, but that's in the evenings after the work is done."

Abby pulled the suede work gloves on her hands and picked up the first bale of hay by the wire holding it together. It weighed a little less than the fifty-pound plates in the gym but still, heaving it up over the end of the truck and sliding it forward wasn't an easy feat.

"So how many cows are we feeding?" she asked.

"We're running about a hundred and fifty head right now. Ten pounds of hay per cow, twice a day. Ezra liked to spread it out over two feedings rather than putting twenty pounds per cow out there in the morning."

Shiloh was huffing after her first bale. "Why should we do it the way he did?"

"He might have been a son of a bitch in y'all's eyes, but he knew ranchin' and he knew cattle. I learned a lot from him that I'm passin' on, because I told him I would. You can like it or stay at the house. It doesn't make me a bit of difference." He pushed his glasses up on his nose and for a minute there Abby thought he might cry.

She picked up another bale and threw it over the side of the truck. Bonnie wasn't even breathing heavily. That scrawny woman must have worked hard her whole life. With that work ethic, she could have made a fine army officer, too.

"We should be completely done with everything by nine thirty with so many hands to help out," Rusty said. "I go to church on Sunday morning. Any of you want to follow me, be ready by ten forty-five. You can drive your own vehicles or ride with me if you want. I have a double cab truck, and I don't mind haulin' you to church, since I'm going anyway."

Well, wasn't that nice of him, but no, thank you. Abby would rather stay on the ranch than go meet the neighbors this week. By her calculations, when they got this truckload of hay unloaded, there'd be another one to do. Then late that evening it started all over again. Forget the running in the morning. She'd be getting plenty of exercise with ranching and she could get an extra hour of sleep—provided that the nightmares stayed away.

"I'll go to church with you," Bonnie said. "I'd like to meet the people here in the canyon and get acquainted since I'm plannin' on bein' here a long, long time."

"I'll honk one time. If you don't come out the door at the count of five, you can find your own way," Rusty said.

"Hard-ass, ain't you?" Abby smarted off.

"Darlin', he's just protecting his interests. He promised to teach us. He didn't promise to like it or to baby us. He and Ezra are cut from the same cloth. He'd probably drown his girl babies," Shiloh said.

Rusty chuckled. "Naw, I'd sell them to the gypsies that come through here in the spring every year. Ain't no use in drownin' something that could bring in a few dollars."

Abby decided right then that she liked Rusty. He had a sense of humor. He didn't turn her insides to mush like Cooper. She damn sure didn't have visions of stripping his clothes off and having wild passionate sex with him. And that was a good thing.

Shiloh threw her last bale on the truck and crawled over the side to get it situated right on the top of the others. "Don't want y'all bitchin' at me because I didn't do the job right."

"Are you ready to go back to Arkansas?" Abby asked.

"Hell, no! I might not be superwomen like you two but that doesn't mean I'm ready to throw in the towel the first day," she said.

"All right ladies, time to move this wagon train out so we can come back and do it again. Who's going to milk the cow and who's going to feed the hogs and gather the eggs? I figure there's a job for each of you. You can keep that job every day, or you can switch off. They're minor jobs, but when it comes to working cows or deliverin' baby pigs, you'll all have to learn that part."

Abby raised her hand. "I'll take care of the hog feeding."

There was no way in hell she was going to admit that she hated chickens and didn't know jack shit about milking a damn cow.

"I'll take the milking every morning. I've done it many, many times," Bonnie said.

"Your trailer on a farm?" Abby asked.

Bonnie's head bobbed once. "My grandparents had a little bit of land and they deeded an acre over to Mama. They're gone now, but they did some small-time ranchin' and farmin'. After they were gone, one of Mama's boyfriends fancied himself a rancher. He had a milk cow and a pen full of goats. He didn't like to take care of them, so the job fell on me."

"That leaves me with chickens. I can do that," Shiloh said. "My grandmother had a henhouse when I was a little girl. I used to gather eggs. I guess it's like riding a bicycle. You never unlearn the art once you get it down."

※ ※ ※

Abby paced from the living room through the kitchen to her bedroom and back to the living room. The house was empty with both Shiloh and Bonnie taking Rusty up on his offer to go to church. Finally she stretched out on the sofa, leaned her head back on the arm, and shut her eyes.

Of course a picture of Cooper popped into her head. He wore that leather jacket and his cowboy hat and snow fell on his sexy facial hair. If only there was a button she could push to delete the damn scene, but it was burned into her brain as surely as if it had been branded there.

"Branded," she groaned. According to Rusty, they'd have to help with that job, too. Her nose snarled at the imagined scent of burning hair.

A knock on the door brought her to a sitting position. The second one took her to her feet. There was no peephole, so she eased it open to find Cooper's smiling face on the other side of the old-fashioned screen door. He held up two butcher-paper-wrapped packages.

"Thought I'd best knock, since I didn't know if all y'all went to church. I figured the chicken was gone, so I brought steaks for dinner. Thought I'd have them all done and on the table when y'all came home, to repay Rusty for inviting me to dinner yesterday. Mind if I come on in and get busy?"

She threw the door open wide. "You cook?"

"Of course, don't you?" His hip brushed against hers on the way through the door, creating a brand-new batch of sparks.

She refused to blink for fear she'd drag up another sexy picture of him. What was standing before her was enough to give her hot flashes. She didn't need any help from her mind.

"Sure, I can make doughnuts that will melt in your mouth and biscuits and gravy, pancakes, and anything that has to do with breakfast. Past that, I do soup from cans and a mean Frito chili pie."

"Well, I'll just make myself at home and get busy."

She followed him into the kitchen, where he laid the packages on the cabinet and went to work. "Can I help in any way?"

He slowly scanned her from toes to eyes. "Are we talkin' about cooking?"

"What else would we be discussing?" She was flirting, but dammit, he'd started it.

"I just wanted to be sure we were on the same page." He moved toward the pantry door with her right behind him.

He picked out five potatoes from a basket and turned around. "Help me. I can't carry them all."

She reached out to take them, and he laid one in each hand, fingertips touching her palms when he did. Desire flushed through her veins like she was hooked up to a moonshine IV. Granted, it had been a hell of a dry spell since the last relationship, but no man had ever made her go weak in the knees just handing off potatoes.

She backed out of pantry and carried the potatoes to the sink, where she washed them. Then he deftly wrapped each potato in foil and put them inside the oven. After that he seasoned the steaks and lined them in a row in a pan he'd gone back to the pantry to get. He wasted no movements, proving that he was as much at home in the kitchen as he was on the jogging trail or probably in the sheriff's chair.

She braced herself on the cabinet and hoped to hell he didn't realize it was out of necessity to keep from sliding right on the floor. Damn! Damn! Damn! Flirting was a bad idea. Anything else could and would be catastrophic. But she wanted him to kiss her, to hold her close. Hell, she wouldn't even say no to a round of sex right there on the cabinet just to put out the fires in her body.

"We'll get out yesterday's leftovers, but steak needs a big old stuffed baked potato to make it good," he said as he worked. "It's still thirty minutes before the preacher winds down. Rusty and I are real partial to medium-rare steaks. You got any idea how your sisters like theirs?"

Hell's bells, she didn't give a shit how they wanted their steak. She wanted Cooper undressed and in her bed, or on the sofa, or the floor. The kitchen table even looked good.

"I like mine seared and hot in the middle," she said.

"Kind of like sex?"

She blushed. Crap! Had she really said those words out loud?

*Hell, yes,* that smart-ass inner voice in her head yelled. *You've been thinking of sex ever since you first laid eyes on him, but it's a bad idea. Back away, Abigail Joyce. Back away right now or you'll be sorry.*

She turned away and looked out the window, focusing on Martha coming back from out near the barn. "Yes, I do like my steak just like sex." She ignored that niggling voice and whipped back around to see what Cooper had to say next.

But he didn't say a word.

He took a step forward and suddenly he was so close that she could count his eyelashes as his eyelids lowered and his lips came closer and closer. He pulled her closer with one arm while the other hand found its way to the back of her head, where he tangled his fingers in her hair and the kiss deepened. It was a kiss, for God's sake, not an earth-changing experience, but the air around them became so thin that she was slightly dizzy. Her arms snaked up around his neck and she rolled up on her toes. Then his tongue found hers and it turned into something a hell of a lot more than a simple kiss. She had a split second to make the decision to step back or not. She chose to press even closer to his muscular body, feeling the evidence behind his zipper that said he was as turned on as she was.

One of his hands was suddenly under her shirt and against the bare skin on her back. Common sense screamed at her to end the kiss and talk dinner. He cupped her bottom with his hands and with a short hop, her legs went around his waist. Without stopping the string of scorching kisses, he carried her to the sofa and sat down with her in his lap.

The pearl snaps on his shirt made a long series of noises when she pulled the top one with enough force to undo them all the way to his belt buckle. One of her hands inched its way inside his shirt, feeling just the right amount of chest hair and muscles on the way around to his back. His hand made its way from her back to cup a breast. Skin against skin and she didn't even remember him unfastening her bra. She felt as if they could light candles off the places where he'd touched her skin. His tongue continued to make love to her mouth as his other hand massaged her back in gentle circles, each one creating another ripple of desire.

"Your skin is like warm water on a cold day," he said.

"And yours is like fire." She laughed.

He unbuttoned her shirt a little at a time until he could slide it off her shoulders. Kissing each piece of bare skin as he unwrapped her body like a Christmas present, he maneuvered her backward until she was stretched out on the sofa with him on top of her.

In the military they had a code. Red light meant stop right now. Yellow light meant to put the skids on it and take a step backward. Green light meant go right ahead at whatever speed worked best.

All she could see was a big green light when she reached to tug the rest of his shirt from his jeans.

"Abby, darlin', if you are going to say stop, do it now, please."

"Cooper, darlin', I'm not going to say stop," she whispered softly in his ear.

"Dear Lord," he rasped hoarsely.

"It's damn sure not a time to pray," she said as she undid his belt buckle and unzipped his jeans.

He jumped up off the sofa and said, "Boots."

She nodded and two pair of boots landed somewhere over beside the door in a pile. In seconds their jeans and underwear joined the boots. She did notice that her bra hung on the door handle and was damn glad that all three dogs were outside. One of them might think it was a new toy.

"I want to play, but it's been a long time," he drawled.

"This doesn't have to be our only playdate." She wrapped her legs around him and arched her back until her breasts brushed against that luscious hair on his chest.

She gasped when he filled her and started a steady rhythm.

"Did I hurt you?"

"No." She rocked with him, matching every stroke with her hips, his kisses on her lips, eyelids, and forehead driving her insane. She locked her legs tightly around him, dug her nails into his back, and tried to melt her whole body into his in that instant.

He brought her to the edge of the most intense climax she'd ever known and then they tumbled over the side together.

"Oh, my God," he whispered in a rasp.

He tried to roll to one side but that only sent both of them tumbling to the floor. His strong arms held her tight as she landed right on top of him.

"You okay?" he asked.

She tried to say something, but there wasn't enough air in her lungs for anything other than panting so she just nodded.

He pulled a throw from the sofa and covered them with it and pulled her close to his side.

When she could finally talk, she gasped. "This was one hell of a big mistake, Cooper."

"Probably so," he agreed.

"It's going to make things awkward and it can't happen again."

"Probably not," he yawned.

"Holy shit! It's past noon. They'll be coming home any minute."

"Guess we'd best go make the tea, hadn't we? Unless you want to take this to the bedroom and have another go at it just to be sure that it was a mistake," he said.

Her hand went to her mouth to see if it was actually as warm as it felt. She was surprised to find her lips were cool to the touch.

"We've got to get dressed," she said. "Church will be over soon."

She pushed away from him, gathered up all her clothing, and headed for the bathroom. He followed right behind her and turned on the shower. "We'd best take one together since we're pressed for time."

She gasped. "We can't do that."

"I'd say we'd have to. They'll be here any minute and one whiff of either of us and they'll know what we've been doing. Oh, and I need a lemon," he said.

"What the hell for?" She turned on the water.

He adjusted it. "To suck on so I can wipe this smile off my face. It might have been a mistake, but honey, that was amazing."

"Shit!" she said. "It is going to be awkward."

"Probably. Want me to wash your back for you?"

"Hell, no! That would start something we don't have time to finish."

# Chapter Five

Cooper had just turned thirty-one and he'd dated since the eighth-grade Valentine's Day dance seventeen years ago. He'd had a couple of relationships but nothing serious since his granddad died. That was the year he'd won the election for sheriff, and he'd been busy with taking care of that business, plus the ranch, so he hadn't had a lot of time for dating. He'd had the occasional fling that usually started in the Sugar Shack on a Saturday night and most of the time ended by Sunday morning when he went home to do chores.

What in the devil had he just done? He'd only known the woman a couple of days. It was too soon even to be kissing her, and yet they'd just had amazing sex. They'd wanted it. They'd had it. Now they had to suffer the consequences.

He kept letting his eyes shift around the kitchen to catch glimpses of her. Sure, she was cute as a newborn baby kitten, but she'd been through a lot the past twenty-four hours. That was probably the only thing that made her vulnerable. It's a wonder she hadn't whipped out some martial arts skills and knocked him colder than an ice cube when he'd kissed her.

"You do realize that there's lots of single guys living in the canyon and in Claude and Silverton," he said.

She brought two casserole dishes from the refrigerator and popped one into the microwave to heat it up. "And that is supposed to mean?"

"Think, Abby. This isn't a big ranch, but it would be a real nice living for a cowhand who'd like to move up in the world. Someone who hasn't got, nor will ever have, the money to buy his own place. I'm sure that Shiloh and Bonnie have already been sized up at church and bets are being made as to which cowboy will make headway with them. Wait until they see you when they come callin' with their hats in their hands." He smiled.

"I'm so sure they'll be fallin' all over themselves to flirt with a woman who lives in her old army camo. And if they did, I've got too much on my plate to deal with a relationship right now. With anyone, Cooper." She looked right into his eyes.

"I get your drift, Abby, but it doesn't have to be strange between us. We can be friends and neighbors even if we don't have sex again," he said.

She inhaled and let it out slowly before she spoke. "I'm like those cowboys you are talkin' about. I've always wanted my own piece of dirt—granted, I never pictured it being as desolate as this. I'm an only child, which means I don't share too well, and I'm not going to play nice with Ezra's other two daughters. Not even if I do feel sorry for Bonnie."

He crossed his arms over his chest, more to keep from wrapping them around her than anything else. "Who are you trying to convince? Me or you?"

"I'm stating fact, not trying to talk anyone into anything," she protested.

"Didn't sound like it to me," he argued.

"Frankly, Cooper . . ." She smiled.

He quickly threw a palm out to stop her. "Don't finish that line. I saw the movie."

"You watched *Gone With the Wind*?" she asked.

"Grandpa loved it. He took Granny to see it on the big screen when they were dating, and every time it was rereleased, they went again. Then when DVDs came around, he bought it for her one Christmas and they watched it together once a year on the anniversary of their first date in 1947. He was seventeen that year and she was sixteen."

"That is so romantic," she said.

"We Wilson men tend to be romantics. He also watched it every year after she passed away on the anniversary of their first date." He grinned.

"That's what I want when I settle down. A love like they had," she said.

"So you're ready to settle down?"

"I have no idea," she said.

❋ ❋ ❋

The minute church was over, Loretta brought her daughter, Nona, up the aisle to Shiloh and Bonnie. "Where's the third one?" she asked.

"Abby stayed home today. Maybe she'll come next week," Shiloh said. "I'm pleased to meet you, Nona. You'll have to stop by the ranch and visit with us sometime."

Nona sure didn't look like she could ever be Loretta's daughter—or her sister, or even kin to her. They were both lovely women, but Nona was a short blonde who reminded Shiloh of Abby in girl clothing. She had big blue eyes and a small frame, a beautiful complexion, and a little bit of sass in her attitude. Yes, sir, she looked more like Abby's sister than she did Loretta's daughter.

"And this"—Nona pulled a man away from a group of people—"is my husband, Travis. We've only been married a few weeks. Y'all ladies want to come to Sunday dinner at Lonesome Canyon with us today? There's always plenty and we'd love to have you."

"Not today," Rusty said. "I got a text message from Cooper that said he was taking steaks over to the Malloy Ranch to cook dinner for us. Maybe we could take a rain check."

"Anytime," Nona said. "Oh, wait a minute. Waylon, come on over here and meet two of Ezra's girls." She motioned toward a cowboy on his way out the door. He turned around and waved, then made his way back through the crowd to where they were standing in a group near the front pew. Shiloh's chest tightened when she saw his blue eyes.

"This is Shiloh and this is Bonnie. The oldest one, Abby, stayed home today, but you'll meet her before long. They all three have Ezra's blue eyes," Nona said.

He shook Bonnie's hand first and then Shiloh's. "My pleasure, ladies. I live across the road from Malloy Ranch. Drop by anytime."

"Guess we'd better be going," Nona said. "Maybe we can have a girls' day out some Sunday afternoon."

"Know where there's a good spa?" Shiloh asked.

"Oh, yes, I do. I'll call you or come by and we'll make some plans," Nona said over her shoulder as Travis escorted her toward the door with a hand on her back.

Shiloh wished Waylon had his hand on her back. As handsome as he was, she would have let him lead her anywhere.

"Steaks?" Bonnie asked Rusty.

"That's what his text said."

"I hope Abby didn't scare him off or kill him. I could sure eat a big juicy steak," Bonnie said.

※ ※ ※

"Sounds like they are here. We'll see how your sisters like their steaks, and then I'll start cookin'. I hope they didn't invite cowboys home with them, because I only brought five."

"I'm not sharing a single bite of my steak. If one of them brought home a gold-digging cowboy, then she gets to share hers," Abby said.

A cold north wind pushed its way inside along with three adults and three dogs when the front door slung open. The dogs headed straight to the rug in front of the fireplace, even though only embers still burned there.

Cooper and Rusty had played on the same football team, had been in Future Farmers of America together, and had tied more than once for the grand champion steer at the county livestock show. Rusty had proven to be a damn fine quarterback for the Silverton Owls even as a sophomore for their six-man football team. He had an arm that could put a ball into the hands of a receiver every single time.

"I just need to know how y'all like your steaks and dinner will be on the table pretty quick," Cooper said. "I'm talkin' to Shiloh and Bonnie. I know that Rusty likes his medium rare."

"Same," Shiloh said.

"Me, too," Bonnie said.

Rusty removed his coat and hung it on the back of a wooden rocking chair that had been drawn up to the fireplace. "While Cooper plays chef, there's something we should discuss."

Shiloh had been on her way to her room but she stopped, came back, and tossed her denim duster over the back of the sofa. Bonnie unzipped her leather jacket but kept it on. They sat down on opposite ends of the sofa and waited.

Abby rested her elbows on the back of the sofa between the other two women and snapped half a dozen pictures of them, Rusty, and Cooper, with her phone.

"What are you doing?" Bonnie asked.

"My best friend, Haley, wants to see pictures of y'all and of the canyon, so I took a few," Abby answered. "Now what did you want to talk about, Rusty?"

"We are about out of leftovers. I promised Ezra to teach y'all the basics of ranchin' so this place wouldn't go to ruin if one of you did stay on and inherit the place. I did not promise to teach you to cook," he said.

"You said we'd fend for ourselves," Abby said.

"I did, and that's fine when there's a refrigerator full of leftovers, but now it's time to amend the rule. We work all day starting tomorrow. There's still some land I want to clear to plant alfalfa on this spring. I need extra hands and I don't want all of y'all trying to fix food at the same time in a one-hour lunch break."

"And?" Shiloh asked.

"And I've laid out a plan. After basic chores, which everyone helps with seven days a week, you three will do a rotation with cooking," he said.

Shiloh raised her hand. "I'll go first."

"Fine, you on Monday, Bonnie on Tuesday, and Abby can have Wednesday and then it starts all over again. Figure out what you plan to cook on your days each week and Sunday afternoons I'll make a trip to the grocery store. The day that you cook, you do basic chores, then you get to come to the house to fix lunch and catch up on laundry and cleaning. Whatever you see needs done, do it. After lunch you go to the fields with everyone else," he said.

"Why aren't you on the rotation?" Abby glanced into the kitchen. She'd rather be in there with Cooper than listening to talk about sharing cooking duties. "Or are you like Ezra and think that the kitchen is for a woman?"

"Hey, now," Cooper protested loudly from the kitchen.

"Abby, if you don't want to cook, you can take it up with your sisters, but we're not wasting time or settling arguments in the kitchen every day," Rusty said.

"Sir, yes, sir!" Abby saluted.

Rusty frowned.

Cooper chuckled. "Think you could get those other two to give you that kind of respect?"

"I wasn't in the army and I'm not saluting anyone," Shiloh said.

"Sundays?" Bonnie ignored the remark.

"No one has Sunday kitchen duty," Rusty said. "Since we don't work other than normal feeding chores on that day, I don't give a shit if y'all kill each other in the kitchen. If you want to go into Amarillo or go sightseeing or out on a picnic with one of the cowboys you met in church, then it's your day to do so," he said.

"And after the work is done at night?" Shiloh asked.

"That's your business, not mine," Rusty said.

"Fair enough," Shiloh said.

"What if one of them can't cook anything but chili pies?" Cooper asked.

"Then I guess we'll eat Frito chili pies every third day. No bitchin' and moanin' about the food, ladies. On a ranch we eat what's put before us," Rusty said.

❊ ❊ ❊

Abby took a deep breath and straightened up, glad that Shiloh had offered to take the first day. Then Bonnie had Tuesday, which meant Abby would be cooking Wednesday and Saturday. She should serve chili pies both days.

*But you won't.* The voice in her head sounded a lot like her mother's.

No, she wouldn't. Her mother had taught her to shoot a gun, change oil, and fix a flat and a million other things, including cooking.

"Thank you, Mama," she mumbled under her breath on the way back to the kitchen.

"Who are you talking to?" Cooper asked.

"The voice in my head," she answered. "I'll put out the rest of the leftovers. The table is set. Y'all drinkin' sweet tea?"

"Yes," Bonnie and Shiloh answered at the same time.

Rusty nodded. "And, ladies, Cooper and I are leaving for Amarillo right after dinner, so be thinking about what you need for your cooking days."

"Just so y'all know, on my mornings to cook, I don't mind dusting or vacuuming or even moppin' the kitchen floor, but I don't clean your rooms and I don't do your laundry. That's your responsibility on your cookin' days," Bonnie said.

Yes, sir, Bonnie would do well in the army and with a little encouragement, she could go far. Abby was reminded of that old movie with Goldie Hawn where she enlisted in the army after a drunken binge. What was that thing called?

She wrinkled her brow, trying to remember and finally blurted out, "*Private Benjamin.*"

"Who?"

"I like that old movie," Cooper said. "It was one of Grandpa's favorites. Never knew him to watch much except anything that starred John Wayne and like I said before, *Gone With the Wind* once a year, but he did like that one."

Bonnie flipped her blonde hair back over her shoulders and suddenly Abby felt downright dowdy. There was Shiloh in a cute little plaid skirt that skimmed her knees, high-heeled dress boots, a dark blue sweater, and big gold hoop earrings. Her makeup was flawless and her hair had been curled that morning. And Bonnie, even in her skin-tight column dress with buttons down the back and those cowboy boots, looked like a French model.

"Are you calling me Private Benjamin because I said I'm not doing your laundry?"

"No, I was thinkin' you'd do well in the army." Abby picked a blonde hair from the shoulder of her black turtleneck and carried it to the trash can. She quickly scanned the rest of her shirt to make sure none of Cooper's hairs had been left behind. When she looked up, he was staring right at her and he winked as if they were thinking the same thing.

"Not me. I'm going to raise cattle, pigs, and chickens and make a garden. I've already been out there and checked it out. I'm thinkin' we should enlarge it by half and put in extra potatoes and maybe some sweet potatoes. I'm here to stay and a bigger garden would cut down on the grocery bills."

Abby had no doubt that Bonnie believed it at that moment. The determination in her expression said that no one could change her mind and they'd best not even try. But if summer in the canyon was as brutal as Abby imagined it could be, come July Bonnie might even beg Abby to suggest a recruiter.

"Y'all ready to eat?" Cooper asked.

"Soon as I get this list finished," Shiloh said.

Abby whipped around to see both of her sisters busy writing down things on notepads they'd pulled from their purses. She hadn't even given a second thought to what she'd cook those two days and there they were handing their lists to Rusty. Crap! She didn't even have a notepad in her purse. For a woman who'd kept entire companies of soldiers in line, she was sure getting slow about getting her ducks lined up in a pretty row on the ranch.

"I'll get mine done right after dinner," she said.

"Should we compare notes so we don't have the same thing two days in a row?" Shiloh asked.

"Rusty said we eat what's put before us," Abby answered. "Don't y'all go makin' chili pies. That's the only thing I know how to cook."

"I hate chili," Bonnie said.

"There's always peanut butter and jelly sandwiches," Abby said.

"Steaks are ready. Food is on the table," Cooper said.

Shiloh raised an eyebrow. "Real plates?"

"It's Sunday," Abby said.

"When my granny was living, we had a special meal on Sunday like this. I always looked forward to it after I went to church with her and Grandpa," Bonnie said.

Cooper nodded. "When my granny was living, we did the same. Invited folks over to dinner after church and enjoyed the fellowship. And she always got her best plates down for that day. So who all was at church? Did I miss anything?"

"Loretta and Jackson invited us to dinner, but I told them you were cooking steaks here," Rusty said.

"We met several people," Shiloh said.

Bonnie continued. "Nona and Travis and a cowboy named Waylon that sure was cute."

"I'll tell him you said that next time I see him. Did he tell you that his spread is out there across the road from y'all?"

"He did," Shiloh said.

Rusty passed the big bowl full of potatoes to Cooper, who handed them to Abby, their hands touching in the transfer. The instant hot sparks let her know that the sex had not ended the attraction one bit. If anything, it had intensified the sparks. She sent the bowl on down the table to Shiloh and tried to focus on the steak on her plate.

Rusty picked up the bread and sent it around. "He's bitten off a chunk, trying to run that ranch by himself until spring when he can bring in a couple of hired hands. He needs a good woman to help him run the place."

"What about you, Cooper? Do you need a good woman?" Bonnie asked.

Cooper picked up his fork and knife, cut off a piece of steak, and held it in the air while he answered, "Jackson beat my time. I've always loved redheads since the first time I laid eyes on Loretta. If I can't have her, I might just be an old bachelor."

"Isn't she older than you?" Bonnie asked.

Cooper popped the bite of steak into his mouth and opened up his foil-wrapped potato and shoved butter and sour cream inside while he chewed. "By about ten years, but I didn't care. I was eight and she and Jackson were both eighteen. That was the year she got pregnant with Nona and they got married."

Abby quickly did the math in her head. "More than twenty years between their two kids and not any between?"

Rusty shook his head. "She and Jackson got crossways when Nona was about three or four. I don't remember much about it since I was just a little kid then, too, but my mama talked about it. Loretta took Nona to Oklahoma and divorced Jackson. Then, last summer, Nona got it in her head she wasn't going to finish college—that she was going to learn ranching from her daddy." He paused to take a bite of steak, then went on with the story. "So here came Loretta, like a class-five tornado. If y'all had been here a couple of weeks ago, you could have gone to their wedding. It was Ezra's last time to get out in public."

"When is she due?" Shiloh asked. "She looked like she could drop that baby in church this morning."

"It's twin girls due sometime in the early spring," Cooper said.

"Ezra said it's in the water down here in the canyon. If a man drinks it, all he's going to throw is girl babies," Rusty chuckled.

"What about when you add tea and sugar? Does that make a difference?" Abby asked.

"Wouldn't know, but it sure wouldn't hurt for us to keep that in mind, Coop." Rusty's light green eyes twinkled behind the thick lenses of his glasses.

"Wonder if a little bit of Jack Daniel's would make a girl baby all sassy and hard to get along with?" Cooper bumped his elbow against Abby's arm.

"Probably that's how you get twins." Immediately she wondered if her mother had shared a shot with Ezra the night that she was conceived. A glance at Shiloh and then one at Bonnie convinced her that most likely all three of Ezra's wives had done a little sipping with him. Hell, that might be what it took for the women to crawl into bed with that man.

*Stop it! You read your mama's letter the day she died, so admit that she loved Ezra and stop making excuses.*

"Loretta told Ezra that it was his white lightning that caused the twins, and with her temper in the mix already, poor old Jackson sure doesn't need twin daughters with extra sass thrown in," Rusty said.

"Oh? So where did Ezra get white lightning and what's that got to do with Loretta and her twins?" Shiloh put two heaping spoonfuls of corn casserole on her plate.

"She came here one time to talk to him for advice and he gave her a glass full of his moonshine. He said he cured her of her problems and she agreed with him, but at Nona's wedding she told him it was the white lightning that caused her to get pregnant. He made it up next to the canyon walls every year—mostly just enough for himself and to share with someone he liked, but that wasn't often."

"I kinda doubt that was the whole cause Loretta got pregnant." Abby laughed and it felt good. The only time she'd sat around a family dinner table in the past twelve years had been when she came home for short visits to take care of business. Her favorite part of the visits had been sitting around the table either at Haley's house or at her parents' place with old folks and kids all talking at once.

"Ezra made 'shine? Was it any good?" Bonnie asked.

"The best," Cooper said.

"You might change your mind if you had some of mine." She smiled.

"You do a little sideline business, do you?" Rusty asked.

"Have in the past. Mama's granddad taught me the particulars before he passed on. At sixteen, I was making a fine apple pie. Good 'shine should have a little flavor, or else it's nothing more than white lightnin'. A woman is known in the holler by her secret 'shine. Mine was apple pie. My granny's had a little taste of peach."

"I've got a jar down in the bunkhouse. Ezra's instructions were to open it up and share it with whoever is still here one year from his death. If no one is, then me and Coop will share it to celebrate my ranch bein' right next to his," Rusty said.

"Darlin' you'd best get out more than two red plastic cups when you open that jar, because I'll be here and it could be these other two won't give up and run away," Bonnie said. "Maybe we'll put in a couple of rows of corn in our garden. I like to work with my own homegrown corn. You didn't tear down the still, did you?"

Rusty shook his head. "It's still back there in an old huntin' cabin built right into the canyon wall."

"Good." Bonnie flashed him a brilliant smile.

"Bonnie inherited Ezra's 'shine ability. What did you get, Abby?" Cooper asked.

"His stubbornness," she said quickly then wished she could cram the words back into her mouth. She should have said that she got nothing from him because she sure didn't want to have even one tiny cell in her body like Ezra Malloy.

"And you?" Rusty looked over at Shiloh.

She pushed her dark hair over her shoulder. "Mama said that I had his temper and his blue eyes. 'His mean blue eyes' is what she actually said."

"I haven't seen that," Rusty said.

"You haven't crossed me."

On the outside Shiloh was the quietest one of the three, but evidently there was a fair amount of grit on the inside. That meant she would most likely fight for her place on Malloy Ranch.

"Shit," Abby huffed.

"What was that?" Cooper asked.

"Thinking out loud," she said.

"Ezra did that. He said *shit* under his breath a dozen times a day when something didn't go the way he wanted," Rusty said. "A part of him will live on with y'all here."

All three sisters looked at each other and rolled their pretty blue eyes toward the ceiling. They could read each other's minds in that moment, because they were all thinking the exact same thing. Each of them wanted their own ranch, but they sure didn't want to be compared to the man who'd made it a possibility.

# Chapter Six

The wind whipped Abby's hair around her face to the point that she was spending more time pushing it back than throwing hay off the back of the truck for Bonnie and Shiloh to cut loose and kick around for the cows. She finally bent at the waist and gathered it up in a high ponytail with her fingertips, then secured it with the rubber band she found in her pants pocket.

Bonnie slapped a cow on the flank to get her to move to one side. That girl had spunk. Yes, she did. She hadn't shown fear of anything since she got there and she spoke her mind. Shiloh was a different story. She'd been reserved, but she reminded Abby of a lit stick of dynamite.

"Hey, Rusty," Abby called out above the whistling wind, "how much does that big round bale machinery cost?"

"Anywhere from three to ten thousand dollars would be about right. We could probably pick up a really good used one for five thousand," he said.

"And how much does a round bale weigh?" she asked.

"From a thousand to twelve hundred pounds."

"That means we could bring two out here in the winter once a day, right?"

He opened the truck door and stepped out. "You'd need a spear to attach to the front of the tractor, which would be another five hundred or so, but yes, that's right. The other thing about the big bales is that you don't have to hire haulers to get it from the pasture to the barn. You can just line them up against a fencerow and they're waiting there for you when you need them."

"I'm buying that stuff next January when these other two sell out to me," she said.

"It ain't happenin', woman." Shiloh's cold blue eyes could have frozen her on the spot.

"We'll have to make small bales this year and believe me, you'll want the machinery for the big ones after a long, hot summer of hauling hay," Rusty said.

"I wouldn't think this red dirt would produce anything but cactus and wildflowers," Abby said.

"You'll be amazed what happens with a little irrigation. There's a shallow creek that weaves its way over here so the water doesn't cost us anything. Most of it's over on Lonesome Canyon, but a nice wide loop comes through Malloy Ranch. That's it, ladies. Time to take care of the pigs, milkin', and chickens and then Shiloh can go to the house until after dinner and you other two are with me," he said. "Don't forget your gloves."

※ ※ ※

Abby could hear the truck coming before she could see it. When the vehicle stopped on the other side of the fence, Sheriff Cooper Wilson crawled out, shook the legs of his trousers down over his boot tops, and waved.

"What is he doing here?" Abby asked.

"I called him," Rusty said.

"In sheriff's capacity?" Bonnie asked.

"Yes," Rusty answered.

Abby fiddled with a small plastic bag in her pocket, took out a lemon drop, and popped it into her mouth. Oh, yes, she was definitely suckin' on the bitter to get to the sweet. Hauling tree limbs and sticks to a brush pile was not her idea of learning how to ranch and take care of cattle, but there wasn't a way in hell she was going to let Bonnie get ahead of her.

She'd been so proud of herself that morning—she'd gone all of thirty minutes without even thinking about Cooper, and now there he was. She looked like warmed-over sin on Sunday morning and he was all sexy in that starched uniform and the distressed leather jacket.

Cooper stopped at the barbed-wire fence and propped his elbows on a wood post. "Looks like y'all got a good runnin' start. So how do you women like ranchin' today?"

"I've cleared land before," Bonnie said.

"It's all work. What are you doing here?" Abby couldn't get the memories out of her mind—the way his hands felt on her body, his lips on hers, or the way his eyelashes lay on his cheekbones when his eyes fluttered shut. It had been a wild, crazy mistake and couldn't happen again. And yet she wanted the thrill of his kisses and his body next to hers again and again. Subconsciously, she'd hoped a one-time stand would take him out of her mind; it hadn't. Consciously, she'd known it would be awkward; it wasn't. He acted like it had never happened, standing there with his legs slightly spread and leaning on the fence post.

*I told you not to shit in your nest*, her inner voice reminded her.

"Earth to Abby," Cooper said.

"What?"

"You asked what I was doing here. I was talking, but you were a million miles away." Cooper pointed at the brush pile. "Rusty called and wanted an opinion about burning this pile of brush. It's polite to call the neighbor if you're about to set fire to something this close to his ranch."

"Fire?" Bonnie asked.

That single word caused Abby to remember the heat of his hands as they roamed over her body, the warmth of those few minutes of afterglow, and the way her heart raced every time his hand touched hers.

"Hey." Cooper reached across the fence and touched her on the arm. "Are you okay?"

"I was just wondering why we needed to burn all this," she said a little too quickly. Hopefully, he didn't feel the delicious little shiver his hand had caused to flutter through her whole body.

Rusty sat down on the biggest log in the pile and nodded toward the brush pile. "It would take years for this to rot and go back to dirt. We'll start the burn after dinner and it should be down to embers by evening. There'll be four of us keeping it from spreading and the wind is still so it shouldn't spark, Cooper."

"I'll come on back and help after I get off work, barring any catastrophic thing at the courthouse," Cooper said.

"I'd appreciate all the help you want to give." Rusty checked the time on his cell phone. "Hey, it looks like it's dinnertime. Shiloh was putting a roast in the oven when we left. You might as well come on up to the house and eat with us, Coop."

"I never turn down a home-cooked meal and it is my lunch hour. See you in a few minutes." Cooper jumped the fence the same way he had before and Abby bit down so hard on the lemon drop that it shattered in her mouth.

*You've tasted the fruit of the evil tree and it was pretty damn fine, but now you have to leave it alone*, the voice in her head said. "Hush," Abby said aloud.

"Are you talking to me?" Bonnie asked.

"I was arguing with the voices in my head," Abby said.

"Happens to me all the time. You know what Jerry Clower said about that?"

Abby frowned. "Who?"

"The comedian Jerry Clower?"

"Yes, I do. He said that if you're arguing with yourself, then you're about to mess up," Abby said.

"That's right. Listen to the voices. They're probably smarter than you think you are," Bonnie said.

"And what's that supposed to mean?"

"I thought my grandparents were old-fashioned and downright mean to me, but believe me, when I listen to the memories in my head, they steer me right," she said.

"And did they tell you to leave Kentucky and come to Texas?" Abby removed her gloves and followed Bonnie toward the truck.

"Damn straight, and they tell me every night not to let you run me off," Bonnie said.

"Me? What about Shiloh?"

Bonnie shrugged. "She don't intimidate the hell out of me like you do."

Abby crawled up in the back of the truck and backed up to the cab before sitting down. She wasn't about to tell Bonnie that she intimidated her, too.

If there was a pothole in the path back to the house, Rusty went out of his way to hit the damn thing. By the time he parked in the backyard, Abby was ready to tear down the blasted vehicle and change the shocks herself. She bailed out of the bed of the truck and saw the sheriff's car sitting in the front yard.

Maybe that was the trick to the whole mistake—think of him as the sheriff and not as Cooper, the man who'd created such turmoil in her heart and life.

She'd pulled the stocking hat off and stuffed it into her jacket pocket. Now her hair was a mess, her face was dirty from piling up the twigs and limbs that had gotten past the blade on the front end of the tractor, and her pocket was empty of candy. That was enough to put any woman in a foul mood.

"Well, Mama, what would you tell me to do right now?" she whispered.

The voice in her head giggled.

The table was set for four, but Shiloh added another setting with a smile when Rusty told her that Cooper was joining them. She was dressed in cute little designer jeans and a Western shirt that she'd tied at the waist, showing an inch of taut belly when she reached for the salt and pepper. Her dark hair was pulled up in a messy bun on the top of her head and she wore white socks on her feet.

Abby went to the sink to wash her hands. "What have you done all day besides put a good meal on the table?"

"Cooked. Cleaned the living room and did my laundry. I figure we can each take a room that we are responsible for keeping clean. I'll do the living room. You and Bonnie can fight over the kitchen and the bathroom. Oh, and talked to my mama. Have you called your mother since you've been here?" Shiloh asked.

"My mother died twelve years ago. I was eighteen and had just finished basic training," Abby answered softly.

Shiloh laid a hand on her shoulder. "I'm so sorry, Abby. I don't know what I'd do without my mother. She's been my support system my whole life—she and her sister, my aunt Audrey."

"Thank you." Abby's hand went up to cover Shiloh's. "Mama was mine until I lost her."

The temperature felt like it rose by ten degrees when Cooper joined them in the kitchen. Abby wished she had one of those church fans with Jesus and the little lamb on one side and a funeral home advertisement on the other. Cooper smiled. "Smells good in here. Roast is one of my favorite meals. Mind if I join you, Abby? I need to wash up, too."

"Ranks right up there next to pinto beans and ham, right?" Rusty said.

"That's what I've got planned for tomorrow." Bonnie smiled. "You should come back then, Cooper."

"Well, thank you, Miz Bonnie. I'd be honored." Cooper's hip was plastered against Abby's. His hands were with hers in the sink and they tangled up together as they rinsed the soap from them. Everything went so quiet that she feared her thoughts were sitting above her head in a bubble like in cartoons.

"What? Why is everyone looking at me?" she asked.

"What's on the Wednesday menu? We were talking about food," Rusty said.

"Frito pie." She flashed a brilliant smile. "If you like it I'll make extra, Cooper."

"Why don't we just issue a standing invitation, Coop," Rusty said. "Anytime you can get away, you are welcome here. There's three cooks, even if one says she can't make anything but Frito pie."

"Thank you, Rusty. I'll try to make it by real often. A bachelor does appreciate good home cookin'," Cooper said.

*Did you hear that?* the voice shouted at Abby. *He said* bachelor *and he was staring at you when he said it. He's content with his life and this wasn't his first one-time stand.*

"So are you one of those self-proclaimed bachelor-for-life-type men?" Bonnie asked.

"Are you about to ask him out?" Rusty teased.

"Not me. He's not my type," Bonnie answered.

"Ouch! What is your type?" Cooper asked.

"I'm not real sure what is, but I know what ain't, and that's a lawman," Bonnie said. "Now let's set down. Shiloh has done too much work for us to let it go cold."

Dinner was served on the table, family style. Shiloh had arranged the roast beautifully with the carrots and potatoes surrounding it. The gravy boat had a matching plate under it for passing ease and to catch the drip. Rolls were in a napkin-lined basket. Leave it to Shiloh to do everything up all pretty. Lord, it had been years since Abby had been responsible for putting a full meal on the table. And now she had to compete with pretty plates and gravy boats?

"If you decide to leave this ranch, I'll hire you to take care of my house and cook for me," Cooper said.

Instant jealousy washed over Abby. If there had been a mirror in the kitchen she would have seen a lime-green face when she looked into it. If she hadn't been so hungry and if roast wasn't on her list of top ten favorite meals, she would have gone to her room and eaten dinner out of her candy drawer. She shut her eyes to get everything in perspective. Then Cooper's arm brushed against hers as he reached for another helping of roast and there was another burst of warmth, making her all oozy inside.

Her eyes popped open so quick that the room was a blur until she could get things into focus. Bonnie bumped her knee under the table and when she glanced across the table, the insolent little shit winked as if she could read her mind.

Abby felt a blush starting on the nape of her neck. She downed half a glass of sweet tea trying to cool down from the inside, but be damned if Cooper's leg didn't touch hers under the table. She inhaled deeply, mentally tore down her Glock and reassembled it four times before she got control. Not once in all her life had a man affected her like Cooper Wilson. Not even the blue-eyed boy who'd been her first love while she was in high school. Or any of the military guys, and she'd always been a sucker for a man in a uniform.

"Save room for dessert," Shiloh said. "I made iced brownies, but I didn't know if everyone liked chocolate, so I put together an apple pie, too. Figured if we didn't eat it for dinner, we'd have it for supper and as a bedtime snack."

"I like both," Rusty said.

"Me, too." Cooper nodded.

"Lord, I'm going to have to take up jogging with Abby if we keep eating like this," Bonnie said.

"I'm not runnin' anymore. I figure as hard as we work, it's as good as any workout program," Abby said. "I'm having ice cream on both my brownie and my apple pie. I could never choose between those two desserts."

Shiloh smiled. "Well, thank you, Abby. There's plenty for everyone to have both. I cut the pie into six pieces and the brownies into a dozen."

"You done good on these dinner rolls, Shiloh. You'll have to teach me how to make them. Last time I tried, Abby could have used them as weapons of mass destruction," Bonnie said.

"It's in the technique, not the recipe. Maybe next Sunday we'll make up a batch for cinnamon rolls just for practice."

It was probably too late in the game for either of those women to be her sisters, but they could be her friends. She'd always made friends at every base she'd been assigned to. In the military a soldier needed friends to have his or her back. Sometimes when she left, she kept in touch with the people she'd known, but most of the time in the transitory world she'd occupied for twelve years, she'd simply moved on. This could be the latter. When the year was up, they might send a Christmas card occasionally or even call once in a while for the first year, but they'd move on. Still, it would make the year a lot more pleasant if they were friends.

Were they both struggling as much as she was? Shiloh had reached out to her, but Abby was the oldest, so she should have made the first gesture. And she should have made Bonnie feel comfortable enough that she didn't feel threatened.

Ezra had caused all of this by pitting them against each other. The smart thing to do if she wanted to thwart him was simply to work at getting along with her sisters. That would make the old fart turn over in his grave and start digging his way up out of that cemetery.

*Even if we all three stick around, it doesn't mean everything will be rosy and peachy,* the voice said.

Her mama had told her often, especially after a big argument, that anytime two people live together every hour of every day there will be disagreements. It didn't matter if it was a mother/daughter, girlfriend/boyfriend, or friend/friend relationship. Hollywood made millions off that very thing, because it was real life.

*Friends like Rusty and Cooper?* she asked herself as she listened to them talking about how much more hay Malloy Ranch would produce with the acreage they were clearing. In that moment she decided that she wanted to be more than Christmas-card friends with her sisters. She wanted a friendship with them like Rusty and Cooper had with each other.

Bonnie reached for the bread basket. "Wouldn't it be great if that mesquite we're uprootin' could be used for something other than firewood?"

"If it could, we'd all be rich," Abby said.

"Now if that didn't sound just like Ezra," Rusty chuckled.

Abby bristled, then relaxed. She couldn't run from her heritage. She didn't have to like it, but it was there forever as surely as the blonde hair she'd gotten from her mother. She glanced sideways at Cooper and for the first time in her life wished she had been born with flaming-red hair and had grown up to be a tall woman.

# Chapter Seven

$\mathcal{A}$ bonfire was a bonfire, whether it was on the beach or on the backside of a ranch in a deep canyon. To Abby that meant s'mores and hot dogs. Since there were no hot dogs, buns, or relish in the house, that left s'mores and she had the makings for those in her snack suitcase: chocolate bars, marshmallows, and graham crackers. Sometimes she had roasted a marshmallow over a candle to make one for herself when she was in Afghanistan.

Bonnie drove the tractor that afternoon and did a fine job of uprooting the mesquite trees. Shiloh, Rusty, and Abby took on the business of cleaning up the debris left behind and tossing it onto the two huge brush piles.

"Are we going to set fire to both of these things this evening?" Shiloh asked.

Rusty motioned for Abby to help him with a big limb. "Yes, we are. When Bonnie gets finished with those trees over by the wall of the canyon, we'll remove the front blade and add a tiller to the back. One of you is going to plow two widths around the whole area. That way the fire won't get loose and jump the fence onto the Lucky Seven."

"Why wasn't this land cleared before now?" Abby asked.

"Not enough help. Ezra was a tight old fart. Until that last two months, he didn't want help and he damn sure wasn't paying anyone but me. Even then, he bitched about writing my paycheck every single week," Rusty said.

"So it wasn't a happy relationship?"

"I wouldn't say that. We understood each other." Rusty flashed one of his rare bright smiles. "Ezra bitched and I bitched back. He was the grandpa I never had and I loved the old shit, even if he was cantankerous, opinionated, and determined, just like his three daughters. And both of you can stop shooting dirty looks at me. You can like it or not, but it's the truth. Every one of you is like him in one way or the other, but all of you got his temper and his determination."

"Hey, I'm glad you didn't start without me," Cooper yelled from the other side of the barbed-wire fence.

Abby spun around just in time to see him put a hand on one of the fence posts and clear the wire by several inches when he jumped over it. He'd changed into a stained work coat and faded jeans that fit tightly over his butt.

Her heart pitched in an extra beat when he got close enough she could see his face clearly beneath his black cowboy hat. He removed his coat and went right to work. The sleeves of his brown-and-yellow plaid flannel shirt strained at the seams when he picked up one of the biggest logs on the ground. She remembered well the way she'd felt when he slipped those arms around her waist—excited, protected, safe—even when they were tumbling off the sofa . . .

God, she needed a bite of chocolate or a butterscotch candy, but her pockets were empty. The s'mores makings were in a bag in the front seat of the truck, but she couldn't dip into those.

Suddenly, the only noise was the chirping of a few birds going to roost and a lonesome old coyote howling in the far distance. The tractor had stopped and Bonnie bailed out, went to the front, and started messing with the attachment in the front.

"Okay, time to change the blade to the plow. Pay attention," Rusty said.

"Will we be tested?" Shiloh asked.

"No test, but you only get one lesson, so learn it well," Rusty said.

"Yes, sir." Abby saluted smartly.

"You do that again and I won't teach you jack shit," Rusty said.

"Why?" Bonnie took a step forward.

"Because she's being insolent just like Ezra, and believe me that was one of the things I didn't like about him. I hated it when he talked down to me," Rusty said. "Understand?"

Abby's head bobbed up and down. If she'd been that pissy to any one of her training officers in the military, she'd have spent time cleaning the bathrooms with a toothbrush. She deserved the dressing-down, even in front of the other two, but it didn't make it sting any less.

"You're right, Rusty. That was rude and disrespectful. It won't happen again," she said.

"I'll show them how to get things changed," Cooper said. "Want me to plow a couple of circles around the fire?"

"No, I want Abby to do that," Rusty said.

"Punishment," Shiloh said under her breath as they headed toward the tractor.

"I deserve it," Abby said.

"Then I'll ride with her and teach her the method." Cooper jogged ahead of them.

"You've done this before, haven't you, Bonnie?" he said when he reached the tractor.

"Couple of times on an older tractor. Not much difference, though."

"It's pretty simple. Just unhitch, push the blade out of the way. Here, Abby, help me," he said.

"How much does this thing weigh?" she asked.

"Somewhere around a hundred and fifty pounds. Too heavy for you?"

"No, I can do it." She bent her knees and on Cooper's count to three, they picked it up and moved it a few feet away from the tractor.

Cooper was close enough that every burst of breeze brought the remnants of his shaving lotion to her, but not so close that their bodies or hands touched. Still, the air crackled around them like it does just before a storm and she had to remind herself that he was there to help as a neighbor and Rusty's friend. He hadn't jumped the fence for her.

"Now, Bonnie, hop back in that tractor seat, turn it around, and back it right up to the plow attachment beside the truck," he said.

Without a word she scrambled back up into the tractor and eased it toward the plow. Cooper jogged over in that direction and motioned with his hand until she was close enough, then he put up a palm.

"Good job," he said. "Abby, we'll have to get it lined up, but she did well enough that we'll only have to move it about six inches to the left. It weighs a little less than the box blade."

Abby picked up one end and he got a hold of the other and together they lined it up so it could be attached. Cooper didn't tell her she'd done a good job like he had Bonnie, but that was okay. The way he squeezed her hand when they got the thing fastened said that he approved.

Bonnie was back on the ground in a minute, everywhere at once, helping get the plow situated. "So how many times do I plow around the bonfire?"

"Rusty says I have to do it," Abby said.

"She's being punished." Shiloh leaned against the tractor tire and watched the procedure carefully.

"What for?"

"Insubordination, and I deserve it," Abby said. "I was being a smart-ass and I got called down for it."

"Takes a big person to take correction," Cooper said.

"Takes a foolish person to need it," Abby said.

"Is that a quote?" Bonnie asked.

"Yes, ma'am. Straight from my mama," Abby answered.

"Okay, Abby, you take the driver's seat and I'll get in the passenger's side," Cooper said.

"What is going on between you and Cooper? There's definite vibes every time he's around," Bonnie whispered when he circled around the back side of the tractor.

"I'm not sure. It's complicated," Abby whispered back.

"I bet it is." Bonnie nodded.

"Ever driven one of these before?" Cooper asked when she was settled.

"Not exactly, but I reckon if I can learn to drive a tank, I can learn this thing," she answered.

She put her hand on the gear stick and he covered it with his. Her first reaction was to jerk it free, but she took a deep breath and reminded herself that this was a driving lesson not a romantic episode. And yet, there was that sizzle that set her insides to yearning for the satisfaction that only Cooper could deliver.

"Not yet," he said. "First make sure the PTO—or power take-off—is on one, because you are pulling a plow, not pushing a box blade. That's the lever over there to your left." He removed his hand and pointed. "It's on one right now, but you want to check it every time and adjust it according to the job. Now, see that lever right there. It's got a high and a low range. High is for when you are driving the tractor home in the evening. You want low range when you are plowing the field."

"Okay, now what?"

"Ever driven a stick-shift vehicle? Maybe one with a trailer on the back?"

"Yes, I have in the army."

"Good, then the rest is pretty much like that. You've got four forward gears and a reverse. You'll probably want to work in first or second, and remember you are never shifting when you are on the move."

It took every bit of her concentration to think about what he was saying.

"Repeat all that back to me," he said.

"This one goes to one when we are plowing. This one is on low and keep it in first or second gear because we want to go slow."

"And use the clutch," he said. "Now it's time to go."

She took a deep breath, clutched, and put her hand on the gear stick. It sounded like she was tearing the thing apart and she looked over at Cooper.

"Clutch is tight. Push it all the way to the floor to engage the damn thing," he said.

She did and the noise stopped. Everything was in place, so she shifted her foot to the gas pedal and they took off so fast that Cooper was thrown backward.

"Slow down. We're going to plow, not run a race," he said.

She pulled her foot back a little. "Like this?"

"Yes, now drop the plow with that lever right there," he said.

It didn't take long to make two rows around the brush pile, but it was a hell of a lot harder than it looked and she was damn glad that Cooper had showed her the ropes. Instead of looking like a perfect square when she finished, it resembled a child's drawing of a circle.

"Now drive the tractor over there on the other side of the truck and park it. Remember to clutch when you put it out of gear," Cooper said. "And Abby, we need to talk about this thing between us."

"Right now?"

"No, but soon."

"I told you it would be awkward," she said.

"But that's just the point. It's not," he told her.

"And that makes it awkward, right?" she asked.

"I don't think so, but it's definitely something we need to discuss. Alone. With more than five minutes to spare."

"Okay, then." She opened the door. She looked forward to talking to him and yet dreaded it at the same time. The last time they were alone, they'd gotten themselves into this situation. She couldn't even control her thoughts now, so it would be a devil of a job to control her actions if they were alone again.

"You'll get better with practice. I should've told you that clutch was tight," Bonnie said the minute Abby's feet were on the ground.

Abby wiped her forehead with the sleeve of her jacket. "How'd you know so much about this?"

"Told you before, my mama's folks had a little farm down in the holler. Grandpa taught me to drive a tractor when I was so young that I had to sit on two pillows. My first plowin' job didn't look a bit better than that."

So Bonnie wouldn't be quitting the race, not when she was more qualified than either of the other two sisters. But that did not mean Abby couldn't learn. Before spring her plowing would be so sharp that she could write messages in the red dirt that could be seen from satellites.

"Since we have to be out here to watch the fires, I packed a picnic," Shiloh said. "I brought leftover roast beef sandwiches, chips, brownies, and a gallon of sweet tea. It's in the truck, so when the fire is lit we could have a tailgate party."

"Bless your heart," Rusty said.

"I brought stuff to make s'mores," Abby said.

"I brought one hell of a healthy appetite." Bonnie laughed.

"Looks like you hardworkin' ranchin' ladies thought of everything, and we thank you," Rusty said.

Cooper had gotten out of the tractor on the other side and smiled as he passed by her on the way to the tailgate supper. Her breath caught with a hitch in her chest. Just watching him walk sent desire spiraling. It wasn't a damn bit fair, but there it was right in front of her and it couldn't be denied. She could attribute it to funeral nerves, to physical attraction, to lots of things, but it still shouldn't have happened. Even if she'd wanted it to and even if she wanted it to happen again—like in the next five minutes.

Shiloh brought out her loaded paper sack and a roll of paper towels. Bonnie carried the gallon jug of iced sweet tea and five plastic cups and Abby picked up the small sack she'd shoved the s'mores items into. While they set up on the old truck's tailgate, the two cowboys lit up the brush piles. In minutes flames reached for the top of the canyon and heat found its way to the tailgate party.

Cooper grabbed three ziplock bags containing sandwiches and poured himself a glass of tea. He sat down on the cold ground, leaned back against the truck tire, and started eating.

Rusty picked up two sandwiches, a bag of potato chips, and a glass of iced tea and sat down on the edge of the tailgate next to the brownies. "Got to protect my dessert here."

"We're havin' s'mores. Didn't you hear Abby?" Bonnie asked.

"I like those things just fine, but not as much as I like these brownies." Rusty grinned.

"Bring your sandwich over here, Abby. You can sit on the running board," Cooper said.

"I told you so," Bonnie whispered.

Abby shook her head at Bonnie. "You have a big imagination."

She rounded the end of the truck and slid down beside Cooper, keeping a foot of space between them. "For a chance to sit down,

I'd latch on to Lucifer's tail. Draggin' brush is backbreaking work. Is all ranchin' like this?"

"Most of it. You ready to pack up your bags and go back to Galveston?" Cooper asked when she'd settled on the narrow ledge.

"Not yet, but it's tempting," she answered.

"Hey, Shiloh, this roast makes wonderful sandwiches," he called.

"Thank you." The response came from the running board on the other side.

"So," Abby said softly, "you ready to talk?"

"Not here," he said.

"What did you say, Abby?" Bonnie leaned around the end of the truck. "Were you askin' me something?"

"No, I was asking Cooper about his day at the sheriff's office," she said quickly.

Cooper raised his voice so everyone could hear. "I was about to tell her what happened today. I lost a damn prisoner. We gave him yard duty, which means he was supposed to pick up trash and that kind of thing. And he walked off the courthouse lawn and disappeared."

"What was he in jail for?" Abby asked.

"Drunk driving. I went out to the ranch where he's a hired hand and they said he caught a ride, packed up his things, and was already headed back to Mexico. His cousin, a truck driver, runs a route from somewhere near El Paso to Amarillo, so they thought he caught a ride with him."

"That happen often?" Bonnie asked.

"It's the timing," Rusty said. "It doesn't look too good when this next year is an election year and there are rumors that Cooper's deputy, Jim Westfall, is throwing his hat into the ring."

"How long is a term?" Shiloh asked.

"Four years," Cooper answered.

"You want to take it on for another four years?" Abby asked.

"Haven't made up my mind, but I'd hate to lose due to mistakes in judgment." Cooper changed the subject. "That's burning fast out there. Y'all might get to go to the house by ten if it keeps on like this."

"Ten?" Shiloh groaned.

"That's better than midnight," Rusty said.

"Ready for s'mores?" Abby asked.

"I'll sharpen up five sticks," Cooper answered. "You city girls know how to roast a marshmallow so it's toasted on the outside and melted in the middle?"

"Who are you callin' a city girl, cowboy?" Bonnie teased.

Cooper was the first one to get his cookie made and he held it out to Abby. When she reached for it, he shook his head. "No, ma'am, I don't give my toys away. But you can have the first bite since you provided the stuff to make it."

She was very careful to bite off a corner without letting her lips touch his fingers. The sparks flying off the burning mesquite bushes wouldn't be anything compared to the sizzle if that happened.

Cooper had called the time just about right. The fires had burned down enough by ten o'clock that they could kick dirt over the ashes and call it a night.

"Now what?" Bonnie asked. "Want me to drive the tractor back to the barn?"

"No, it can stay here—we'll plow the whole pasture tomorrow. It's time to go home and get some rest. Tomorrow will be another long day," Rusty said.

"Good night, everyone," Cooper said.

"Thanks for the lesson," Abby told him, wishing they had found a private moment to talk. Until they did, different ways that conversation could go would play through her mind on a continuous loop.

"You are very welcome. You're a quick study, Abby." Cooper slipped something in her hand when he passed by on his way to the fence. She quickly tucked the piece of paper into her pocket and joined the others at the truck.

Rusty dropped them at the house and went on to the bunkhouse. Abby made a mental note to walk back there sometime just to see where he did stay, but not tonight. As soon as she was in the house, she intended to call first shower and then fall into bed. Even a twenty-four-hour guard duty hadn't worn her out like working out there in the fields all day long. She was so tired candy didn't even sound good.

"I'm showering right now," she said as soon as they were in the house.

"I want a bath," Bonnie said. "Soon as you get finished in the shower, I'll start it. When it's done, Shiloh can get her shower while I'm in the tub. Organization is the key to getting to bed faster."

"What if I don't want to be in the bathroom at the same time you are?" Shiloh asked.

"Your choice. I'm calling second and I'm going to soak some of this grime off my body," Bonnie said.

Abby left them to their argument, gathered up her things from her room, and went straight for the bathroom. Ten minutes later she came out with a towel around her head and one around her body. She nodded at Bonnie, waiting in the hallway, and carried her dirty clothing toward the utility room, where she intended to start a load of laundry before she went to bed.

She crammed all of her things into the washer, added detergent, and was about to shut the lid when she noticed a piece of paper on the top of her camo jacket.

"Cooper's note!" she mumbled as she grabbed for it.

The only thing on it was a line of ten numbers, presumably his cell phone number, since he'd said they needed to talk. Strange as it was, they'd had sex, but neither of them had the other's phone number. That had to be the most ass-backward way of doing things.

She carried the number to her bedroom, where she dressed in plaid pajama bottoms and an army-green T-shirt, brushed her hair out, and sat down in the gold chair. The door squeaked when Martha pushed her way into the room. She curled up beside the recliner.

"Too late to call a man?" Abby dropped her hand over the side and rubbed the dog's ears. "It's only ten o'clock. What do you think, Miz Martha?"

The dog's tail thumped against the floor.

"I'll take that as a yes," Abby said.

Her phone was on the table beside the chair, so she picked it up and only hesitated a second before pushing the buttons. It startled her when he picked up on the first ring.

"I hoped you'd call tonight. Too tired to meet me at the cemetery?"

"Right now?"

"Or on your front porch?"

"Where are you?" she asked.

"I'm at home, but I can be on your porch in two minutes if I jump the fence and about seven if I drive over," he answered.

"It's cold and my hair is wet. We can talk in your truck," she said.

"I'll bring it in dark," he said.

She smiled at the military lingo meaning he'd turn off the lights and coast into the driveway to avoid any noise. Not that he'd have to do that with all the music on and the shower running in the bathroom, but still, it was considerate of him.

The truck was sitting beside hers when she reached the porch. She eased out the door with Martha right beside her and hurried across the cold ground, wearing her combat boots loosely laced and flopping on her feet.

She hopped inside the truck, leaving Martha outside. The dog ducked her head and ambled back to the porch to wait.

"Sorry," she said.

"For what?" Cooper asked.

"Martha came out with me. Now she has to wait in the cold."

Cooper's smile lit up the cab of the truck. "You could have put her in the backseat. Sometimes Delores—that's my grandpa's dog—rides back there."

"I'll remember that for next time," she said. "You called this meeting, Cooper. What do we need to talk about?"

"The fact that we got the cart before the horse."

"We sure did and it is making things weird. Do you have a girlfriend? If you do . . ."

He put up a palm and quickly said, "No, I'm not involved with anyone. I haven't dated in a year because I've been so busy. Did you ask because you have a boyfriend?"

She shook her head. "No, not in a long time."

"I really had a good time working with you tonight, but why are you learning to do any of this if you aren't planning to stick around?" he asked.

"It's in case I do decide to stay and become a rancher. I brought Mama's ashes with me and I want to scatter them somewhere in the canyon before I leave, but I want to do it in the spring when the flowers are blooming. Past spring, Cooper, I don't know what I'll do," she answered. "I want a place, but I want it to be the right place. I want to own property but I don't even know if I want a ranch or just a big yard with a white picket fence around it. Can't hurt to learn while I'm thinking about things."

"I see," he said.

"How could you? You were born and raised right here in the canyon. You've got roots so deep that a tornado couldn't uproot you. How could you understand all these conflicting emotions I'm having?" She turned in the seat to see him better. The moonlight defined half his face; the other half remained in shadow.

"Don't underestimate me, Abby. That quickie was as unlike me as it was you. I don't want you to think I'm a horndog. You don't want me to think you are loose legged. I vote that we put our mistake behind us and be good neighbors and maybe work on a friendship." He pushed a strand of blonde hair behind her ear.

"We're already that. Only a friend and a good neighbor would spend his whole evening helping burn mesquite," she said. He had no idea that his hands brushing against the side of her face sent quivers of desire to the depths of her insides. Or that sitting this close to him made her want to be more than a neighbor or a friend. But she couldn't offer more and he didn't appear to want more, so that's all she was going to get.

"Thank you. Maybe I'll see you tomorrow at dinner?"

"Yes, Bonnie is cooking. If she can cook like she does everything else, it should be good." She reached for the door handle, thankful the dark hid the slight trembling of her hands. "Good night, Cooper."

"Good night, Abby. I'm glad we settled this."

# Chapter Eight

Abby really wanted to get the hang of plowing down so that she could move on to the next lesson in ranching. That morning she checked everything three times before she fired up the engine. The first and most important thing was to know the machinery. That done, she'd work hard on technique.

"I can do this," she declared as she started off with less of a grind than she had the night before.

Shiloh and Rusty had left her to do her job and gone off to walk the fencerow, tightening up the barbed wire where it sagged and making sure the posts were secure. She tried to keep the furrows straight as she drove from one end of the pasture to the other. Her corners left a lot to be desired, but by the time she'd plowed under all the ashes from the brush fires, the furrows were getting straighter. Pride filled her heart. She hoped Cooper stopped by so she could show him how much she'd improved after just one lesson.

Speak of the devil—or the cowboy, in this instance—and he shall appear. She looked out ahead of her to see Cooper leaning on the fence separating the two ranches. He waved and her hands got all sweaty inside her work gloves. She jerked them off and tossed them over on the passenger seat. The stocking hat came off next and joined the gloves. Too damn bad she couldn't remove her boots and socks.

When she reached the end of the row, he jumped the fence and motioned for her to stop. When she did, he stepped up on the running board and waited for her to roll down the window.

"How does it look?" she asked.

"Doing a fine job. Little crooked there on the first run, but it won't affect the way the wheat or the alfalfa seeds sprout. Rusty said you were going to plow this morning and I was out dropping hay off for my cattle, so I thought I'd stay long enough to make sure you remembered all the gears and basics. Looks like you took to this part of ranchin' like a duck to water. See you later if I don't get tied up at the office and have to stay through the noon hour." He stepped off the running board.

She shut her eyes so that she couldn't see him walking away, but it didn't help one bit. That jittery feeling every time she was around him was still there. She opened them just in time to see him turn around and wave at her.

She waved back and started plowing again. Like she'd told Bonnie, it was complicated. Everything, it seemed, about her and Cooper was jam-packed full of twists and turns. One minute she thought she could be friends and neighbors with him; the next minute, when he was so close she could have leaned out the window and kissed him, she wanted so much more.

☀ ☀ ☀

Cooper was getting out of the sheriff's car when Rusty parked the work truck in the backyard. Cooper threw up a hand in a wave and headed for the front porch at the same time Rusty, Shiloh, and Abby went for the back one. They all met in the kitchen, where Bonnie was putting the final touches on dinner.

"I'm hungry," Shiloh said.

The house smelled wonderful, like ginger and ham and fried potatoes with onions. Abby's stomach growled loudly and she looked up to see Cooper smiling.

"Driving a tractor all morning is rougher work than it looks, isn't it?"

She nodded. "And I forgot to load my pockets with snacks, so I hope Bonnie made a ton of food."

"Y'all get washed up and I'll put it on the table," Bonnie said.

Rusty headed for the bathroom.

Shiloh raised an eyebrow at Abby. "Mind if I use your bathroom?"

"Sure, I'll take the kitchen sink," Abby said.

"Kitchen sink is big enough for two, don't you think?" Cooper asked when the others had disappeared.

"Probably for four since it's a double sink," Bonnie answered.

Abby squirted a small amount of liquid soap in her hands and rubbed them together. Cooper did the same, his side plastered against hers just like the last time they'd washed their hands together. He hip butted her to one side. She came back with her own hip and he chuckled.

"Bonnie, she's not playing fair," he tattled.

"You kids best behave or you won't get dessert."

Abby flipped water at him before she dried her hands. "What's for dessert? Maybe it's not good enough to be nice for."

Bonnie pointed toward the bar. Abby squealed. "Hot damn! That's pecan pie. What kind of cake is it? Doesn't look like chocolate."

"It's gingerbread and there's warm lemon sauce to go on top."

"And I thought you were just a country girl who only knew how to make beans and potatoes," Abby said.

Bonnie's giggle sounded as high-pitched as a little girl's. It didn't match the gravel in her voice or the look in her blue eyes that said she'd seen far more than anyone ever should. "A pot of beans in our house was a delicacy, darlin'."

"Ours, too. Mama made them in the slow cooker, but they weren't as good as the ones that simmered all morning on the stove, like these," Abby admitted.

"Do I smell something with ginger?" Rusty appeared in the doorway with his nose in the air.

"It's gingerbread with lemon sauce," Cooper answered. "I'm glad I didn't have to give up dinner with y'all like I thought I would."

"Why?" Rusty asked.

"Had a call that a rancher out between Silverton and Goodnight thought some kids were trying to run a meth lab out at the back of his property. My deputy and I went out there, but all we found was beer bottles and signs of lots of parties," Cooper said.

As he talked, Abby scanned him from boot tips to pretty brown eyes, spending an extra second or two on his belt buckle. She was tired of apologizing to the voice in her head for wishing that his lips were on hers again or that his hands were splayed out on her back. Fiery heat put high color in her cheeks. She hoped everyone thought it was a combination of the cold wind outside and the hot kitchen inside rather than her scorching thoughts about Cooper.

*Friends*, her inner voice reminded her.

*With benefits?* she argued.

*Don't start something you can't finish.*

"Abby, did you get that plowing down to an art?" Cooper dried his hands on the end of the same towel she used.

"Workin' on gettin' used to it. Don't know that I'm learnin' to enjoy it yet," she said.

"Okay, folks, sit down and let's get started. Noon hour is sixty minutes," Bonnie said.

They took their chairs and started passing food around from one to the other. Since Cooper sat right next to Abby, every time he handed off a bowl or platter to her, their arms bumped against each other or their hands brushed. It was both misery and exciting at the same time every time a fresh new jolt shot through her.

"I'm feelin' bad about comin' here for dinner, so I'm goin' to make y'all a deal. I'll provide dinner on Sunday. Either steaks right here when you get home from church since that's the only thing I can cook, or else I'll take the whole bunch of you out to dinner up in Silverton at the little diner there," Cooper said.

"Deal!" Abby stuck out her hand.

That way she'd cook on Wednesday and Saturday every week. Her days would be set and she'd never have to interrupt her Sunday sleep-in mornings to plan a meal.

"Deal," Bonnie agreed. "Abby can shake for all of us since you are closest to Cooper."

His hand engulfed hers and held a moment longer than necessary, even for a hearty shake. So she was special in his eyes now. He had to be crazy as an outhouse rat if he wanted to take friendship to a new level. Ezra was her father. That should tell him she'd make a lousy spouse and a horrible parent.

Cooper dropped her hand and smiled. "This is really good cookin', Miz Bonnie. You ever think of puttin' in a café of your own?"

"Hell, no!" Bonnie said quickly. "I can cook and I don't mind doin' it, but I damn sure don't want to cook every day."

"You want to make some extra money and cook for my poker night this Friday night?" Cooper asked.

Bonnie shook her head. "No, thank you. Pour up some chips and dip and put out the stuff for them to make sandwiches."

"So we're still on for poker and at your place later this week?" Rusty asked.

"Seven sharp," Cooper answered.

"Waylon and Travis?" Rusty asked.

Cooper nodded. "And Jackson if he can drag himself away from Loretta. I swear he's so happy about those twin girls, it's unreal."

"I could bring the leftover gingerbread to the poker game," Rusty said.

"Like hell you will," Abby declared. "If we don't get to play cards with the boys, then the boys don't get our gingerbread."

"Y'all play poker?" Cooper asked.

Bonnie giggled.

"What?" Shiloh asked.

"I would bet dollars to cow patties that she's played before and that she's damn good at it. She might own your ranch and maybe even your boots before the night was over if you played with her," Abby said.

Bonnie beamed. "I'm not that good."

"We'll take y'all on Saturday night, right here at this table," Rusty said.

"I'll bring the dessert for that night," Abby said.

Cooper laid a hand on her shoulder and their eyes locked across the space between them. "I thought Frito pies was all you knew how to cook."

"I know how to open a container of ice cream, squirt caramel sauce on it, add a dollop of whipped cream, and put a cherry on top." Abby smiled sweetly.

He quickly removed his hand and cleared his throat. "Saturday night it is. Seven o'clock unless I have an emergency. You ladies best go on and bring your Friday paychecks. You can just sign the backs when I win them from you. Rusty, did you tell them why Ezra's land is set so far back off the road?"

Rusty put a thick slab of ham on his plate and passed the ham to Cooper. "Story has it that Ezra and Jackson's grandpa got into a poker game. They were the only two left and Ezra thought he had a good hand, so he bet half his ranch on the win. Grandpa

Bailey put up half of his, which was a damn sight more acreage than Ezra had. Ezra spread out a straight flush and figured he'd just landed half of Lonesome Canyon. Grandpa Bailey had a royal flush and gave Ezra a choice. Front half or back half of Malloy Ranch. Ezra chose the back half because it was better land and had the house and the family cemetery on it. Grandpa Bailey gave him the easement if he kept up the road, so he could get back here to his ranch."

"And story has it that was the last time Ezra played cards. If you got his card-playin' genes, y'all might do well to leave the poker to the big dogs," Cooper said.

"Maybe none of us got our poker faces from Ezra. Maybe we got them from our mamas," Shiloh said.

"Or our maternal grandpas," Bonnie piped up.

Everyone looked at Abby, who shrugged. "Who said I have poker sense? I just offered to bring dessert, not wipe out the whole lot of you."

"That one will bear watching," Bonnie said.

"I agree," Cooper nodded. "Fantastic dinner, Miz Bonnie. I still think that you and Shiloh could put a restaurant in either Claude or Silverton and make a fine living."

"Haven't got time," Shiloh said. "I've got a ranch to run."

"And I done told you, I'm not interested," Bonnie said.

Abby felt eyes on her again as she reached for a second helping of ham. "What? I'm hungry. It takes a lot of food to make enough energy to work like we do."

"Chili pie for real? Twice a week?" Rusty said.

"It's kind of like poker, Rusty. Sometimes you'll get a good hand. Sometimes it'll be a real bitch. Pass the cucumber salad, please. We didn't get much of this kind of fresh stuff where I've been for three years."

"What was your job over there?" Shiloh asked.

"I commanded a company of soldiers. Only two people on base were higher ranked than I was."

"Wow! Now that would be a dream job, to get to command men and make them do what you said," Bonnie said.

"It was male and female soldiers," Abby said.

"I guess I just normally think of soldiers as men."

"Times have changed," Abby said.

Cooper cocked his head to one side. "Did you ever make decisions that you regretted later?"

"Of course," she said. The little girl in the window of that building came back to haunt her. In an instant her life was wiped out, but she would live forever in Abby's mind and in her dreams.

"You look like you just saw a ghost. We should change the subject," Shiloh said. "I'm ready for dessert. I'll bring it to the table if Bonnie will clean off a spot for it."

"I'll help Bonnie," Rusty said.

Cooper's hand rested on her shoulder again. "Sorry if I brought up bad memories," he whispered.

The warmth of his touch was welcome and almost put the little girl's dark eyes out of her mind. He squeezed gently and she managed a weak smile.

"Sometimes they appear at the craziest times," she said.

"Who wants which dessert?" Bonnie asked.

"I'd like gingerbread with lemon sauce. Mama used to make a gingerbread doughnut with a lemon-flavored glaze. I always begged her to save me one for an after-school snack. But I want pecan pie, too, and I'm too full for both. Bring me the gingerbread because I want it more," Abby said.

"I want a piece of each," Cooper said. "I'll share a bite of my pie with Abby so she can have a little bit."

Bonnie put two pie plates in front of Cooper. One held the pie, the other the gingerbread.

Abby glanced over at him and a big bite of pecan pie was heading straight for her mouth. There was nothing to do but open up. Eating from the same fork was almost too intimate.

"Well?" Bonnie asked.

"Heavenly," Abby said.

"Taste the gingerbread now and tell me which is best," Bonnie said.

Abby made sure there was plenty of lemon sauce on the bite she put into her mouth and nodded, giving Bonnie a thumbs-up sign. "Fantastic."

Neither dessert affected her like sharing a simple dessert fork with Cooper. Butterflies fluttered around in her stomach and she could scarcely keep the smile off her face. No one wanted to see gingerbread or pecans in her teeth, though, and she didn't want to explain why she was grinning like a Cheshire cat during dessert.

"Really good," Rusty said. "You could make both of these for the poker party."

"Nope. Abby is making dessert that night. She already volunteered," Bonnie said.

# Chapter Nine

 coconut crème cake chilled in the refrigerator along with a banana pudding. Abby would have made tiramisu, but she'd forgotten to put ladyfingers on her list when Rusty went to the store. If someone didn't like coconut or bananas, then they could have ice cream for dessert. The lasagna was ready to pop into the oven and homemade Italian bread was rising on the back of the stove with a towel over it. Salad makings were ready to toss together at the last minute.

She shouldn't have made a big deal about not knowing how to make anything but chili pie, but dammit, she hadn't planned on cooking for a family when she left Galveston. It felt as if she was losing control, being told to cook two days a week and to clean while she had the half day off from the ranch work to boot. And Abby did not like the feeling that loss of control brought into her heart and soul.

With the last load of laundry in the washer, she was ready to tackle the bathroom. It didn't look too messy at first glance, but neither had the communal ladies' room in the barracks in basic.

"So you belong to me on Wednesdays." Abby carried a bucket of cleaning supplies into the bathroom. "And I bet you've never been military clean in your life. Looks can be deceiving—if my old sarge put on the white glove, you'd find out you were filthy."

Starting at the far side with the toilet itself, she scrubbed the whole thing until it shone. She frowned at the apparatus holding the seat and lid onto the potty. She could see bits of mold down in the crevices and could hear the drill sergeant yelling at her as she stuck her white-gloved pinky finger into a valley just like that.

She needed an old toothbrush to get that area really clean, and she found one in the medicine cabinet above the sink, along with a dozen half-full bottles of prescription medicines, all with Ezra Malloy's name on them. She carried Ezra's toothbrush back to the potty and cleaned out those pesky little grooves.

"I can hear you doing flips in your grave, Ezra." She laughed. "Well, this is just a little bit of the punishment you deserve for your sins."

She checked the clock when she finished and smiled. It was exactly eleven thirty—time to remove the lasagna from the oven and set it on the table and put the Italian bread in the oven to bake. Mama always said that good lasagna had to blend flavors for thirty minutes after it was cooked, and Mama had been a fabulous cook.

Fifteen minutes later the salad was tossed in a chilled bowl. The whole house smelled like baking bread and the table was set.

The phone rang. She located it by following the sound into her bedroom and there it was, an old black rotary shoved under the edge of her bed. Thank God that thing had never rung before or she'd have gone into instant cardiac arrest. She sat down on the floor and answered it cautiously.

"Hello?"

"Hey, Abby, this is Cooper." As if she needed him to tell her his name. "I didn't want to ask in front of the whole family, but could I please have your cell phone number? You have mine and I figured yours would be in my phone in the recent calls area, but it has disappeared. I'd like to call you sometime," he said.

The phone smelled like cigarette smoke and there was a dirty ashtray under the bed, along with several cardboard boxes. Why hadn't she noticed those boxes before now?

*Because you haven't vacuumed your room or dropped anything close to the bed that you'd have to pick up*, that sassy voice in her head said.

"You still there, Abby?" Cooper asked.

"I'm sorry. Yes, I'm here." She rattled off the number.

"Thank you. Are you talkin' on the phone in Ezra's old bedroom?"

"I found it under the bed."

"I shoved it up under there when we took out the hospital bed. He kept the phone on the bed with him until he died. There is also a phone outlet in the living room if you want to move it in there. And you might want to know that he did not have a long-distance plan," Cooper said. "I'm leaving the office now. Be there at noon for my chili pie and ice cream."

She left the three boxes alone, but carried the ashtray and the phone with her to the living room. It wasn't hard to find the outlet for the phone because there was a light spot on the wooden table beside the rocking chair that testified the phone had sat right there for many years. The ashtray went into the trash can—butts, ashes, and all.

At five after twelve, Bonnie came through the back door into the utility room right off the kitchen with her nose in the air. "That is not chili. I was dreading coming home for dinner because the smell of that stuff gives me the dry heaves worse than drinkin' too much."

"Why?"

"Mama likes chili and Mama likes to drink. The morning after isn't too pleasant," Bonnie said.

A cold blast of air preceded Cooper from living room to kitchen. "That's Italian. I know oregano and basil when I smell it."

"And fresh-baked garlic bread," Rusty said.

Shiloh pushed Abby out of the way so she could wash her hands at the kitchen sink. "You lied. You can make more than chili pie."

"Disappointed?" Abby asked.

"I'll wash up in the bathroom since no one is using it today," Cooper said.

Abby's heart did a flip when she realized that he hadn't gone to the kitchen sink to wash his hands with Shiloh.

Shiloh shook her head. "I'm not a bit disappointed to have Italian for dinner today. I can get a chili pie at a fast food place or make it in five minutes anytime I want it."

"You can pop frozen lasagna in the oven anytime, too," Abby said.

"Darlin', Mama's people are Italian. You can't fool me. That's the good stuff, and that bread is not store-bought either."

"So that's where you got the black hair," Abby said.

"Yes, it is and half of my temper." She smiled.

"I haven't seen much of that yet."

Cooper returned from the bathroom. "Can I help put anything on the table?"

"We've got it, Cooper. And Abby, you haven't pushed me into a corner. If you ever do, you might get a taste of that temper," Shiloh answered.

After the funeral, they'd sat down randomly, but now they had their appointed places around the table—Rusty on one end, Shiloh on the other. Bonnie across from Cooper and Abby.

*Why does she get to sit at the head of the table? I'm the oldest,* Abby wondered as she settled in next to Cooper, the sparks flitting around the room like butterflies in the spring.

"You are left-handed," she spit out without thinking.

"Been that way my whole life," Shiloh said. "That is why I always sit where my elbows don't create a problem for the person sitting next to me."

"So was Ezra. Guess that's another thing you inherited from him. This is amazing, Abby. If Ezra had realized that hiring three women would make meals appear on the table like this, he might have parted with a few dollars to run the place," Rusty said.

"Damn fine food. Olive Garden can't hold a candle to this," Cooper said. "You can make this anytime you want, Abby. Oh, before I forget. The poker game is off for this weekend, Rusty. I've got to transport a prisoner down to San Antonio. Want to do a ride along to keep me company?"

"Stayin' the night?" Rusty asked.

Cooper nodded. "Leavin' at six o'clock Saturday morning. We need to get him to the station there by five o'clock and processed in. Then we'll stay the night and come back Sunday. We'll be home by bedtime."

"You women able to run this place for the weekend without me?" Rusty said.

"I reckon we can feed cows and gather eggs without you lookin' over our shoulders," Bonnie answered.

"Think you could get those two pastures plowed on Saturday without tearing up the tractors?" Rusty looked down the table at Shiloh and Abby.

"If we do tear up a tractor, I'll get out my toolboxes and have it all fixed by the time you bring your drunk ass home," Bonnie told him.

"Oh, yeah?" Cooper raised a dark eyebrow.

"Saturday is my day to cook, but we can always eat leftovers if Bonnie needs me to help her fix a tractor. Which reminds me, you will owe us big-time for not being here to cook dinner or take us out on Sunday, but I'm sure you will make it up to us the next week, right?" Abby said.

"Sure, I will." Cooper smiled.

"Then I vote that Sunday after church we go to Amarillo for shopping. We will have our paychecks before you leave, right?" Shiloh asked Rusty.

"Cash or check?" he asked.

"Cash," they all three said in unison.

"Pass the bread and salad. What kind of dressing is this anyway?" Cooper said.

"Homemade Italian," Shiloh answered for Abby. "And a good cook never gives away her secrets. This has a touch of something I don't recognize, but it's awesome."

Cooper bumped his shoulder against Abby's. "It's not bad for chili pie."

She bumped him back, not a bit surprised what it created. "Some days I get it right. Some days, the pigs wouldn't touch it."

His hand on her knee said that he didn't believe a word she'd said.

❄ ❄ ❄

The boxes under her bed nagged at her all afternoon as she cleaned out the barn, sweeping each stall and putting down fresh hay in case it was needed for calving season, which Rusty said would start any day. She hoped to hell Bonnie knew something about being a cow's midwife in an emergency.

She leaned the rake against the gate and sat down on a bale of hay to catch her breath. Why hadn't Rusty taken those boxes out of the room? He'd removed everything else but one ashtray and the telephone. The bed had even been stripped down, and there were no towels in her tiny little half bath. He had been thoughtful and left a couple of dozen hangers in the closet, and the place did smell like it had been sprayed down with a mixture of disinfectant spray and that stuff that takes away odors.

Switching thought tracks from her bedroom and the boxes back to the barn, she picked up the hoe and rake and carried them back to the tack room. Sucking in deep lungfuls of barn scents, she instinctively reached for a piece of hard candy. It was a trick she'd learned in the war zones, and it came in handy with her snack habit. If she was eating something, then her sense of smell wasn't so acute. But her pocket was empty and it was all Cooper's fault.

If he hadn't set her hormones into overdrive, she would have remembered to make a side trip back to the bedroom for her normal pocketful of anxiety prevention after dinner.

Think of the devil, and the cell phone will ring.

She fished it out of her pocket and hit the "Talk" button. "You are in trouble."

"What'd I do?" he chuckled.

"It's your fault I didn't put candy in my pocket and this barn smells like cows and rat piss," she said.

"What's candy got to do with that and how is it my fault?"

"We were talking about Italian food and I forgot to get my candy. Candy dulls the smell," she said.

"It does not. That's a psychological trick that they tell you over there to keep you from puking when you smell bombs and dead bodies."

"You are full of shit," she said.

"Not me, darlin'. I was in the National Guard for ten years and they pulled our unit for a nine-month tour in Iraq five years ago. I was not impressed enough with my extended vacation in the sand and sun to want to reenlist. But if you'd been there to cook lasagna for me, I might have."

"Five years ago I was in Afghanistan. Are you flirting with me? I thought we were just friends," she said.

"If I'd have known you were that close, I would have popped over for a beer." He laughed. "I called to fuss at you for lying about not being able to cook. And what would you do if I was flirting?"

"I'd tell you that you were making a big mistake," she said.

"Why? Flirting isn't falling into bed with each other again."

"Because it could lead to that, and you have roots and I have wings. I'm not sure they work too well together," she said.

"Maybe you could put down roots."

"Maybe you could grow wings."

"I'll never leave this ranch," he said.

"And I don't know if I'll stay on this one."

A long pause preceded his next statement. "The canyon has a way of getting into folks' blood. Loretta could tell you all about that. Once you've been here for a while and then leave, it haunts you and beckons you to come back home."

"Only if you left something behind," she said. "Loretta left Jackson behind and that's what haunted her."

"Be careful, Abby. It can sneak up on you. Want to go to the Sugar Shack with me some weekend for a beer?"

"Maybe. If you don't find a little brown-eyed doll in San Antonio this weekend who takes your eye. If you get a new girlfriend, she might not understand your friendship with the neighbor," she said.

"Jealous?"

"Not even a little bit!" she lied.

"I'm hurt," he chuckled. "I just knew you'd be all jealous and that would give me my ego trip for the whole day."

She crossed her fingers behind her back. "To be jealous would mean I am more than a friend."

Cooper's chuckle turned into laughter. "Now I'm really hurt. I might even be bleeding from a cutting remark like that."

"I've got another stall to clean and I'm sure you've got a county to save from drug dealers, cattle rustlers, and outlaws. See you tomorrow at noon. It's Bonnie's turn to cook and she might be making Italian too," Abby said.

"I'm not complainin' one bit. See you then."

Holy shit! She'd just agreed to go on a date with him. Her hands actually trembled at the thought of dancing with him.

*You are going to the local bar for drinks. You'd go with Haley and not think a thing about it, so why not with Cooper?*

*Because*, she argued with her conscience, *I'm not attracted to Haley and I am to Cooper. I'm going, but . . .*

She stopped and thought about all the thousand *but*s she should consider before she opened that can of worms.

Number one, the biggest *but* in any equation, was never start something that couldn't be finished. It showed poor judgment. It didn't matter how his touch made her feel—nothing could last between them. Her fault, not his. She had a deep fear that she'd be like Ezra when it came to a permanent commitment and parenthood and another fear that she'd demonstrated exactly the latter when she blew up that building with the little girl inside. Cooper deserved better than that.

*But* number two stated that it was better to nip something in the bud. If she stayed in the canyon, Cooper was and would always be her neighbor.

"But the flirting and the bantering is so much fun," she whispered. "I like him. I really do. He's a decent man."

She finished the last stall seconds before she heard two tractors and a truck pulling up outside the barn. Rusty's glasses fogged over when he left the cold and came into the tack room.

"Time to call it a day," he said.

Without the glasses, his eyes weren't nearly as big and there was a softer look about his face. His lips weren't as firm and hard looking, yet his chin was stronger. Standing with his feet apart, his jeans tight, his boots scuffed from work, wearing his standard mustard-colored work coat, he'd make any woman take a second look. Yet not one single spark flickered between them. She felt like she was looking at a cousin.

"What?" he said as he put his glasses back on.

"Nothing. When do we get to see the bunkhouse?"

"Anytime you want to after you've been here a year and run me off the ranch," he said. "Until then, by the will Ezra left behind, it belongs to me. I will tell you that it's small and only houses six men at the most. Oh, and when it's my time to host poker, we play down there."

"Rusty, I don't think any of us will be firing you. As far as I'm concerned, you'll have a job on the ranch as long as you want it," Abby said.

"Thank you. We'll have to see how long I want it. Now, let's call it quittin' time. Even old slave driver Ezra knew a body needed rest after long days of hard work." Rusty smiled.

She stopped long enough to make a ham sandwich out of yesterday's leftovers, put it and a handful of chips on one plate, and use a second one for a huge slab of coconut crème cake. With a can of beer under her arm, she made her way to her bedroom with barely a nod at Shiloh, whose head was thrown back on the sofa, or Bonnie, who'd let all three dogs into the house to lie on the rug in front of a cold fireplace. When she started down the hallway, Martha got up and meandered toward the bedroom with her.

"Let me grab a shower first," Bonnie groaned. "No, I'm having a bath—a long one to get the aches out of my poor body."

"I'll go second. I'm halfway into a romance book I want to finish tonight," Shiloh said.

"See y'all in the morning." Abby carried her food to her room.

She sat cross-legged on the floor, her food spread out around her. Martha plopped down beside her and she fed her bits of cake, sandwich, and even chips. Bonnie hadn't said that anything but chicken bones would hurt the dog, and the old girl seemed to really like cake.

She could see the corner of one of the boxes. They probably contained exactly what was advertised on the end: three sets of Corelle dishes in that old modernistic gold pattern that was popular when the dishes first came out. There were even a few of them left in the mismatched set of plates in the cabinet. But right there in bold Sharpie letters on the end of each box were her initials—AJM—and she wanted to know why. How in the world had he even known her name? Her mother had said that he hadn't wanted to see her or to know what she'd been named.

She pulled all three boxes out to find numbers on the tops. One, two, and three—evidently she should start with one, since Ezra had made it easy. It had to be his handwriting, but the perfect numbers and letters had an almost feminine slant to them.

"So he was a perfectionist?" she said.

Pushing her half-eaten sandwich to the side, she decided she would give the rest to Martha. She upended the beer, taking several long gulps.

"Maybe I need some of his white lightning before I open the boxes," she mumbled as she pulled number one closer.

The tape was yellowed and peeling on the first box. The second one had started to turn colors, but it was still stuck down fairly well. The third one looked fairly recent.

"So he closed them up and never looked back?" She frowned.

She slipped a fingernail under the tape on the first one. It tore lengthwise, leaving some of it stuck firmly. After three tries, she pulled a knife from her pocket, flipped it open, and slit the tape.

"Files?" The frown deepened as she pulled them out. All neatly kept in manila file folders with years printed on the outside in the same slanted hand.

She started with the first one, dated 1984. It held her mother and Ezra's original marriage license and a copy of her birth certificate. She'd weighed seven pounds and seven ounces, had come into the world at twenty inches long on November 16, 1984, at seven thirty a.m. There was a picture of her in the hospital nursery that had begun to fade and one of her in a bassinet on a sun porch.

"Mama, he threw us out. Paid you to leave and promise you'd never come back to the canyon and you sent him pictures of me? What was wrong with you?" Her voice caught in her throat and it took the rest of the beer to swallow down the lump.

There was one folder for each of her first ten years in the box with the number one on the top. Each one held newspaper clippings, report cards, and awards that she'd gotten at school. It ended with a picture of her building a sand castle on the beach with her mother.

Box number two covered her life for the next ten years. It wasn't until she got to the end and found the copy of her mother's obituary in the local newspaper that reality dawned.

"Mama didn't do this. We were stalked." Goose bumps the size of the canyon wall raised up on her neck and arms. "But why? He didn't want me because I was a girl, so why would he even care what I did?"

The third box covered from ages twenty-one to thirty, ending with her separation papers. Lord, the man had copies of every commendation and promotion she'd gotten. The only thing missing were actual pictures of her in Afghanistan and Kuwait. Evidently it had cost far too much to hire an investigator to go that far.

It was all surreal, sitting there looking at her life. "But he only knew what I did and what I looked like; he didn't know who I was. Mama knew the important things."

She returned the smoky-smelling folders to their proper boxes and shoved them back under the bed, unwound her legs from sitting cross-legged and went straight to the closet for a bag of miniature candy bars. It might take every one of them to get her through the next hour until bedtime and then she wasn't sure she would be able to sleep.

Her phone rang and she dropped the candy like she'd been caught stealing money from a bank vault.

"Hello," she answered cautiously.

"Abby, are you okay? Your voice sounds strange."

"Hello. Did you know about the boxes under the bed?" she asked abruptly.

"No, was I supposed to? Is this some sort of a horror movie?" Cooper asked.

"Did you know that Ezra stalked me my whole life and that he kept files on everything I ever did?"

"No, I had no idea."

"Well, he did."

"You want to talk about it?"

"I don't know. I'm in shock and I don't understand why he'd do that if he didn't want me."

"Meet me in the hay barn. I can hop the fence and get there faster than if I drive over," he said.

She started to say something, but the television noise behind him had stopped. When she looked at the phone, she realized he had ended the call. She picked up the disposable plates and headed toward the kitchen, glad to see that both Shiloh and Bonnie were in their rooms.

With one leg propped backward against the wide barn door, he looked more like one of those old Marlboro men than a sheriff. He dropped his boot to the ground and opened his arms. She walked right into them.

He drew her close and she could hear the steady beat of his heart thumping in there against his broad chest. "My God, Abby, you are trembling."

She'd had those symptoms before, on her first deployment. It had happened when she and another vehicle were on their way to check out some intelligence. By a strange twist of fate, she'd been in the second sand-colored patrol car. The first one hit a bomb and went straight up into the air. Her driver stopped and backed up as fast as he could. Then bodies came floating down from the sky.

She'd made it back to base before she went into shock, but she recognized the symptoms very well.

"I feel violated," she said.

"Why?"

"He didn't want to know me, but he sent someone to spy on me. It's . . . it's . . ."

"Crazy? That was Ezra. He was a controlling old fart. He might not have wanted you on the ranch to undermine a son he might have later, but you were his as much as this ranch was," Cooper said.

"I was just a pile of hay or dirt or a cow?"

He kissed the top of her head. "Darlin', I can't explain Ezra or his crazy notions. He was old-school, back when old school was the only school, if you know what I mean. His ideas went back to the time that Texas was settled. I liked him. He was honest, opinionated, and funny. But that doesn't mean I agreed with him. We had some damn good arguments."

"About round bales of hay?" she asked.

"Among a whole raft of more serious issues, believe me." His arms steadied her nerves as he tipped her chin up with his fist and his lips settled on hers like they belonged there. It wasn't one of those steamy kisses full of passion and heat but it calmed her, grounded her in reality. Then he drew her closer to his chest and wrapped his arms around her and she felt protected from everything. Not even the boxes under the bed mattered anymore.

"I'm not sure that was a wise idea," she said.

"What? The kiss?" She nodded. "Maybe not, but it happened," he said. "Let's take a drive. Have you been to Silverton?"

"Just through it on my way to the funeral, and I was running late."

"Then let's go get a soft drink at the convenience store and I'll show you the courthouse and the police station and the diner. It's a nice little Texas town."

It wasn't a date. It was two friends going for a cola or maybe a beer. She could damn sure use one more that night and Cooper would be driving.

❄ ❄ ❄

Cooper had lived next door to Ezra, gone to church with him, talked to him over the fence, but he hadn't actually known the man. When it came to Ezra, no one really knew what made him tick or think the way he did. So there was no way he could help Abby understand the man who'd fathered her.

If Abby had grown up on the ranch next door, he might have fallen for her when they were teenagers. But she hadn't and like she said, she had wings. That meant she could fly away at any moment. He liked her, liked her spunk and her determination to learn the business, but . . .

And therein was the problem—a woman who hated the ground she walked on would never be happy for a whole lifetime in the canyon, and he'd never be happy with a lifetime out of the canyon. He wished things could be different, that she'd stand still long enough to grow roots, but that hateful voice that argued with him said that wasn't likely to happen.

"It'll be pretty in the spring when the wild daisies are in bloom," he said.

"That's what I hear. According to the marriage license, Ezra married Mama about this time of year. Now I wish I'd asked more questions about why she was even in Texas."

"Why don't you ask your living relatives in Galveston?" he asked.

She shook her head. "Don't have any. Mama was adopted at birth by an older couple who died before I was born. Mama didn't marry until she was past thirty and then she married Ezra, who was even older."

His truck drove on, coming out of the canyon north of Silverton. Land reached out to touch a sky full of twinkling stars with a big round moon taking center stage. "Ezra said once that he met his first wife at a wedding, the second one at a church picnic, and the third one was a waitress in a truck stop between Claude and Amarillo. Does that help?" Cooper asked as he drove down Silverton's wide Main Street.

Abby slapped her knee. "Georgia!"

"This doesn't look a thing like Georgia," Cooper said.

"No, Georgia was Mama's best friend when she was a kid. She had a picture of Georgia on the bookcase in the living room. It was taken on Georgia's wedding day and Mama was in the wedding party. She told me about the wedding in the little white church that was in the background and how beautiful it had been with all the poinsettias and Christmas decorations. That must have been where she met Ezra, but that means they got married a month later. Holy shit!"

"Georgia who?" Cooper asked.

"Mama never told me her last name. She married a soldier and after the wedding they went to England. Their friendship had faded with the distance. I found Mama crying one day and she said Georgia had died," Abby said.

Cooper laid a hand on her shoulder without a word. She reached up and squeezed it and then her hand went back to her lap. He moved his to the steering wheel and turned into a parking spot beside the courthouse.

"This is where my day job is located," he said.

"That's one big courthouse for such a little town."

"It takes care of the whole spread-out county. Want something to drink now?"

"I thought I wanted a beer when we left home, but I've changed my mind. What I really want is a pint of ice cream—rocky road or praline—if there's a place still open. I'd even share it."

"Happy to." He grinned. A rooster crowed, cutting off further comment about her ice cream habits, and she cocked her head to one side.

"That's Rusty's ringtone," he said. "I'll only be a minute . . . Hello, don't tell me you are backing out of our trip."

"No, this is a business call. Abby never came back from her walk. Her truck is here, and her sisters are on the verge of hysteria. Would you come over here and help us locate her?"

"She's right here in the truck with me. We drove up to Silverton for ice cream," Cooper said.

"I'm not hysterical," Shiloh said in the background.

"Here." Cooper handed the phone to Abby.

"Hello," she said cautiously.

"Give me that phone," Shiloh said.

"Oh, shit!" Abby whispered.

"Abby Malloy, we were worried about you," she said.

Cooper could hear every high-pitched word coming through the phone. Shiloh was not a happy woman right then and Abby would have some explaining to do.

"I'm a big girl. I can leave the house without telling either one of you," she protested. "Don't wait up for me. And don't bother to lock the back door. I could open that thing in ten seconds with nothing but a hairpin."

She hit the "End" button and handed the phone back to Cooper. "Maybe you'd better make it two pints of ice cream."

# Chapter Ten

"You think Bonnie and Shiloh will get out a shotgun and make me marry you?" Cooper teased as he parked the truck near the yard gate.

"I haven't reported to anyone since I was eighteen years old. I'm not starting now. Good night, Cooper, and thank you for the drive and the ice cream. But most of all for talking to me about Ezra."

He leaned across the console and brushed a soft kiss across her forehead. She would have liked very much for the next one to hit her lips square on, but the living room curtain pulled aside, framing two faces peering out, and she was glad she and Cooper were both sitting upright in the truck cab.

"Please don't walk me to the door. They'll think it's a date," she groaned.

"And that's bad?"

"No, but it is personal. And after less than a week, I'm not ready to share any more of my personal life with them," she said.

"I understand." He nodded. "I'll see you tomorrow, then. Got any idea what's on the dinner menu?"

"It's Shiloh's day to cook and I have no idea what she's planning. She likes the kitchen better than outside, but I got to hand it to her, she's pulls her fair share on the ranch as well as in the kitchen," Abby said.

"And you?" Cooper asked.

"I don't mind cooking or cleaning, but I'd rather be outside. I'd best get on inside or they're liable to come out here," she said.

He brought her hand to his lips and kissed her knuckles. "Good night, Abby."

"Good night, Cooper."

Martha's old head popped up from Ezra's chair where she'd been sleeping and she hopped down to the floor with a fluid movement, ambled across the living room, and stuck her cold nose into Abby's open hand. Her tail wagged and Abby could've sworn the dog grinned when she dropped down on her knees to pet her.

Bonnie held out her hand. "Give me your phone."

Abby shook her head. "I don't think so. I'm thirty years old. That's too damn old to get my phone taken away because Cooper took me to Silverton for ice cream."

"I'm not taking it away from you. I'm programming your number into my phone and then I'm putting mine into yours."

"And"—Shiloh piped up from the sofa—"Rusty went through the roof when I said that about him killing us off to get the ranch. I might have given him an idea, though, so we have to watch out for each other."

Abby handed the phone to Bonnie. "Y'all are paranoid. Rusty isn't capable of murder."

"But Cooper might be, or maybe Jackson. I can see them coveting this place, and what better way than to offer Rusty a big price after we all disappear," Shiloh said.

"I thought you read romance books," Abby said.

Bonnie put the phone back in Abby's hand. "What's that got to do with anything? I read romance, too."

"It sounds like you've been reading murder mysteries. I'm going to bed now and FYI, ladies, I will not tell you I'm leaving every time

I step out the door. We are grown adults, not teenagers, and I do not answer to either of you."

Martha followed Abby as she started toward her room.

"No attention for Vivien and Polly?" Shiloh asked.

"No," Abby answered.

"Why?"

"I like Martha better, and those two dogs belong to y'all, not me. Martha is mine. You want them to have attention, then it's your job to provide it. I'm going to take a long, warm bath. Y'all have permission to use my half bath if you need it while I'm in the big bathroom. Just don't knock on the bathroom door."

"The queen gives orders but we can't," Bonnie said.

"Oldest child rights," Abby said.

"And we get permission to enter the holy quarters." Sarcasm dripped from Shiloh's tone.

"Don't get bitchy. Neither of you have invited me into your rooms," Abby threw over her shoulder on the way down the hallway.

❉ ❉ ❉

Ranching was never done.

Period.

No one ever said, *If we get this fence fixed, it will be done for a week.* Not once had she heard someone yell, *And we finished plowing half the state of Texas, so we get to sleep until noon tomorrow.*

*But* didn't exist in ranching, not even for a nice excuse like, *but I broke my fingernail and I have blisters on my toes.* And no one ever uttered the words *when I get the barn cleaned and the cows milked and the eggs gathered, I can read for the rest of the afternoon.*

Thursday and Friday were long, exhausting days on Malloy Ranch. Two forty-acre fields were now planted in ryegrass and by spring the cattle would be eating green grass rather than hay. Two more fields were planted in winter wheat and next week the place where they'd burned the brush would be planted in a different kind of rye.

Cooper had been so busy with the sheriff's job that he missed dinner on Friday and that made her cranky.

*You are acting like a hormonal teenager*, she fussed at herself.

Abby and her sisters had finished the evening chores and she'd sat down on the porch with Martha at her side when her phone rang. Haley started in the minute she answered it.

"Sorry I haven't called sooner but the twins had a stomach bug and all I've gotten done for the past three days is change stinky diapers and rock them. Tell me what's going on and don't stutter around. I feel something in my bones," Haley said.

"And your bones never lie?" Abby laughed.

"Not when it comes to you they don't," Haley answered. "Trust me. Well, shit! Got a baby waking up. I'll call later and we'll talk some more about it. Big hugs," Haley said.

Abby shoved the phone back into her pocket and said, "Well, Martha, at least I don't have to change your stinky diapers."

She reached out to pet the dog and the phone rang again. "That didn't take long," she said.

"What?" Cooper asked.

Just hearing his voice put a smile on her face. "I thought you were someone else."

"Oh, got another boyfriend who calls often?"

"Another?" she said slowly.

He chuckled. "I called to tell you that I missed you at dinner, but I had to forget the lunch break if I was going to get through by five and get this pasture seeded."

"Bonnie made fried chicken."

He groaned. "I'd just about kill for good homemade fried chicken."

"Then you should have taken a lunch break," she said.

"Is your other boyfriend there now?"

"No, he is not and no, I do not have a boyfriend. How about you, Cooper? How many girlfriends have you got who are just your friends?" she said.

"I haven't done a head count lately, but I will tell you that not a single one is here right now offering to help me plow until midnight when the rain is supposed to reach the canyon."

"How many tractors do you own?" she asked.

"Two big ones and a little one that Grandpa bought for Granny to use when she got the urge to help. It hasn't been driven in years, but I can't bear to sell it."

"Since you were good enough to teach me how to drive a tractor, I'll drive one of them for you tonight. Tell me how to drive to your place. I don't have any idea how to get there except over the fence. But why don't you ask Rusty to help you?"

"I'm not attracted to him," Cooper said.

"And you are to me?" she asked.

"Honey, that question doesn't even need an answer. I'll pay you if you're serious about plowin'," he said.

"I'll take it in ice cream instead of dollars."

He told her exactly how to get from Malloy Ranch to the Lucky Seven. She pulled her boots back on, tucked the laces into the tops, and then braided her hair into two ropes that hung down the sides of her shoulders.

"What are you doing? Going for another walk?" Shiloh came out of the bathroom with a towel around her head and a long terry bathrobe belted around her waist.

"Actually, I'm going for a drive, and I won't be back until midnight or after, so don't wait up for me. And if my phone rings, somebody better be dead."

"Surely to God you aren't going on an ice cream date looking and smelling like you do. Don't you own anything other than camouflage?" Shiloh asked.

"I don't think I smell bad enough to fog the inside of a tractor cab. The rest is none of your business," she answered.

Bonnie came out of her room and stopped in her tracks. "Where are you going?"

"She hasn't had enough of tractors. She's going to go plow up something until after midnight," Shiloh answered.

"And I'm taking the leftover fried chicken with me," Abby said.

"Sounds like a midnight picnic to me." Bonnie smiled.

"Sounds like a woman who's lost her mind to me. Not even Cooper Wilson would be able to talk me into getting back into a tractor cab, especially at night," Shiloh said.

"Maybe I want to get that field ready where we cleared off the mesquite. Or maybe"—she wiggled her eyebrows—"I'm on my way to the bunkhouse to seduce Rusty."

Shiloh popped her hands on her hips. "I'm not blind. I can see the way Cooper looks at you and you aren't doing one thing to discourage it. Yes, he's interested in you, Abby, but have you ever stopped and considered maybe he's even more interested in this ranch? It would sure be a nice addition to his place, now wouldn't it?"

"I'm not having this conversation right now. Good night, girls," Abby said.

Bonnie stepped around them and said, "Take the rest of the cookies if you want to. Tomorrow you have to cook and you can make more."

Shiloh set her full mouth in a firm line and shook her head slowly, muttering the whole way into her bedroom. "Don't you dare take all those cookies. I'm having a few for a bedtime snack."

"Nosy little shits. Can't even sneak out without telling them," Abby told Martha as she slipped out the front door.

Abby had been raised in a tiny apartment with her mother; Ezra had lived like a king. She figured Cooper must have a similar setup on Lucky Seven, but when the big two-story white house came into sight, she gasped. Several turned porch posts supported a sleeping porch that wrapped around three sides of the house, with doors that opened out of bedrooms on the second floor. Several cats lazed against the railings.

Cooper was sitting in the first of a line of rocking chairs lined up on the wide porch. He waved and said, "Welcome to this side of the barbed-wire fence."

"You scared the shit out of me," she said breathlessly. "I figured you'd be in the field and I'd have to call you to tell me how to get there."

He chuckled. "Sorry about that. I waited on you so we could take my old farm truck. Come on with me and we'll drive out to the back of the ranch. It's on the southwest corner of the property and I'd hate for you to drive your good vehicle down the rutted path."

She held out a paper bag. "Chicken, cookies, and half a dozen leftover biscuits stuffed with strawberry jelly."

"You are an angel straight from heaven," he groaned.

"You might have trouble convincing Shiloh and Bonnie of that." She laughed. "Show me the way. I'm still a rookie, but I'll do my best."

"Long as the seed gets in the ground, I'm not complainin'." He helped her into the old truck with a blanket thrown over the wide bench seat. No console between them. No fancy dash or CD player.

It looked like it might fall apart any minute, but when he started the engine, it purred like a kitten.

"Radio doesn't work, either," he said when he caught her scanning the inside. "Grandpa bought it used in the sixties. It's like an old mule. Still got a lot of good in it, if you baby it just a little and don't use it like a hot rod. And Abby, you don't have to work until midnight. When you get tired, just call me and I'll drive you back to the house. Weatherman says it's going to rain cats, dogs, and baby elephants tomorrow, so I wanted to get the seed in the ground. It'll be too muddy to get the tractors in the fields if it does rain."

"A wise man I know told me once that friends help friends. I think his initials are CW." She smiled.

"Imagine that," Cooper said.

They were both quiet on the way to where the moonlight lit up two big green tractors sitting at the edge of a freshly plowed field. With darkness surrounding them, they looked like monsters instead of machinery.

"Here we are. We've got about five hours and that should get the job done with both of us working," he said.

She turned toward him and nodded. "Just tell me what to do and I'll do my best."

She was in the tractor cab making the first round exactly like Cooper told her when she realized what he'd said about the weather on Saturday. He and Rusty would be in a patrol car transporting a prisoner to San Antonio. She and her sisters—when did she start thinking of them as sisters, anyway—would be doing chores. If it was raining all that hard, there was no way they'd be able to plow or plant that last field that Rusty mentioned. That meant a day off and she planned dozens of ways to use the time as she drove the tractor up and down the field by the scanty moonlight.

All the light disappeared behind clouds after a couple of hours and she had to depend on the headlights, instinct, and hope. She could see the lights of Cooper's tractor across the fence from where she worked and he seemed to be going faster than she was. Afraid that she'd mess up, she kept her speed steady. She'd seen the cost of the seed they'd planted on Malloy Ranch and there was no way she'd waste that much money by not doing the job right.

*Besides, you want to please him, right?* It was Haley's voice in her head that time and Abby's eyes were too heavy to even argue with her friend.

She reached into her pocket and pulled out a ziplock bag full of candy, opened it with one hand, and dumped all the pieces on the seat beside her. The sugar rush woke her up, but talking to Cooper on the phone for an hour was what really helped.

"So what is your favorite kind of music?" he asked.

"Country."

"I'm shocked. I figured you for a hard rock girl like Bonnie."

She laughed. "Then prepared to be double shocked. Bonnie listens to country music, too."

"Your favorite artist?"

"Travis Tritt and Blake Shelton. It's a toss-up," she answered.

"And female artist?"

"Miranda Lambert and or the Pistol Annies. How about you?"

"Male artist is George Strait. Female would be a tie between Martina McBride and Patsy Cline."

"Did your grandpa introduce you to Patsy?" she asked.

"Oh, yeah. He loved her and Loretta Lynn. We've still got a turntable in the living room and dozens of vinyl records that I play sometimes."

His roots really did go way, way down into the ground.

"Favorite food?" he asked.

"Don't laugh at me, but I love good old greasy hamburgers made on a charcoal grill. Not one of those gas ones, but real charcoal," she said. "Your turn."

"Steaks on a charcoal grill."

A few rain sprinkles dotted the windshield, but they didn't last long. Maybe the weatherman had been wrong or perhaps the storm blew right over the top of the canyon and went on its merry way.

"Got to take this call. If I lose you, I'll call back," he said.

She waited a couple of minutes before his voice returned. "That was the dispatcher. She knows that I'm plowing and wanted me to know that the bad weather is comin' in the next twenty minutes. If we want to get out of here before it hits, we'll have to stop now. It's pouring down in Silverton and we could get stuck in the mud if we don't leave. We'll leave the old truck and take the tractors back to the barn. Just follow me."

"I'm on my last round. Let me finish it first," she said.

"Hurry. The dispatcher said it's got some power behind it. They are blowing the sirens to warn folks in town to take shelter," he told her.

She finished that round, whipped around the corner, and saw red taillights coming across the end of her field. The lights stopped and Cooper was suddenly out of his tractor running to open the gate for them to pass through. When both tractors had cleared enough space, he stopped and jogged back to shut the gate, waving at her on the way.

Lightning split the dark sky and thunder rolled off the edges of the canyon. The old work truck would be stuck out there until the mud cleared up, but there was no way they could drive three vehicles back to the ranch.

She pulled in beside where he'd parked and could see him coming toward her. In the semidarkness, with the eerie aura of a storm surrounding him, his swagger was even more pronounced than usual. He'd removed his coat and the plaid shirt he'd worn over an oatmeal-colored thermal undershirt was unbuttoned, flapping in the wind like Superman's cape. The sleeves were pushed up to his elbows and his broad chest stretched the knit shirt so tight that she could see the ripples of stomach muscles.

"Thank you, Abby. You are a lifesaver." He threw an arm around her shoulders and together they walked the short distance to her truck.

The big rolling black clouds brought more bursts of lightning and deafening thunder, but she felt safe with his arm around her. She shivered and he drew her near as he opened her door.

"Cold?"

"I hate storms. The static in the air reminds me of a hurricane."

He drew her closer. "We don't get hurricanes in this part of Texas. Maybe a tornado, but never a hurricane. You seen many?"

"Not a lot. I was deployed when that big one hit several years ago, but the one I do remember hit us when I was about fourteen. We lived on the strip above the store in an apartment. The wind damaged our roof and the water got into the shop, but it didn't ruin any of the equipment. After the power was restored we were able to get opened up in a couple of weeks, but it was pretty scary."

"At that age, you probably thought the sky was falling."

"You'll laugh, but I thought the ocean was coming to get us," she said.

Actually, a hurricane hadn't been a lot different than the feeling she had when he touched her or kissed her, or even shared pecan pie with her. Different circumstances arranged the nerves in different ways, but when it was all said and done, it took her breath away and made her heart race.

"Good night, Cooper."

He leaned into the truck and cupped her face in his hands. Thumbs rested on her jawbones. One of his pinky fingers traced her lips, sending jolts of electricity far greater than the lightning through her body. His eyes closed slowly as if he wanted to look at her and kiss her at the same time, and then his lips touched hers, gentle at first. His hands moved to the back of her head to hold her steady as he deepened the kiss. Ripples went from her scalp to her toes and, defying gravity, traveled right back up her legs to her spine and right up to her lips. She wrapped her arms around his neck and moved closer to him, biting back a moan the whole time.

"Good night, Abby," he said hoarsely when he broke the kiss. "See you Sunday when we get home. I'll call you over the weekend."

He slammed the door and the first drop of rain hit the windshield. She slapped the steering wheel and fussed at herself for not stopping this thing in the beginning. Now it would be ten times— no, a thousand times—harder to end.

"Friends, my ass. Friends don't kiss like that," she said.

Years ago, with raging teenage emotions and desires, she had known the excitement of that first kiss, that first sexual experience with the boy she'd thought she'd marry someday, and the misery of the first major breakup. On her first deployment, afraid of being killed in a foreign country, there had been a tall, dark soldier whom she'd thought she was in love with for a brief time. The sex had been better; the breakup hadn't been as devastating. But the sex with Cooper was a thousand times hotter.

She started the engine and turned the truck around. When she reached the end of the lane and turned north, the rain got more serious. As she drove under the Malloy Ranch sign, the wind picked up and a streak of lightning split the pregnant clouds wide-open. Forget about raining cats and dogs or even baby elephants, this was hurricane-quality wind right there in the middle of the canyon.

Visibility was so limited that she slid to a greasy stop mere inches from the yard fence. There was no doubt she would get wet from truck to house, so she opted to go through the back door. She could leave her wet boots and clothes in the utility room and not track mud all over the living room carpet.

The cold rain, blown with gale-force winds, stung her eyes and face and even her underpants were soaked by the time she grabbed the doorknob—only to find it locked.

"Well, shit!" She turned to jog around the house to the front door. The porch would offer some protection while she picked that lock. The stoop at the back didn't stop a bit of the rain from pelting the hell out of her.

A sudden burst of light blinded Abby and the door flew open. She blinked several times before she could focus.

"Shiloh?"

"You look like a drowned rat. Surely you've got enough sense to come in out of the rain. There's clean towels in the dryer. See you in the morning."

Standing on the rug just inside the door, Abby shucked out of her coat and hung it on one of a line of nails. "Did you wait up for me?"

"I did not! A clap of thunder woke me and then I saw a couple of headlights through the rain. Looked like aliens. I got up to be sure we weren't about to be abducted," she yawned. "You do look a little like E.T. Are you sure you are Abby Malloy?"

"Right now I'm not sure about a damn thing, but thank you for opening the door," Abby said.

Shiloh waved off the comment with a flick of her wrist. "See you in the morning for chores. It's going to be so much fun in the rain."

Martha was lying in the hallway beside her door when Abby reached her bedroom. The dog wagged her tail and stood, meandered inside the room as soon as Abby opened the door, and went straight for the gold rocking chair, where she curled up.

"Do you want a blanket?" Abby laughed.

Martha laid her head down and shut her eyes.

Abby pulled a small throw from the back of the chair and wrapped it around Martha's body. Then she dropped down on her knees and scratched her ears. "I'm going to take a quick shower. He kissed me again, Martha, and I'm not sure what to do with all these emotions," she whispered.

# Chapter Eleven

All three Malloy sisters crowded into the front seat of the work truck the next morning. Abby drove over the muddy pathway in steady rain to where the cattle waited for breakfast. The hay would be like soggy shredded wheat, but it would be one of those eat-it-or-leave-it situations.

"Okay, are we ready to get wet?" Abby parked the truck and the cattle started coming toward it.

"Might as well be. The clouds aren't parting," Shiloh said.

"Next July we'll be praying for this kind of weather. When it's so dry the lizards start carrying canteens," Bonnie said.

Abby was slow to get out in the cold rain. "How do you know?"

"Mama talked about the summer she was pregnant with me. When she got really good and drunk, she'd tell me about that miserable summer and how hard she worked only to have fall come late that year. I was born the third of November and she said the first frost hadn't even hit the canyon."

"Your mama drank?" Shiloh asked.

"No, my mama drinks. Might as well get this work over with." Bonnie threw open the door, scrambled up over the fender, and tossed three bales out on the ground before the other two could get the clippers out of their hip pockets.

Abby snipped wire as fast as she could and Shiloh crawled into the truck bed to help Bonnie toss the bales out. The lightning bolt that ripped through the sky at the top of the canyon wall was behind them so they didn't see it. But all three women ducked and covered their heads when the thunder sounded like the whole canyon was falling in on itself.

"Holy shit!" Abby yelled. "Where did that come from?"

"My heart almost jumped out of my chest," Shiloh said. "I hate storms."

"Me, too. Let's get these chores done and go home," Bonnie said.

"One more load of hay, then you'd better drive the truck to and from the barn so you can get the milk to the house. The hens might get mad at getting wet when Shiloh gets the eggs, but the hogs won't care if their feed is a little soupier than normal," Abby said.

If someone had told her a month ago that she'd be working on a ranch with her sisters and enjoying it, she would have thought they were batshit crazy. But there she was, in the middle of a canyon, in the winter, doing chores with siblings and hoping to hell neither of them left.

"And then we get to stay in the rest of the day until chores tonight, right?" Shiloh asked.

"Yes, ma'am. Can't plow mud, and the barn is clean and ready for whatever happens. Let's hope we don't have a problem with a pregnant cow. Either of y'all ever pulled a calf?" Bonnie asked.

"Have you?" Shiloh asked.

"Couple of times, but it's been a while."

"You might have to show us if that happens," Abby said.

Instead of being jealous that her younger sister knew so much more than she did, Abby breathed a sigh of pure, unadulterated relief. Shiloh might throw in the towel after a day like this, but hopefully Bonnie would stick around long enough that Abby could learn from her.

A deep sense of loss hit Abby in the gut at the idea of Shiloh leaving. It was a new feeling and she analyzed it carefully as they finished up the chores the next hour. It had to be blood calling to blood, because she hadn't felt that way when she left Haley behind every time she went home from a deployment. Similar and yet very different from the loss of her mother, the feeling still caused her to reach inside her pocket for a miniature candy bar. She brought out a handful and offered Shiloh and Bonnie one.

"Thank you," Shiloh smiled.

"I love plain old chocolate without any nuts or caramel to mess it up," Bonnie said.

"I just love candy." Abby laughed.

An hour later, Bonnie took the keys from her oldest sister and slid into the driver's seat. Abby went straight to the hog shed, loaded two big buckets with feed. Pigs were a grunting and snorting lot when they ate or when they knew the food was on the way.

"The whole bunch of you will look better to me when you are wrapped up in the freezer as pork chops and bacon," she said as she poured the food into the troughs. Her nose curled at the scent. "You guys could use some heavy-duty deodorant. Shiloh better be glad that I hate chickens. She'd have run the first day we were here if she'd landed a job with y'all."

Martha yipped at her feet and she reached down to rub the dog's ears with her gloved hand. "What are you doing here? I figured you'd go on home after helping us feed the cows."

She made a mental note to ask Rusty if Ezra had cured his own pork or if he'd had it done. Maybe there was a smokehouse somewhere on the property. "I bet you Bonnie will know how to process the bacon and hams. She can teach me how to do it, so next year . . ."

*Whoa.* She quickly stopped the thought process. *When did you start thinking about next year instead of spring and one day at a time?*

Martha wagged her tail and trailed along behind Abby, both of them soaked to the skin when they reached the house, and Abby still hadn't figured out how she'd even begun to think about staying at the ranch.

Shiloh was busy putting her clothing in the washer when Abby pushed into the utility room and stopped to drip on a rug. The smell of laundry soap, the sweet scent of shower gel, and warmth met her, but it all quickly disappeared when Martha shook from head to toe. Eau de wet dog blanketed the room.

"Use this to get her dried off." Shiloh pitched a towel toward her. "I already took care of Vivien and Polly. Thank goodness I came in the back door and they didn't do that on the living room carpet. Tile can be wiped up, but I'm not sure I'd ever get the smell out of the carpet."

"It would give us a good excuse to get it replaced," Abby said.

"But could we ever agree on what color?" A towel was twisted around Shiloh's head and she wore a thick terry robe, belted at the waist.

Right then, at that moment, Abby envied her that robe more than anything because it looked so warm. She peeled off her wet, muddy clothing and tossed it in a pile on the floor. Wearing only her bra and underpants, she shivered and headed through the kitchen to the hallway.

"You can have the washer next," Shiloh said. "I only brought two pair of old work jeans, so it's a tough job keeping them clean."

Abby stopped and looked over her shoulder. "Me, too."

"I tossed what was just wet in the dryer and put my muddy jeans and coat in the washer. I'll put your stuff in next. This rain is so cold that I feel like I fell into a frozen lake even yet. I'm making hot chocolate and starting a fire. Shall I make three cups? I feel sorry for Bonnie. That little leather jacket is all she's got."

"Sounds good to me. I've got an extra camo jacket. Think she'd like to wear it?" Abby asked.

"You could ask her. Hey, what's for dinner?" Shiloh asked.

Abby had forgotten all about it being her day to cook. "I was planning on meatloaf, but since it took twice as long to get the feeding done in this weather, how about vegetable soup and cornbread and maybe a pan of chocolate chip bar cookies for dessert?"

"Sounds wonderful. I'm going to my room and catch up on e-mails. My friends in Arkansas probably think I've died," Shiloh said.

Abby finished undressing and tossed the pile of wet clothing toward the washing machine. Shiloh had piled her things on top of the dryer, so Abby grabbed them and headed toward her bedroom. She tossed them onto the bed; picked up her shower kit, a pair of pajama pants, an oversized T-shirt, and underwear; and headed toward the bathroom. If she hurried, she could be finished by the time Bonnie arrived. Martha curled up in the rocking chair and shut her eyes.

"Kind of nice being in out of the rain, isn't it, old girl?" Abby said. "You just stay right there. You don't need to protect me in the shower."

She could have let the water beat down on her back for an hour, but the minute she felt warm blood flowing through her veins instead of ice water she turned off the faucets and threw back the curtain. Steam had fogged the mirror and hung above her head like smoke in a cheap honky-tonk. It felt so good that she would have sat down on the edge of the tub and soaked more of it in, but she heard Bonnie talking out in the hallway. Abby hurriedly threw a towel around her body and motioned Bonnie inside when she stepped out into the hallway.

"I left the steam," she said.

Bonnie smiled. "Milk is strained and in the refrigerator. Poor old cow probably thought my hands had been dipped in ice water. I hope this is the last of winter."

"Shiloh is building a fire and making us all a cup of good hot chocolate. I'm making vegetable soup for dinner. You'll feel better in a little bit."

"Thank God we don't have to go back out until evening," Bonnie said.

Abby found Shiloh curled up on one end of the sofa with a quilt thrown over her legs. She wore a pair of dark blue knit pajamas printed with bright red high-heeled shoes and had a book in her hands.

Martha, Vivien, and Polly were sprawled out in front of the fireplace. Abby eyed the old, worn leather recliner. No one had touched Ezra's chair since they'd first arrived. It was just a chair, for heaven's sake.

Shiloh drew her legs up to make room. "You can sit here beside me. Your chocolate is right there on the end table."

Abby shook her head. "No, I'm sitting in this chair."

"You are a braver woman than I am. I've avoided that chair because it smelled like smoke until I used a whole bottle of leather cleaner on it last week and then sprayed underneath it with disinfectant. At least that's the story I kept telling myself until now. I'm actually afraid the chair will make me more like him."

Abby picked up the plush throw from the back of the chair and plopped down before she lost her courage. "It's just a chair."

"Maybe it is to you, but you've fought wars. I haven't. Do you ever fear that you'll be the kind of parent that would turn your back on your child like Ezra did?" Shiloh asked.

"It scares the shit out of me," Abby said.

"Me, too," Shiloh said. "And that fear gives me severe commitment issues. I get close to a man, then I create a problem so either he breaks up with me or else he gets angry and that gives me reason to break it off with him."

"Never thought of it like that, but I guess I'm in the same boat with you."

"Not a very pleasant boat, is it?" Shiloh said.

"No, but at least we know why we are the way we are," Abby said.

"Why we are what?" Bonnie joined them, worming her way through the dogs until she could pull the extra rocking chair up to the fire and hold her hands out to warm them. Her chambray shirt was faded and her flannel pajama pants were two sizes too big. "Lord, I hate bein' wet and cold both. A nice summer rain with a sexy cowboy under a big old cottonwood tree can be nice. But feeding cows in mud and milking in a cold barn is miserable. Now what was it that we were talkin' about?"

"Afraid of commitment. Afraid we'll be sorry mothers," Shiloh said.

"I just figured that all came from my mama, but I guess I got a double dose with the Ezra genes," she said. "So y'all have the same feelings."

Both Shiloh and Abby nodded.

Martha and Polly sat up at the same time, growling and eyes darting around the room. Vivien slowly went into a crouch and did a belly crawl across the floor.

"It's just thunder and it's a long way off," Shiloh said.

Martha barked loudly and Polly ran to the back door. Vivien put her paws on the doorknob and whined.

"What's gotten into them? It thundered . . . oh, my God! Why is the house shaking?" Shiloh covered her ears.

"It's an earthquake in the middle of a rainstorm," Abby yelled.

Bonnie shook her head and rushed to the kitchen window overlooking the backyard. "That's not an earthquake. It's a stampede.

They just broke down the back fence and here they come. They're splittin' around the house, so that should slow them down."

Shiloh and Abby raced to the window. Three women watched a black sea of cattle break when they saw a house in front of them. The ground trembled beneath so many hooves and the thundering got louder the closer they got. The fence hadn't even slowed them down. They'd come right through it and they didn't come to a screeching halt until they reached the back porch.

"Whew. For a minute there I thought they might plow right through the window," Bonnie said. "Y'all okay?"

"That was wild. It was like a car wreck. I couldn't take my eyes off it but I knew I should run for cover," Shiloh answered.

Abby just nodded in agreement. A dozen thoughts went through her mind, beginning with hoping that Bonnie knew how to repair fences and herd cattle in hard rain.

"Abby?" Bonnie asked.

"We've got lightning, rain, and scared cows," Shiloh groaned.

"The key word is *we*. We might not know everything about runnin' a ranch, but if we stick together, we can take care of this." Abby's tone sounded a hell of a lot more confident than she felt, but she had faith in her sisters.

In a few minutes the yard was completely full of bawling cattle stomping over every blade of grass and breaking down all the rosebushes. Their rolling eyes and heaving sides said they were still spooked, but one section of fence was all that was destroyed . . . if the yard and flowers weren't counted.

"I bet there's fifty head out there and best I can see, they've all got the Lucky Seven brand."

"What happened?" Shiloh asked.

Bonnie took a deep breath. "Scared me, I'll admit it. I don't know for sure, but my guess would be that a streak of lightning spooked the shit out of them and caused a stampede. They're not our cows, girls. They belong to the Lucky Seven, which means there's a busted barbed-wire fence between our property and Cooper's. So much for staying in the house. We've got to round them up and get them back on his side of the fence."

"Shit! Shit! Shit! My coat isn't near dry and Abby's is still soppin' wet," Shiloh said.

"That must've scared you." Abby finally smiled. "I haven't heard you cuss like that before."

"Yes, it scared me, and it's days like this I want to pack my bags and head back to Arkansas," she said.

Bonnie started for her room. "I guess these dogs will get to show us how good they are. Thank God I know how to mend a barbed-wire fence. I'll get the things from the tack room and we'll herd cattle with the truck and the dogs."

"And Rusty's four-wheelers," Abby said.

"He didn't say we couldn't use them. Keys are on the rack," Bonnie said.

"I have no idea how to drive a four-wheeler," Shiloh said.

"Then you can drive the truck," Abby told her. "We can get this done in a couple of hours and still have the afternoon to rest."

※ ※ ※

The dogs did a fine job of herding the cows back through the broken fence, but then the cattle decided to veer off seven ways to Sunday. Shiloh kept the biggest part of the herd moving across the pasture toward the fence a mile away with the help of Martha on one side and the other two dogs on the other.

Bonnie rode one of the four-wheelers on the west side of the main herd, cussing loud enough to blister the hides of any heifers that strayed.

Abby manned her post on the east side and the area behind the truck with enough swearing to earn her a thumbs-up from Bonnie a couple of times. Using the torn-up ground as a guide to drive them toward where she hoped they'd find the broken fence, Shiloh drove with the window down, screaming at the cows as loud as both her sisters.

They were making progress until the truck got stuck in the mud about halfway across the pasture. Shiloh turned off the engine, motioned toward her sisters to keep moving, and started herding cows on foot.

"Where in the hell is a burst of thunder when we need it?" Abby yelled over her shoulder at her sister.

Shiloh, bless her heart, looked miserable with her hair hanging in her face. Abby was glad she couldn't see herself, because she probably looked even worse.

As if answering her prayers, lightning sliced through the rain, hit a mesquite tree dead-on and set it on fire. The blaze didn't last long, but the crack of the hit echoed through the canyon like a kid yelling down into a deep well. Then the thunder rolled right over their heads. The lead bull rolled his eyes and doubled his speed, the cows following right behind him. At the fence line, he tried to turn and go back the other way, but Martha nipped his heels and made him keep going.

"Good dog," Abby said.

That's when the front tire of the four-wheeler hit a gopher hole. The engine stalled out and Abby went flying over the handlebars to land in a nice mushy pile of cow shit. Instinctively, she tried to get rid of it by wiping her hand on the leg of her pants but all that did was smear it. Shiloh ran over to make sure she was all right, only to slip in the mud and go sliding a good five feet on her belly before coming to rest at the four-wheeler's back tire.

When Abby extended her clean hand to help her up, she took it, but the ground was so greasy that Abby lost her footing again. One minute she was looking at her sister, trying her damnedest to keep from laughing; the next she was staring up at gray skies with rain beating down on her face and a black cow the size of a barn running toward them.

At the last minute, Martha got between them and the cow and steered her off in the opposite direction. Abby's heart pounded so hard she could feel it in her ears. Her pulse throbbed behind her eyes and the cows were breaking from the herd faster than Bonnie could take care of it on her own.

"Help me get this damn thing pushed out of the hole and you can ride on the back with me. You're not doing a bit of good out there on foot anyway," Abby said.

"If y'all are through horsin' around, I could use some help," Bonnie yelled.

Abby couldn't believe her eyes when Shiloh flipped her off.

Lightning took out another mesquite tree and the rain came down even harder. It slowed the herd down, but kept them together better than before. The dogs were able to keep the rest of them headed toward Cooper's fence and the four-wheelers on each side deterred any straying.

They marched right through the busted fence and huddled up not far into the Lucky Seven property like a bunch of football players on Friday night. Bonnie pulled out a roll of barbed wire, a pair of cutters, and a stretcher from the saddlebag on the back of the four-wheeler and headed for the fence.

She barked orders and Abby and Shiloh followed them without arguing. "Y'all keep the cows from coming back through or any of ours from going over into Cooper's pasture while I get the first strand up. Then y'all can help me with the last two strands."

Abby was sure glad that Bonnie knew something about everything because she didn't know jack shit about how to fix a barbed-wire fence. She could probably blow one up, but putting one back together was a whole different ball game.

At the end of the repair job, Abby had a barbed-wire scratch on her wrist, her camo jacket was torn, and she was standing ankle-deep in water. Bonnie had a scratch across her cheek where the barbed wire had popped back and bit her and Abby's loaned jacket had a long slit down one arm. Shiloh's jeans had a tear in the thigh with a red bloodstain outlining it and the tennis shoes she wore were completely covered in cold water.

"If we don't have pneumonia or gangrene tomorrow morning, it will be a miracle . . . oh, no! No! No! No!" Abby stomped, sending a splash all the way to Bonnie's eyes.

Bonnie wiped at her eyes and pushed limp strands of soaking-wet hair behind her ears. "What the hell? If there is another damn Lucky Seven cow on Malloy land, Cooper can take care of it later."

"Look. I'm counting at least four head of Malloy cows over there and we've already fixed the fence." Abby pointed.

"So much for Rusty and Cooper not knowing that we had trouble." Shiloh brushed fresh blood from her leg and wiped her hand on the seat of her jeans.

"I'm not cutting this fence. Cooper and Rusty can take a cattle trailer over there later and get them," Bonnie said.

"Let's go get that truck unstuck and go home," Abby said.

"Let's just go home and forget the truck," Shiloh said.

"And let Rusty think we can't function without him on the place?" Bonnie asked.

"Okay, okay, we're already wet anyway," Shiloh groaned.

"And the lightning hasn't struck us yet, so that makes us lucky," Abby said.

Shiloh pointed a long slender finger at Abby. "You can shut up. You said this wouldn't take long and it's already past dinnertime. I'm tired. I'm wet. I'm hungry and I'm cold. And besides that my leg is cut open, so don't you say anything or else lightning is liable to flash out of the sky and set my hair on fire."

"Fate is a hormonal bitch on steroids. And honey, it was me that said it wouldn't take long, not Abby." Bonnie laughed.

"Bonnie is a prophet with that saying about fate. Get her one of them gold chest plates and a fez with a tassel on it," Shiloh said.

"You did a good job, Bonnie. I wouldn't have had any idea how to fix that fence. Does Rusty carry tools in the four-wheeler all the time?" Abby asked.

"I doubt it, but most ranchers keep tools in their truck. When Shiloh got stuck, I grabbed the tools and shoved them into the four-wheeler's saddlebag," Bonnie answered. "We're standing here in the rain, ladies, when we could be talkin' in front of a nice fire. Mount up and let's go."

Abby threw a leg over the four-wheeler and Shiloh climbed on behind her. Bonnie led the way back to the truck and looked at the situation. She might have experience with fixing a fence but Abby had gotten more trucks out of sandpits than she could count. Surely getting one up out of a mud puddle couldn't be a bit more difficult; however, she wasn't saying a word. Shiloh looked like she was about to cry or throw a hissy, and she was the mildest-tempered one of the three. Abby had learned long ago that the quiet ones were deadly when they'd had enough.

"Bonnie, can you go back to the house and either get some chain or one of those boards the cows broke on the fence?" she asked.

"Sure thing," Bonnie said. "Hey, Shiloh, crawl up here behind me. You can go on and get cleaned up. This only takes two people, anyway."

Shiloh did not argue. She moved from one vehicle to the other and they left Abby standing in the rain. She quickly crawled inside the truck and slammed the door.

Abby pushed her blonde hair from her face and envied Shiloh that warm dry robe. In minutes she heard the roar of the four-wheeler coming back and thought about the fact they would have three vehicles and two drivers when they got the truck back on the road.

"Shit fire!" She shook her fist at the sky when she was out of the truck.

"What now?" Bonnie asked.

"Two drivers. Three vehicles."

"We can't get no wetter. Shiloh looked like she was about to blow a gasket, though, so I thought she'd best go on to the house."

"Who died and made you boss?" Abby asked.

"Ezra died and right now we are all three the bosses. You got a problem with that?" Bonnie asked.

Abby smiled and then chuckled. That turned into laughter that floated out across the canyon through the driving rain. "This is what that old fart wanted."

"Have you gone crazy? Did lightning strike you while I was gone?" Bonnie asked.

"No, can't you see it? Ezra wanted us to get into a situation where we disagreed and fought so we'd leave one by one and Rusty could have the ranch."

"Bullshit! This is my ranch," Bonnie said.

"It's *our* ranch right now. We needed Shiloh, but if you thought she'd wimp out and leave, then you did the right thing. We can manage and Ezra loses."

A smile covered Bonnie's face. "Then let's get to it and go home while he turns over again in his grave."

"We'll have to drive the truck and one four-wheeler back to the barn and both ride back through the muddy fields."

"We're tough." Bonnie smiled.

A length of fence, ragged on both ends, stretched out across on the handlebars in front of Bonnie. Abby grabbed the board.

Bonnie yelled over noise of the storm. "Got another problem in the yard. A Lucky Seven bull has parked his fat ass on the porch. He's lying there like he owns the house and all that's in it. Reminds me of those fancy places that has a big concrete lion out by the fence."

"Well, dammit!" Abby said. "We'll have to keep him penned up to be sure he doesn't breed any of our cows."

"How are we going to do that? All three of us together can't budge him off the porch. It's like he's found a refuge, I tell you."

"I've got an idea if we can get this truck to moving. We'll use the truck to block the part of the yard fence where the cattle broke the wood down and came through. It doesn't have to fill all the hole, just enough that the bull can't get out."

"The dogs are having a fit, but he's ignoring them," Bonnie reported. "Shiloh let them in the house. She's going to wipe them down and get them warmed up by the fire."

Abby nodded. "Okay, you get in the truck. When I give you the signal, back it out slowly."

Bonnie nodded.

Abby shoved the board into the wet earth and gave Bonnie the thumbs-up sign. The tire spun a couple of times and then it caught and jerked backward with so much force that the board went flying. Abby fell backward again and more mud splattered all over her.

Bonnie applied the brakes and Abby waved at her to take the truck on to the ranch and block the hole in the fence with it. She didn't even try to wipe her face clean but climbed on the four-wheeler and followed Bonnie, who must be pretty damned good at parallel parking because she maneuvered that truck right into the hole. Abby would bet there was less than six inches of space on either end.

When she finished, Bonnie trotted out and settled in behind Abby. In twenty minutes both four-wheelers were parked back in the barn. They looked like shit, but then they'd been run through mud and manure and dodged lightning bolts. If Rusty didn't like it, he could damn sure wash them down all by himself.

They jogged through the cold rain to the house and the minute they were inside they started undressing, throwing coats and socks in a pile together. Shiloh had put another log on the fire so they were greeted with a toasty-warm and, more importantly, dry house.

"Does the leg need stitches?" Bonnie asked Shiloh.

"I'm accident-prone, so I carry a first-aid kit with me. I just cleaned it and bandaged it," Shiloh answered. She'd put her cute little pajama top back on, but now she wore plaid boxer shorts with it and the scratch on her leg had been covered with gauze and tape.

"You go first," Abby told Bonnie when they were inside. "I'll get dried off, throw the jackets and socks in the washer, and change into dry clothes. Then I'll start some dinner. Hamburgers all right with everyone?"

Bonnie padded down the hall in her bare feet. With no makeup and her hair hanging in strings, she looked young enough to be carded at any bar. The only thing old about her was her eyes, and they left no doubt that her life had been the roughest one of the three.

Abby loaded the washer, started it, and headed down the hall to her room, where she stripped naked and dried off. She grabbed a pair of flannel pajama pants from the dresser drawer along with underpants, a bra, and an oversized T-shirt. She dressed in record time and carried a pair of socks to the living room, where she flopped down in Ezra's chair. Clean, dry clothing had never felt so soft or good.

"So, hamburgers?" she asked Shiloh.

"I'm so hungry, I'll take a knife and carve a chunk out of that son of a bitch on the porch if we don't have enough hamburger thawed out," Shiloh said.

Abby couldn't hold back the laughter. She wiped at her eyes and said between hiccups, "I can't believe that just came out of your mouth. I can see Bonnie doing that, but not you."

"Oh, sister, you've got a lot to learn about me. I'm tough as nails on the inside even if I'm not brave enough to sit in that chair," Shiloh said.

The conviction in her voice told Abby that she could definitely be a force to be reckoned with even if she hadn't helped get the vehicles out of the muddy fields.

"We can have ice cream sundaes for dessert and you can make cookies later for our nighttime snacks," Shiloh said.

"Thank you. I'll put the burgers in the skillet, so I can make the cookies while they're cooking. We can eat them warm with the ice cream." Abby left the chair and padded to the kitchen in her socks.

She peeled an onion, sliced it thin, and laid it on one side of a plate while the burger patties cooked. Then she chopped lettuce and sliced a tomato. When she finished that job she took the pickles, mayonnaise, mustard, and ketchup from the refrigerator and set everything on the cabinet. Her stomach growled loudly and she looked at the clock. Two thirty! That meant they had to go back out into the weather in two hours and feed the cows again. And they'd have to use her truck since the work truck was now serving as a barricade.

The cookies were in the oven. The hamburger patties were about done and everything else was ready, so Abby went to the living room and leaned on the back of the sofa. The blaze in the fireplace licked at the logs, consuming them to make heat. Was that what love did? Those flames would fade and die like Ezra's love for his three wives?

Bonnie came out of the bathroom decked out in mismatched pajama pants and a shirt. She took one look at the chair and, after sucking in a long lungful of air, sat down on it.

"That rain and all that work made you brave enough to sit in Ezra's chair?" Abby asked.

"Not brave at all," Bonnie said. "But Ezra is not going to have power over me where this chair is concerned."

Vivien left the fire and curled up at her feet. Martha stretched to take up the room Vivien left behind.

"Kind of funny how they know which woman they should take up with, isn't it?" Bonnie rubbed Vivien's ear between her thumb and forefinger. "Strange thing is that I like this old hound more than I do my mama most days. Don't get me wrong, I'd fight to the death with anyone who said a word against her, but some days I don't like her too well."

"I understand," Shiloh said.

"You? I thought you had a perfect life with your mama and aunt," Bonnie said.

"There's no such thing as perfect. My mama said that when you live with someone twenty-four-seven, you will fight occasionally. It doesn't matter if it's a parent-kid relationship or a husband-wife one, because nobody agrees every minute of every day on everything. Take this stupid carpet. I think it should be taken out and some kind of tile put in here," Abby said.

"We do need new carpet, but it should be a nice neutral color that doesn't show dirt or dog hair," Shiloh said.

"I think it should be bright orange to liven up the room," Bonnie said.

"Point proven," Abby said at the same time the oven timer dinged. "Cookies are done. Meat should be cooked, so let's eat."

Poor sisters! They looked like they were about to cave in. Bonnie had done 90 percent of the actual work, but Shiloh had given it her all and couldn't be faulted one single bit. Abby had lived in horrible situations for days on end but her sisters hadn't. They deserved a break.

"I'm doing the feed by myself tonight, ladies. My truck only seats two people. It's still raining and neither of you are riding in the back and I damn sure don't want my passenger seat to get wet, either," she said.

"No argument from me, but why don't one of us go?" Shiloh asked.

"And get my passenger seat wet? No, thank you," Abby said.

"What about the driver's seat?" Bonnie asked.

"I intend to take that quilt you are using and pad it really well," she told Shiloh.

"If I don't have to go back out there, you are welcome to it. There's a brand-new shower curtain still in the package in the linen closet. You could put it down first and then the quilt," Shiloh answered.

"I'll get all the towels washed up and put away after dinner," Bonnie said.

"I know where Ezra hid the whiskey and tequila. I'll have drinks ready when you get back," Shiloh said.

Abby nodded. "I'll be ready for a dry towel and a drink."

"Hamburgers have never looked so good," Bonnie smiled.

She still had an hour after dinner to go to her room, sit in the old gold rocking chair, and relax. She leaned her head back and had dozed off when she heard Bonnie and Shiloh arguing.

"What?" she asked.

Bonnie was in front of the fireplace, arms folded over her chest, glaring at Shiloh. Her book had been tossed to the end of the sofa and Shiloh was firing back dirty looks at Bonnie.

"I think we should call Rusty," Shiloh said.

"I don't. We took care of the problem. It's our ranch anyway," Bonnie shot back.

"Not for a year," Abby told them.

Their mean looks took a ninety-degree turn and landed on Abby.

"You are going to cast the deciding vote. Yes if we call him. No if we don't," Shiloh said.

"I don't give a shit either way." Abby would love to hear Cooper's voice, but she really could care less whether they told Rusty about the stampede or not.

Bonnie shifted her gaze back to Shiloh. "You're just wanting to brag that we took care of it on our own."

"Oh, for God's sake!" Abby fished her phone from her pajama pants and dialed Rusty's number. She hit the button for speakerphone and laid the phone on the coffee table.

"Hello to you. Is it still raining?" Rusty asked.

"Cats and dogs and baby elephants," Abby said.

"Well, sunshine is on the way. We've outrun it and I heard on the radio that it's moving out of the canyon in the next couple of hours. Everything going all right?"

"We've got it under control. This is on speakerphone and we're all here," she answered.

"Good. Coop wants to talk to you, so I'll put this one on speaker, too."

"Hey, it's come a real toad strangler, hasn't it?" Cooper said.

"Something like that. Y'all got the prisoner delivered?"

"Just now did and now we're on the way to the hotel."

"So you can go drinkin' and flirtin' with the pretty ladies?" she asked.

"We're both exhausted. We've decided to buy a six-pack of beer and a pizza and watch hotel movies in between naps," Cooper said. "What have y'all been doin' all afternoon? Paintin' your fingernails and readin' romance books?"

"You wouldn't believe it if I told you, but it hasn't involved pizza and naps," she said.

"Okay, now you've got my curiosity workin' double time. What did you do?" Cooper asked.

"Well, there was a stampede and we had to put most of the cows back where they belonged, and then we had a busted-up fence and then there was a big old bull lyin' up on the porch like he owned it, so the dogs had to come in the house," Shiloh said. "And tell Rusty that his four-wheelers look like shit."

Cooper chuckled. "And then the aliens landed in their flat little spacecraft and carried you all away to examine your brains. I know it's been raining like hell up there and y'all couldn't even get out of the house, so don't spin yarns to me."

"The real story is that we laid up in front of the television, got drunk on Ezra's moonshine we found hidden in the pantry, and painted our toenails, just like you said," Abby said.

"Are you mad? You sound angry," Cooper asked.

"Just how drunk are y'all to call me with a cock-and-bull story like this?" Rusty asked.

"Nope, just hurt that you don't believe our story. I was going to ask you to show me how to fix barbed-wire fence, but now I don't have to. Bonnie gave us a lesson and I can do it underwater," Abby answered. "Hell, I might join the navy so I can be a SEAL when I leave the canyon."

Cooper laughed again. "See you tomorrow. Don't forget we're going to the Sugar Shack on Saturday night."

"Come rain, shine, or snow, we—as in Abby, Shiloh, and I— are going to Amarillo tomorrow for dinner and to shop. If we're not back by evening, Rusty, the cows and feeding belong to you," Bonnie said.

Rusty laughed. "Your hangover should be gone by evening, but I'll take care of things for you since you want to get away from the ranch. Maybe you'll all be gone for good."

"Not in your wildest dreams," Shiloh said.

"And you can get the bull off the porch if he's still there when you get here," Bonnie said.

"I sure will and I'll shoo all those aliens away, too," Cooper said. "Y'all might want to stop drinkin' now, or you are going to hurt tomorrow. Good night, ladies."

Abby picked up the phone and shoved it back in her pocket.

"Well, we've told him," Shiloh said.

"And a hell of a lot of good it did. Neither one of them believed us," Bonnie said.

"They will tomorrow. I'm going to go stretch out on my bed and get a twenty-minute power nap. You both going to be here when I come back?"

"I'm not going anywhere," Bonnie said.

Shiloh picked up her book. "Wild horses couldn't drive me away."

"Good," Abby said.

Martha followed her into the bedroom and settled down on the rocking chair. Abby plopped down on the bed and pulled the side of the spread up over her feet, but instead of falling asleep instantly, the back of her eyelids became a never-ending slideshow, all of Cooper. There he was at the funeral, jumping over the barbed-wire fence, feeding her pecan pie, sitting beside her in the truck on the way to Silverton. And the one that she settled on at the end of the show was the one of his naked backside that Sunday when they'd had sex.

"Dammit," she said without opening her eyes. "Not a bad picture in the whole lot."

# Chapter Twelve

*W*e have half a bottle of tequila, a full bottle of Jack Daniel's, three beers, and whatever the hell is in this pint jar. If we open it, it'll be like we're inviting Ezra to the party." Shiloh set it all in the middle of the kitchen table.

"Do we need to take a vote?" Bonnie asked.

"If Ezra wants to come to our party, I'll even let him have his chair. I bet he won't stay long when we all tell him exactly how we feel," Abby said.

A deep-throated mooing sounded right outside the kitchen window.

"The bull has spoken. We will toast the three of us getting through this day with Ezra's stump liquor. Women doing a tough job and drinking his liquor. I'd say he won't even show his face," Bonnie said.

Shiloh twisted the ring from the jar and set it beside the rest of their meager bar. "Maybe the bull was calling out to his heifers rather than expressing an opinion."

It started as a chuckle, grew into a giggle, and exploded into laughter, with Abby wiping tears with the tail of her dark brown T-shirt.

"What the hell is so funny?" Shiloh frowned.

"Think about it. The rangy old bull calling out to his heifers. Ezra leaving half a pint of moonshine and naming his bitches after his ex-wives. Was he calling out to his women like that lonesome old bull?"

"I still don't think it's that funny, but then after what I found under my bed this afternoon, I'm not sure anything is funny," Bonnie said.

"Three boxes with your initials on the ends?" Shiloh asked.

Bonnie nodded. "Kind of creepy, isn't it? How'd you know about it?"

Abby felt their gazes turn to her. Suddenly, the moonshine and the lonesome old bull were not humorous. A chill that had nothing to do with the north wind whistling around outside on a moonless night chased down her spine.

"I found the same thing under my bed," she said. "I suppose that's why Rusty more or less assigned our rooms when we first got here."

"Seems like a year ago, doesn't it?" Bonnie whispered.

"How did going through those things make y'all feel?" Abby asked.

Shiloh poured whiskey into three glasses. "Angry, violated in a strange sense of the word, and empty at the same time." She threw hers back like an old cowboy in a Western movie.

Bonnie picked up the whiskey and sipped it. "Just mad as hell. He knew what was happening to me and he didn't give a shit. This drink is my one for the night. I've lived with it my whole life and seen what it can do to a woman. I'll see to it you two make it from living room to your bedrooms, but I do not clean up if you get sick."

Shiloh went to the refrigerator and brought out a two-liter bottle of Coke. She poured a couple of fingers of whiskey into a glass, added ice, and filled it with the Coke. "At first I was mad at Mama for sending him all those things. I called her and pitched a bitchin' fit. She listened for a couple of minutes and when she finally figured out what I was sayin', she was every bit as angry as I was."

Abby didn't mix good Jack Daniel's with anything, not water, not Coke, and she didn't throw it back. She sipped it, letting each tiny mouthful lie on her tongue for a few seconds before she swallowed. "Did you call your mama, Bonnie?"

She shook her head. "Mama is complicated. Sometimes I like her better drunk than sober. At least she's not a mean drunk and she is a mean sober person. I lived with her right up until I left Kentucky—the bills had to be paid and someone had to put food on the table for her."

"Who does that now?" Shiloh asked.

Bonnie shrugged and went to the refrigerator to pull out the sweet tea. "Like I said, it's complicated, but everyone has to learn to take care of themselves at some time in their life."

"Tough love," Abby said.

"You should know all about that. Haven't you been on your own since you were eighteen?" Shiloh asked.

"I have. I joined the army right out of high school and was in training school when I got the news Mama was gone. So I went home, took care of things just like she asked, leased out the doughnut shop for ten years, and rented a storage unit. I only missed a week of my schooling and the army let me make it up when I got back rather than making me start all over. I was nineteen a few weeks later. Couldn't even buy a drink or rent a car legally and I was on my own."

"Enough melancholy. I shoved the boxes back under my bed. I don't know what I'll do with them, but tonight we're celebrating. We have run this ranch for one day all by ourselves and we did a damn fine job of it." Shiloh raised her glass and the other two touched theirs to it, making a clinking sound in the quiet room.

"To the fastest learners in the state of Texas," Abby said.

"To the Malloy daisies." Bonnie smiled.

"Daisies?" Shiloh asked.

"Ezra must have thought about us as daisies or he wouldn't have told Rusty to give them to us to put in his casket," Bonnie said.

"I don't want to be a daisy. I want to be a rose," Shiloh said.

"Well, I want to be a bloomin' cactus, like what blooms in the desert," Bonnie said.

They looked at Abby.

One shoulder raised in a semishrug. "I like daisies. They're my favorite flower—but not the kind we pitched in the casket. I like the wild ones. They are hardy and free spirits."

Bonnie said, "I'll be a daisy, even if I do prefer those pretty, bright-colored blooms on cactus plants."

"I was a wild and free daisy today out there in the rain, chasing cows and mud wrestling with Abby," Shiloh said.

Abby laughed. "I've finished my drink so hand me that moonshine and we'll see how free my spirit can get tonight."

Shiloh slid the pint jar across the table to Abby. "Sowing wild oats on Saturday night means you have to go to church tomorrow morning."

She picked it up and carried it to the living room. "Sowing wild oats does not have anything to do with whiskey, tequila, or moonshine."

"Why?" Bonnie followed Abby.

"Why what? That it doesn't have to do with liquor or why don't I have to go to church?"

Bonnie sat down on the end of the sofa and set her glass on the coffee table. "Both, and where are the dogs?"

"I put them outside in their pens and I'm sure they are disappointed that they have to be in their doghouses rather than by the fire, but they won't leave that damned bull alone even from inside the house," Shiloh answered.

"What's wrong with the liquor?" Abby poured two fingers into her empty glass. "I'm just drinking, not sowing wild oats. Sowing means seed . . . think, Bonnie."

"Oh! If that's the reason, then I don't expect none of us need to go to church, because we haven't had time to sow wild oats this week," Bonnie said.

"Abby did." Shiloh joined them with another Jack and Coke in her glass.

"When?" Bonnie asked.

"I do not kiss and tell." Abby immediately wished she could cram the words back into her mouth. God Almighty, what was wrong with her? She couldn't be drunk on that little bit of liquor.

"Aha!" Shiloh pointed. "Was it good?"

"Curled my toes." Abby turned up the moonshine. Sweet Jesus, that shit had some kick and a hell of a lot of fire. It burned all the way from throat to gut and hopefully scalded her vocal cords so she couldn't talk.

"Tell us more," Bonnie said. "We want details."

"I won't tell any more than that. This is some potent shit, girls. You've got to at least taste it. It's got kick like vodka and for moonshine, it don't taste bad. I think I got a hint of peaches."

Bonnie headed back to the kitchen and returned with a red plastic cup. "I'm the 'shine expert. Let me have a taste."

Abby could hold her liquor. Hell, she'd put lots of big strong soldiers under the table, but that 'shine put a fuzzy halo around everything. The little diamond stuck on Bonnie's nose was twice as big as normal.

"And it sparkles like what floats around my head when Cooper kisses me," she muttered.

"What was that about kisses?" Shiloh asked. "One more drink and you'll be giving us a play-by-play of what happened when you fell into bed with Cooper."

"We're not talkin' about men tonight and it wasn't in a bed," Abby answered. "I've never done drugs, but I swear this must be the way they make you feel."

Shiloh tossed back what she had in her glass and gasped. "Dammit! That stuff really is pure fire." She fanned her mouth with her hand.

Bonnie sipped it slowly. "Not bad. My peach has more body, a hint of cinnamon and brown sugar, and less grit, but this would knock you on your ass just the same if you had very much of it. Here, Abby, you can have the rest of mine."

Abby's hand reached for it as if she had no control. That time it didn't burn as badly as the first but she had to concentrate to keep her wits about her. "Shit! That's some good stuff."

"This is at least a hundred and ninety proof and eight ounces will knock a seasoned drinker on their ass. You'd best not have any more or we'll be throwin' daisies on your casket in the mornin'," Bonnie said.

"Then get me a little bit of whiskey to cool down my throat," Abby said. "And why would this be worse than whiskey or too much wine?"

"A direct result of the floor coming up to meet your head when you stand up too fast. You've both had enough 'shine," Bonnie said.

"Bring the jar to me. I can drink as much as Abby any day of the week," Shiloh said.

"You'll be sorry, but if you want it, you can have it. Remember what I told you about cleaning up after yourselves," Bonnie said. "And if I'm bartending, you've both got to tell me a story."

"About what?" Abby tried to focus on the fireplace, but the flames wouldn't be still. They moved out of the fireplace and danced across the floor. Damn, but they were scorching when they reached her feet. She tossed the throw from her legs onto the floor and looked around for her dog. Why wasn't Martha in the house? Shiloh had put her in the pen. She didn't belong out there in the rain; she should be in the house, not in an old cold doghouse made of scrap metal and used wood. Martha was a sophisticated dog who knew how to herd cattle. If she got pneumonia, Abby was going to beat the shit out of Shiloh.

*Remember not to throw whiskey on that throw if the blaze catches it on fire,* she thought. *Lord, I'm drunk, and I've only had the equivalent of three drinks. Maybe I shouldn't drink any more. What do you think, Mama? You're usually in my head bitchin' at me when I drink. Where are you tonight?*

Bonnie handed Abby a glass with a finger of whiskey in the bottom and then put a glass with the rest of the 'shine in Shiloh's outstretched hand. "Which one of you is going first?"

"First with what? Oh, we have to tell you a story, right?" Shiloh turned up the moonshine and sipped it. "You're right, Abby, it kind of makes me glow from the inside out."

"Sounds like a personality drug." Bonnie laughed.

"I'll go first," Shiloh said. "A story. Let's see, which story. Does it have to be true?"

"The bartender has changed her mind. Tell me if you ever fantasize about how your life would have been different if you'd been raised right here," Bonnie said.

Shiloh sipped again. "Yes, I do, but I can't imagine having Ezra as a father. Lord, can you see him if I came in wearing a strapless prom dress that was cut up to my hip on the side?"

Abby slowly shook her head from side to side.

"What are you thinking?" Bonnie asked. "You are definitely disagreeing with the voices in your head about something."

"This shit isn't so bad after the first initial burn. I was thinking about the look on Ezra's face if I'd told him I was joining the army the week after graduation," Abby said.

Bonnie curled up on the end of the sofa, the throw from the floor over her legs.

"What about you?" Shiloh asked.

"I like to imagine his expression when I told him that it was past time for me to go on birth control. With his views . . . hey, now I'm wondering if y'all's mamas were virgins. I can't imagine my mama being one, not as wild as she was," Bonnie said.

Abby tilted her head to one side. Jesus, Mary, and Joseph! Thinking about her mother's sex life gave her the willies. Or maybe it was the combination of such thoughts added to the moonshine.

"What are you snarling your nose about?" Bonnie asked.

"What you just said about our mamas. Y'all know that Ezra thought we'd take the money and run, don't you?"

"No, I don't know that. I think he wanted us to know each other," Shiloh said.

"He wanted us to fight and bicker and disagree about everything," Bonnie said. "But we're getting our revenge on him by working together."

"The sober one tells it like it is." Abby reached across the recliner arm and patted her on the shoulder.

"I hope he's miserable. At least part of me does. The other part is glad that he made this decision." Shiloh slurred the last word and tried to say it right three times before she gave up. She finished off the 'shine in one last gulp. "Are you sure that's all of it? We could go down to the bunkhouse and steal the jar that Rusty says he's savin' for the year anniversary of Ezra's death."

"Bonnie, darlin', you will have to make a batch before the second anniversary of our dear papa's death so we can celebrate again." Abby's speech was even worse to her ears than Shiloh's.

"You have my promise," Bonnie said. "When the wild strawberries are ready, we'll pick a bunch and I'll try my hand at making a batch with a strawberry flavor."

"It'll be wonshurful," Abby said.

"What was he thinkin', spyin' on us like that? The room is spinning. It's been years since I've been drunk," Shiloh said. "I'm going to just lie down here and prop my head on the arm of this ugly-as-shit sofa. I'm going to throw it out in the yard for the dogs to sleep on when this ranch belongs to me. And I'm getting a nice neutral brown carpet. I'm not putting orange in here. God, it would look like a cheap hippie place."

"Well, thank you so much. Just for that smart-ass remark, I'll buy bright orange carpet for the whole place when the ranch is mine. And then I'll buy baby-pink leather furniture and paint all the walls turquoise," Bonnie said.

"Are you trying to make us puke?" Abby groaned.

"If you throw up, you clean up. I've done enough cleaning up after Mama in my lifetime. I'm not takin' on you two to raise at this late date."

"Oh, hush. I'm going to be here when both of y'all are long gone. Listen to that damned old bull wailing about his harem bein' gone," Shiloh giggled.

Abby reached for the lever to throw the chair back to a reclining position, but it was gone. "Shit fire! The bull ate the switch."

Bonnie got up and pulled the lever for her. "That make the room stop spinning?"

"Yes, ma'am. Thank you, ma'am. Now can you do something about those spiders on the ceiling?" Abby asked. "And Shiloh, I don't know what was in that old codger's mind about us. I think maybe he drank too much of this shit and it fried his brain cells. But I sure can't see him raisin' us three indie . . . pensh—shit, girls. God, Bonnie, get a flyswatter and kill them damn spiders."

Shiloh threw her hands over her eyes. "I see the spiders. Kill them, Bonnie. I hate spiders. Why would Abby put spiders on the ceiling? It's just to make us leave so she can have the ranch and this butt-ugly sofa. I bet she plans to have sex with Cooper on it."

Abby shut her eyes and there were her favorite pictures of Cooper again. She'd have to tell him to stay away from that god-awful moonshine when he got home. That shit would knock even a tough cowboy like him square on his butt. And if that happened, not a single wild seed would get sown, so they wouldn't need to go to church. Had he asked her to go to church with him next week, or was it to a candy factory? She remembered something about a sugar shack. Surely to goodness the church wasn't named that. It had to be a candy place. She hoped they sold good chocolate and maybe even peanut butter fudge like her mother used to make.

"I'm going to bed," she announced loudly. "Bonnie, throw the switch to get me out of this chair, please."

Thank God for furniture and walls and Bonnie, who performed some kind of magic to get her out of Ezra's chair. She slowly made her way from doorway to chair, which she missed when she tried to sit down and slid down to the floor.

"Ass okay," she slurred.

The doorbell rang and she tried to stand up, but the walls kept moving toward her. On the third ring she figured out it was coming from her hip pocket, which meant it was her phone and not the doorbell. She fished it out and dropped it on the seat of the chair.

"Damn slippery little thing. I bet Shiloh greased the sucker down." Finally she got control of it and answered, "Hello."

"Did I wake you?" Cooper asked.

"Nope, the bull was ringing the doorbell. Pesky old fart learned a new trick but I'm not going to charge you for it," she said.

"Are you high or drunk?"

"I. Do. Not. Did. Drugs," she said emphatically.

"How much of that moonshine did you drink?" Cooper's voice was so loud that she held the phone out from her ear and scowled at it.

"Don't holler at me. I can hold my liquor," she said.

"I wasn't yelling. I was actually talking low because Rusty is asleep."

"Bullshit. That's what's all over the porch and the roses are gone and I hate roses. Did I tell you that? I do not like roses. Don't bring me roses when we have sex."

"Abby, you are drunk."

"I'm not drunk. Do you need glasses? I told you I can hold my liquor."

"Why would I need glasses?"

"To see that I'm not drunk. Did I tell you that the bull rang the doorbell and that I think you are sexy and it would be easy to fall in love with you and good night, Cooper?"

He chuckled. "Good night, Abby."

"Don't laugh at me."

"I'm not. I'm laughing at that bull on the front porch. I think he's teaching the cows to two-step," Cooper said.

"You're the one who is drunk. Bulls can't dance." She hit the "End" button, tossed the phone on the chair, and crawled to the bed, but after three tries she gave up trying to get on the bed. She slept on the floor, covered with the spread she'd pulled off the bed sometime in the night when she got cold.

# Chapter Thirteen

*A*bby's nose twitched at the smell of bacon and coffee. She opened her eyes slowly, only to focus on the three boxes under her bed.

"Go away, Ezra." Her mouth felt like someone had made her eat alum.

She pulled the cover over her aching head and shut her eyes. A bull bellowed from right outside her bedroom window and she sat up too fast. The room did a couple of spins, but her stomach did one more past that. She lay back down on the floor, facing away from the boxes. She managed to get to her feet and to the living room, one slow step at a time. Nothing looked like they'd had a wild party the night before, but her head and eyes said otherwise. Shiloh was on the sofa, snoring like a lumberjack, and that rascal of a bull was out there in the yard, calling for his women.

"Calling?" She frowned. Someone had called her on the phone. She remembered thinking it was the bull ringing the doorbell.

"Wake up, ladies." Bonnie's voice rang through the kitchen and out into the living room.

Abby cut her eyes around to the sofa, where Shiloh was sprawled out as much as its narrowness allowed. One arm dangled toward the floor. She'd die right there if she could see that granddaddy longlegs spider not six inches from her fingertips.

Bonnie flipped on the light.

Shiloh raised her head, dark hair completely covering her face. She plopped back down with a moan. "Shit! There's a drum playin' in my head."

"That's called a hangover. I had a headache this morning from just sipping that shit and a little whiskey. I can't imagine what you two are feeling, but I've got the cure. Sit up and take your medicine, ladies," Bonnie said.

"If I ever look at moonshine again, shoot me," Abby said.

Bonnie shoved a spoonful of something toward her mouth and she opened up.

"Honey?" Abby asked. "What good is that shit?"

"You will be surprised. Your turn, Shiloh." Bonnie stepped on the spider and didn't even mention it when she refilled the same spoon and made Shiloh eat the honey.

"It's not working," Abby whined.

"That's because it's step one. The next step is strong black coffee and then you are eating eggs. Whatever that shit is in eggs helps break down the alcohol. And after that you will each eat a banana," Bonnie said.

"Not me. I'm going to crawl to the bathroom and pee and then I'm going to bed," Shiloh said.

Bonnie raised her voice. "We've got chores to do and then we are going to church."

Abby covered her ears. "Don't yell anymore. I don't want to smell pig shit and hear a preacher yell at me. It's all Ezra's fault. He shouldn't have died before he used up all that moonshine."

Bonnie pulled the covers from Shiloh and tapped Abby on the shoulder. "If you don't both get on your feet, I will start singing at the top of my lungs, and believe me, I cannot carry a tune. So on your feet and to the table for coffee. When that's in your stomach, you'll have scrambled eggs, toast, and bacon. Then a banana. After that you could whip a whole passel of grizzly bears."

"How'd you get so damn smart about hangovers?" Abby held her head all the way to the kitchen, where she melted into a chair and laid her face on the cool wood table.

"When I was about thirteen, I got tired of dealin' with Mama, so I went to the library and looked up cures for hangovers and toyed with them until I found one that worked. We might not have had money for a hamburger, but I saw to it there was always honey, coffee, eggs, and bananas in the house," Bonnie said.

"I will puke if I eat a slimy banana," Shiloh said.

"No, you won't. Here's the coffee and two aspirin for each of you. I'll get the eggs ready."

"You are not my boss. I'm not going to church," Shiloh said.

"Yes, you are, because afterward we are going to Amarillo for dinner, shopping, and maybe even a trip to the Walmart beauty shop for our hair and a mani-pedi, if they have them. Believe me, by the time church is over, you are going to be ravenous. And would you look at your fingernails? Waylon won't look twice at you with fingernails like that. And Abby, Cooper is not going to bed with a woman who has straw for hair," Bonnie said.

Abby popped the pills in her mouth and washed them down with coffee. "Now she thinks she's our damn therapist."

Shiloh's chin quivered. "Are my nails really that bad?"

Abby leaned back to get a better look and nodded. "They are."

Shiloh's hands went up to cover her eyes. "Well, your hair looks like hell."

"No fighting this morning. Eat and then we're doing our ranchin' business and then we're going to Amarillo. Besides I've never had the money to blow on a mani-pedi and I want one," Bonnie said.

"Let's skip church," Abby said.

"No, ma'am," Bonnie answered.

Shiloh held her hands out in front of her face. "Never had a mani-pedi?"

"No, I had to buy eggs, bananas, coffee, and honey, remember. I wasn't spoiled bitches like you two," Bonnie said.

"We can't go in my truck. There's only room for two and don't call me a spoiled bitch. I've never been spoiled a day in my life," Abby said.

"Well, my poor old truck got me here on a prayer and four bald tires, so Shiloh, your van will have to take us," Bonnie said.

Abby wasn't going to argue. If her head would stop pounding, she'd let the bellowing bull in the yard drive them to town.

❋ ❋ ❋

The congregation was already singing the first song when the Malloy sisters entered the church. They slid into the first place with room for three people and Shiloh picked the last hymnbook from the pocket on the pew in front of them. She looked over at an elderly woman's book to find the number and flipped pages until she located the right place.

Abby held her hands in her lap to keep from slapping them over her ears to blot out the loud singing. Did everyone have to sing at the top of their lungs? Couldn't they be quieter? It was a church, for goodness' sake, not a rock concert. Every single piano note reverberated in her head, bouncing off aching brain cells like thunder in the canyon. It even felt like the pew was shaking.

God was punishing her for drinking Ezra's moonshine or maybe for mixing it with Tennessee bourbon, because he'd chased all the clouds away that morning and brought out bright—ultrabright—sunshine.

Bonnie elbowed her in the ribs. "Take off those sunglasses. You are in the house of God and that's rude."

Abby put them in her lap and her cell phone vibrated in her pocket. Would lightning rain down upon the church if she opened her phone discreetly to see if some catastrophe had happened on the ranch? They had, after all, left it completely unmanned and that damn bull might have decided to tear the porch down looking for his harem.

She slipped her hand in her pocket and laid the phone on the cushion between her thigh and the end of the pew. Very carefully, she touched the screen and brought up the messages from Rusty and Cooper.

*Why didn't Bonnie make* them *come to church?* she wondered and then remembered that they'd taken a road trip with a prisoner. They'd be home today and they could take care of the bull roaming around the house, bawling for his lady friends.

Bull. Doorbell. Phone. It came back to her in a flash. Holy shit! Had she really told Cooper that she could fall in love with him?

She checked the messages, hoping that she had not said those words out loud.

*On our way home. Can't wait to see you. I do believe Ezra's moonshine melted your wings last night.* That was from Cooper.

From Rusty: *Call me!*

She sent one back to Cooper: *In church. Hangover. Moonshine is made in hell.*

And one to Rusty: *Later!*

Bonnie elbowed her again. "Turn that off."

When did that little shit become the boss? Just because she could almost cure a hangover, that didn't make her God. Abby shut it off and shoved it back into her pocket.

She felt as out of place as a hooker on the front row of a tent revival, anyway. For one thing, it had been years since she'd been in a church. For another, it had been nearly a year since she'd worn anything other than jeans or a uniform and the long skirt felt confining. Shoes with heels weren't as comfortable as her combat boots and the bright blue sweater itched. She had nicked her knee twice shaving that morning. Now her legs looked like she'd run through brambles, but at least the long skirt covered most of that.

She fidgeted with the collar of the sweater when the preacher started his sermon about forgiveness. She'd rather forget Ezra than forgive him, especially after all that stuff under her bed.

Her headache slowly faded as she let her mind drift back to the ranch. It wasn't nearly as desolate as it had seemed when she'd first arrived. Bonnie wasn't quite the brazen hussy that she'd thought her to be at first either, nor was Shiloh a prissy bitch. In the worst-case scenario, she could possibly run the ranch with them—as long as nobody ever brought out another jar of moonshine.

The sermon wound down on a louder note than it began, but by then Abby's head had settled down and she was hungry. Bonnie was right. She could probably put a buffet out of business. She reached into her pocket, but she'd forgotten her normal stash of candy. Damn that moonshine.

"Hungry?" Bonnie asked the minute the last amen was said.

"Starving," Abby answered.

"I had my heart set on Italian, but I can't make it to Amarillo. Rusty mentioned that little diner in Claude. Let's go get a burger or a chicken-fried steak or something really fattening," Shiloh said.

"Where's the cowboy she's eyeballing?" Abby whispered to Bonnie.

Bonnie nodded toward the back of the church. "The one in the green shirt. Dark hair, blue eyes, brooding look."

"I see him. He is one delicious hunk, isn't he?"

"Stop it," Shiloh hissed.

"Not my type. Too serious for me," Bonnie said as they moved out into the center aisle.

"What's his name?" Abby asked.

"Waylon. He's a cousin to Nona's husband," Bonnie said.

"Hey, ladies. Where's Rusty this morning?" Loretta and Nona made their way from the other side of the church to talk to them.

"He went with Cooper to deliver a prisoner somewhere," Bonnie said. "Good morning."

"I need my sunglasses," Abby said.

"They got into Ezra's moonshine last night," Bonnie whispered. Nona gasped. "Sweet Jesus."

"What do you know about Ezra's moonshine?" Loretta looked down at her short, blonde-haired daughter.

"Enough to know I don't want to try it a second time." Nona smiled and stuck out her hand toward Abby. "I'm Nona. You must be Abby, the oldest one of Ezra's girls. Y'all should come to Lonesome Canyon for lunch today."

"We are going to Amarillo to get our nails and hair done and do some shopping. You should come with us," Shiloh said.

"I'd love to, but the in-laws are here for the day." Nona tilted her head toward the other side of the church. "Maybe next time."

"Sure thing. Come on by the ranch this next week if you have time," Shiloh said.

"And y'all have an open invitation to come to Sunday dinner or come visit at Lonesome Canyon, too," Loretta said.

"Thank you," Bonnie said and nudged Abby.

"I'm sorry. This hangover is a bit—bitter sucker." She smiled. "I'm pleased to meet you, Nona. Like Shiloh said, come on over and see us or come around about dinnertime any day of the week."

Abby turned her phone back on while they walked from the church to Shiloh's van. She had two more messages from Cooper. The first one said: *Did the aliens come get the bull last night?*

The second one said: *Home by three.*

There was another one from Rusty that said: *Will take care of evening chores. Have fun in town.*

She slipped her phone back in her pocket. "How far did you say it was to that café?"

"It's at the top of the north end of the canyon. Not very far," Bonnie said.

"You can get there in about twenty minutes," a voice said behind them.

They all turned at once.

"Hello, I'm Waylon Stephens. I met these two last week." A man stuck out his hand toward Abby. "You must be Ezra's other daughter. I can tell by the eyes."

"Abby Malloy," she said.

His handshake was firm and his eyes kind. His dark hair feathered back and had been cut recently. No wonder Shiloh was smiling so big. He was a very handsome cowboy. Not as sexy as Cooper, but if beauty was in the eye of the beholder, then sexiness probably was also.

He dropped her hand and nodded. "All y'all will have to come over to my little spread sometime. It's right across the road from Malloy Ranch."

"Drop by our place. We have dinner every day at noon. Be glad to have you," Shiloh said.

Abby heard a bit of breathlessness in Shiloh's voice. Maybe by the end of the year, Shiloh would have something more than a ranch to keep her in the canyon.

"Hey, Waylon," Loretta said. "You comin' to Sunday dinner?" She and a whole group of folks had filed into the aisle behind Abby.

"Of course, he is." Nona was hugged up to her own cowboy. "This is Travis, my husband, Abby."

"Pleased to meet you," she said.

Lord, did she have to meet the whole canyon before she could get out of the church? Her stomach was growling and she really, really needed to put her sunglasses on. The fluorescent lighting mixed with the sun's rays pouring in from the windows didn't do a thing for the remnants of a lingering headache.

"I can't imagine having a married daughter and expecting twins at the same time," Shiloh said.

Abby wanted to strangle Shiloh. Another conversation just meant longer in getting out of the church and to the food.

"Me, either. Fate has a wicked sense of humor," Loretta said.

That day she wore a cute denim dress with pleats at the top and bright red buttons down the front and red cowboy boots. Her red hair was pulled up in a messy twist with curls on the top, making her look even taller.

No wonder Cooper had fallen in love with her when he was a boy. A woman who could look that good pregnant had probably been movie-star pretty at eighteen.

"Ain't that the truth about fate," Shiloh said. "I never expected to be here at my age trying to learn how to run a ranch."

"From what Rusty and Cooper say, you're all doin' a fine job to only have been here a week. In a year, it'll all be old hat." Loretta smiled. "We'd best get on out of here if we're going to have dinner before suppertime. Remember now, our door is always open."

"Thank you," Shiloh said.

"I can read your mind." Bonnie poked Abby in the ribs.

"Oh, yeah, what was I thinking?"

"That Cooper said you were doin' a good job. It made your eyes go all soft."

"Oh, hush. You might know a little about hangovers, but you aren't an expert on love, and besides, Rusty said it, too. Did that make your eyes go all soft?" Shiloh said.

"No, ma'am. I am not here to catch a husband and I don't need praise from Rusty or Cooper," Bonnie answered.

Everything reminded Abby of Cooper, from comments to pictures in her head. From the delicious little shiver down her spine when she thought of his touch to the smile on her face right then at Bonnie's comment.

✺ ✺ ✺

The Sunday special at the café was turkey and dressing with cranberry sauce, green beans, yeast rolls, and pumpkin pie for dessert. They managed to snag the last available table and all three ordered the special with sweet tea to drink.

"It's like Thanksgiving," Shiloh said.

"Not for me. Thanksgiving was working an extra shift so the folks with kids could be home for the day. Christmas was the same," Bonnie said.

Abby shrugged. "The army served turkey and dressing on the holidays. It wasn't what Mama made, but it tasted pretty damn good."

Since it was a special and only had to be dipped up and served, they weren't long getting their meal. Abby shut her eyes on the first bite and made appreciative noises. "This is so good. I may eat here every Sunday."

"And break Cooper's heart?" Bonnie asked.

"Hey, now! One night of drinking together does not make us all bosom buddies or BFFs or whatever the hell it's called these days." Abby waved at the waitress, who came right over.

"I want this plate all over again," she said.

"Did you remember that we do have pie for dessert?" the waitress asked.

"Yes, I'll have two pieces, whipped cream on both. What about you, Shiloh?"

She blushed. "I shouldn't, but . . . yes, and go away before I change my mind."

"Bonnie?" Abby asked.

Bonnie shook her head. "Just an extra piece of pie will do me."

"So that's two more specials and five pieces of pie, right?" the waitress asked.

"You got it," Abby said.

"I'm having ice cream when we finish with hair and nails. You two are going to be moaning and groaning about still being too full," Bonnie said.

"Not me. By the middle of the afternoon I'll be ready for ice cream," Abby said.

"My God, how do you stay so small?" Shiloh asked.

"Damn fine genes. Mama wasn't a big person."

"Well, my granny was as wide as she was tall and every bite of food I eat goes straight to my thighs and butt," Shiloh said. "But after that wicked, evil stuff last night, I'm starving."

"It burned all the calories right out of your body," Abby said. "Anything you eat today doesn't even count."

"You are full of crap," Shiloh leaned forward and whispered.

The waitress returned with more plates of food and slices of pumpkin pie with whipped cream, taking the dirty dishes back away with her.

Bonnie picked up the clean fork on the pie plate and cut a bite-size piece off. "Oh. My. God! This is delicious. Y'all can eat Cooper's cookin'. I'm not the one kissin' on him, so I don't give a shit if I hurt his little feelin's or not. I'm comin' here for pumpkin pie next Sunday if I have to walk."

"If Cooper doesn't want to cook, maybe we can all come back here with him and Rusty next Sunday," Abby said.

"And if he does?" Shiloh asked.

"Then I'm eating a steak and you can borrow my truck, Bonnie. I'd hate to see you walk that far. You'd be too tired to take care of the milkin' the next day," Abby said.

"And you don't know how to milk a cow, do you?" Bonnie's blue eyes danced when she joked.

Abby took a deep breath and told the truth. "No, I don't, and I don't like chickens."

"Well, I hate hogs," Shiloh admitted. "And I can't milk a cow, either."

"Looks like it might take all three of us to run that ranch after all." Bonnie grinned.

The waitress refilled their tea glasses. "Y'all must be the Malloy sisters. I heard you'd come to the canyon. Ezra used to come in here pretty often for our Sunday special and he always took an extra order home with him. Y'all sound like him when you talk. You all from Texas?"

"Galveston," Abby said.

"Arkansas, but I lived in Texas until I graduated high school," Shiloh said.

The waitress looked at Bonnie. "Kentucky after leavin' Texas."

"I knew I heard the good old Texas drawl in your voices," the waitress said as she walked away.

"Wonder how much she won on that pot?" Abby whispered.

Shiloh had been studying her ragged nails but she looked up.

"I bet they were betting in the kitchen that she couldn't find out where our mamas moved to after Ezra sent them packin'," Abby said.

"We probably are the headlines of the rumor mill," Shiloh said.

"Well, hot damn!" Bonnie grinned. "I always wanted to be in the headlines."

Abby's phone vibrated in her pocket. She removed it and read the text message from Rusty saying they would be home earlier than they'd planned.

"Cooper?" Shiloh asked after she'd finished.

"No, Rusty. They are making better time than they thought. They'll be home by two." Abby smiled.

"He's about to find out the truth about the bull?"

She nodded. "Even when I'm drunk, I do not lie."

A dozen cuss words filtered through her mind when she thought about not lying. She hoped for the millionth time that she had not told Cooper she could fall in love with him. And if she had said it, what was she going to do about it? She still wasn't ready to commit to the canyon, much less to a man, even if he was a damn fine-lookin' cowboy.

※ ※ ※

Forty-five minutes later, they were on the outskirts of Amarillo and Shiloh pointed at a sign. "Look! Nails and hair both done and they're open on Sunday and they take walk-ins. And it even gives the exit number."

"Just tell me where to turn," Bonnie said.

"My truck has a GPS system," Abby said.

"Your truck seats two people. Why didn't you buy a club cab?" Shiloh asked.

"Because there was only me and I didn't need it. I shouldn't have ordered that second plate. Now I'm too full and when I overeat, I get sleepy."

Shiloh pointed at an exit. "That's it right there. Turn off and then it said to turn left. I'm too full, too, but you are not taking a nap. You're going to stay awake and enjoy the afternoon."

Bonnie tapped the brakes and made the turn. "It must be in that shopping mall."

Abby pointed. "There's a wonderful parking spot. Let's go get our hair and nails done and do some serious shopping. If we're going to do this church thing so our wild oats don't take root, I need a couple more civilian outfits."

❊ ❊ ❊

"Holy shit, Coop! I thought Abby was joking when she said she traded some of my cows for your bull. Guess they have gotten into a lot of trouble in just two days," Rusty said.

Cooper pulled out his phone and called Abby.

"Why didn't you tell me my bull was in Ezra's yard?"

"I did. Several times, if you will remember. Both when I was sober and when I was drunk off my ass," she answered.

"How did this happen?" he asked.

"You figure it out," she said and hung up on him.

He called her right back. "For someone who could fall in love with me last night, you sure are bitchy today," he said.

"I was drunk. You can't believe a damn thing a woman says when she's drunk any more than you can believe what a man says when he's having sex."

He hit the "End" button, and immediately redialed her number. When she didn't answer he tried both Shiloh and Bonnie, but there was no answer there either.

"I'll hitch up the trailer," Rusty said after Cooper had put his phone away. "We'll load him up and see how many of my cows are at your place."

"Cows at my place?"

"I thought she was teasing, but she claims she traded some cows for him."

"That's not funny," Cooper said.

"I didn't think so either, but they were all laughing like a bunch of crazy people. Leave them alone for one day and look what happens. None of them are ranch material."

They started walking toward the barn when Cooper pointed to the back fence. "Looks like they started drinkin' pretty early in the day. They've knocked out a whole section of fence with the old truck. Too bad they were on private property or I could haul them all into jail for drinking and driving."

"Must've been one hell of a party. Couldn't you just take them in for a few hours and scare the hell out of them?"

"I don't think even jail would scare Bonnie or Abby."

"And Shiloh is smart enough, she'd probably play like a lawyer and talk them all three out of bail," Rusty said. "Oh, shit! I knew I was missing something. Where's the dogs? If they gave away those dogs, I'll shoot all three of them."

Rusty tipped his cowboy hat back and squinted out toward the pens. "They must have penned them up to keep them from tormenting the bull. But how in the devil did that bull get in the yard?"

"We'll figure it out, but I'm not asking Abby another thing. She's in a pissy mood today. Let's get this job done and then I'll fix us some steaks after we finish up the evening feeding chores. Your place or mine for supper?"

"Mine. That way we'll be there when they come in with all their explaining," Rusty said.

# Chapter Fourteen

"Magic has happened," Abby said when Bonnie parked the van between the silver truck and the poor little faded red one.

"We do look better, don't we? Course, now I feel guilty for spending money on my hair and nails when I could have done both myself and sent the money to Mama for the electric bill," Bonnie said.

"Tough love, remember," Shiloh said.

Abby pointed. "I wasn't talkin' about the magic of our nails and hair. Look, the yard fence is fixed and the bull is gone."

"Poor roses still look bad. Looks like he did manage to uproot a few bushes completely," Shiloh said.

"You any good with flowers?" Abby asked.

Shiloh nodded. "Mama says I have green thumbs."

"Then taking care of the flowers is your job. If I breathe on a plant, it dies."

"Silk flowers die in my care, but I can make a garden produce, so I'll take that job," Bonnie said. "Next week we should put the onions and potatoes in the ground."

"Reckon Cooper has made supper to pay us back for taking care of his bull?" Shiloh changed the subject.

"I wouldn't count on it, but I am hungry again. We forgot all about stopping for ice cream," Abby answered. "Pop the back door so we can unload our bags. I sent a text to Rusty letting him know that we were doing the grocery shopping and I'd bring the receipt for him to repay me."

"That was so much fun in the grocery store. Getting to buy what we wanted to cook with instead of having to make do with whatever was on sale," Bonnie said.

"And all those lovely things we found in the mall. I can't wait to go to church next Sunday just so I can wear that cute little dress I found," Shiloh said.

"You're not foolin' me about wanting to go to church—you want to get all gussied up for Waylon Stephens. You could do worse, though. And he's a real cowboy," Bonnie said.

"How do you know that?"

"Woman, when you've been around as many cowboys as I have, you can tell the wannabes from the real ones a mile away. It's the way they walk in boots and the way they settle their hat on their head," Bonnie answered.

"And the way they wear their jeans," Abby chimed in.

"You're so right. Tight as a hide across the butt and bunched up on their boot tops," Bonnie added.

Abby crawled out of the van. She couldn't wait until next Saturday night so she could wear her new designer jeans and cowboy boots at the Sugar Shack. She should have bought the red boots, but the brown ones with that phoenix done in relief on the front had called out to her, and they'd been on sale, half price.

*Are you going to get all gussied up and torture Cooper?* The voice in her head was her mother's. *Or are you thinking about boots to keep from remembering what you said about falling in love with him?*

"What are you frowning about? One minute you were all smiles and now you look like you sucked on a lemon," Bonnie said.

"I was analyzing why I bought these boots," Abby said.

"So you could wear them to the Sugar Shack and show Cooper that you are a sexy woman and not just GI Joe with boobs," Shiloh said.

Abby couldn't argue with the truth. She had been thinking that very same thing—well, maybe more about how Cooper would react to her in something other than camouflage.

"Well?" Shiloh said.

"You are right." Neither of them needed to know that she'd also been worried all day about telling him that she could fall in love with him.

Cooper and Rusty were sitting on the sofa watching an old John Wayne Western on television. Cooper looked up and waved. Rusty didn't even acknowledge them.

"We could use some help with the groceries," Bonnie said.

"We did the feeding chores. You can bring in the food. What's for supper, Abby?" Rusty asked.

"It's Cooper's day to cook. But I did buy corn chips, chili, and cheese so you can make chili pies. And there's ice cream in the freezer to chase it with," she said.

"Sounds good to me. Call us when it's ready." Cooper didn't take his eyes off the television.

Bonnie pointed her finger at both of them and said, "This is Sunday. What did you tell us about the food? Get up and make your own chili pies."

"Don't you want to know what happened while you were gone?" Shiloh asked.

"You don't need to explain a thing to us. We figured out exactly what happened," Cooper said. "It was stormy and that bull of mine hates storms. I should have put him in the barn before I left. He broke through the barbed-wire fence and created a stampede. He's got a couple of scratches on his chest to prove it, and the herd didn't stop running until this house slowed them down. Y'all used the truck to block the fence and you are lousy at mending barbed wire. I will have to give you some lessons in that. Now will you please go on about your business and let us watch this movie?"

Bonnie's hands popped onto her hips and she glared at both of them. "I did a damn fine job of fixing that fence. Neither of you could have done better and you are so welcome for us keeping your precious bull corralled for you."

"It's going to be y'all's ranch in a few months. You just did what you should have done and you don't get someone kissing your pretty little asses when you do that," Rusty said. "Y'all go on and enjoy your chili pies. We grilled a steak and made us a skillet of fried potatoes. We're good until tomorrow morning. Now move so we can watch the rest of the movie."

Abby picked up her bags and carried them to her room. Then she went out the back door, rounded the house, and brought in the groceries. There was more than one way to teach those two cowboys a lesson.

Shiloh and Bonnie were on the way to the van to help carry groceries as she was taking in the first four bags. She smiled and said, "It's time to kill snakes."

"Where's a snake?" Shiloh looked like she was about to bolt and run.

"It's an expression Mama used—there's more than one way to kill a snake. Y'all just play along with me. I'm about to make supper, ladies. If I remember right, those two smart-ass cowboys do like their desserts, but they told us they're good until morning, according to Rusty."

"How long until we eat? I didn't have a double dinner like you two," Bonnie said.

"About half an hour. I'll start cookin' if y'all put away the groceries," Abby said.

While Bonnie and Shiloh emptied bags and filled the pantry shelves, Abby got out the biggest cast-iron skillet she could find. She set it on the stove and turned on the oven to make peach cobbler. It was a quickie recipe that called for crescent rolls out of a can, peach pie filling, and spices. Separate the crescent rolls, put a peach slice on the top, add a pat of butter, half a teaspoon of brown sugar, and a shake of cinnamon, and roll it up. Lay it in a cake pan and repeat until two cans of rolls were done. Then pour the juice from the pie filling over the top and bake until the bread was done.

While that cooked, she put a pot of rice on the back of the stove and poured olive oil into the cast-iron skillet. She diced two chicken breasts and an onion, which sizzled when they hit the grease.

She handed a wooden spoon to Shiloh. "Keep that stirred while I get the rest ready, please."

"I love stir-fry," Shiloh said.

The sizzling onions sent a wonderful aroma all through the house. By the time the rice was done and fluffy, the cobbler had finished. She added bell peppers and broccoli to the skillet, waited a couple of minutes until the broccoli was bright green, and tossed in chopped cabbage.

"Let the cabbage wilt just a touch and then we'll need a few dashes of soy sauce and a lid for three minutes and we're ready to eat," Abby said.

"And to think I believed you when you said you couldn't make anything but chili pies." Bonnie stuck a finger in the edge of the cobbler and licked it. "You should have made two. I could eat every bit of this one all by myself. Shopping and being pampered is hard work."

Cooper poked his head around the corner into the kitchen. "Hey, just wanted to tell you that I'm leaving. Got a desk full of work to do tomorrow, so I won't be here for dinner. Is that peach cobbler over there?"

The sound of his voice sent Abby's senses reeling and his eyes boring into hers melted her insides. Sparks flew around the room. The temperature shot up at least ten degrees. Her hands itched to touch him, even if it was just for a brief hug.

"It is, and Abby is making stir-fry. Too bad y'all are too full to even taste it," Bonnie said.

"I'll miss it. And I've got a deputy with the flu, so I'll be in the office all day tomorrow," Cooper said.

Now he wasn't coming the next day for dinner, so that would be four days since they'd sat beside each other. She wanted to stomp her foot and throw a hissy like a two-year-old who didn't get her way.

"I'm off to the bunkhouse," Rusty yelled.

"See you tomorrow morning, unless you want to sleep in and let us take care of the feeding," Bonnie hollered back at him.

They helped their plates right off the stove and had barely sat down at the table when Abby felt her phone vibrate in her pocket. She pulled it out and smiled.

"Which one is it?" Bonnie asked.

"Did we make them suffer with this food?" Shiloh asked.

"Cooper. He says I'm wicked, evil, and downright mean. That Chinese food is his favorite and he has to go all the way to Amarillo to get anything decent and that it wouldn't be as good as what he smelled in the kitchen."

"Success!" Bonnie threw up both hands to high-five with her sisters.

❀ ❀ ❀

Abby studied a huge formation that looked vaguely like a chimney from the porch. It changed colors as the sun settled behind it and dusk came to the canyon. She'd tried calling Haley, but it had gone to voice mail and she'd just spent the whole day with Shiloh and Bonnie. They wouldn't want to hear about her restlessness that night or to take a walk with her, either, but she had to do something. She couldn't sit still and yet there was no place to go.

When she was in the army, she ran when she felt like this. And after that enormous dinner and then an equally big supper, she should either go for a run or take a long walk, but she wasn't doing it in a skirt. She went back inside and changed into her comfortable pants and a black turtleneck, put on her heavy jacket, a stocking hat, and gloves. Before she left, she made sure her phone was tucked into the cargo pocket on the side of her leg. She eased out the front door and Martha followed her off the porch and out of the yard.

Her intentions were to walk all the way to the road, but the moonlight reflected off the granite tombstones and reached out to her, so she opened the creaky little gate and went inside. Starting at the front side were names like Hiram Malloy and his wife, Rachel, both of whom had died in 1865. She touched the stones and wondered if Hiram had been young enough to fight in the Civil War and which side he'd defended.

These were her ancestors, whether she liked it or not. Their lives had molded and made the next generation right down through time until Ezra's day. His decision to push her and her mother away had made Abby who she was as well. Her therapist in the army had said she'd probably enlisted to prove she was as good as a son would have been. She touched the tombstone at the head of the mound of wet red dirt. "I was trying to make you understand I was as good as a son. I could and can do anything a boy can do."

She perched on Ezra's tombstone and tucked her hands into her pockets. Somewhere over in the vicinity of Cooper's ranch, she could hear a lonesome old coyote howling at the sky, telling Mother Nature he was tired of winter and wanted spring to push the cold weather into the history books. The wind rattled the bare limbs of the misshapen scrub oak trees outside the cemetery fence. In a few weeks the trees would be decked out with green leaves and the ranch would take on a whole new look. She was deep in thought about Bonnie's garden and Shiloh's roses when she heard the rustling of dead leaves behind her.

"Coming to grips with it?" Cooper asked from the shadows of a big scrub oak tree.

She wasn't sure what to say. There was the man whom she'd told she could fall in love with him not ten feet from her. She remembered the commitment issues she and Shiloh had talked about and it still scared the hell out of her.

"Maybe. I don't know if I am or not. It's easier to accept that these other people were my ancestors than to acknowledge that he was my father. And I was very drunk last night when you called." She blurted out the last line.

"There is no doubt about that," he said.

"What are you doing here?"

"I went for a walk," he said. "I should keep going. See you later."

"Enjoy your walk." She wanted him to stay, but then she wanted him to go. That comment about falling for him was between them and she wasn't sure how to get rid of it.

"Thanks," he said stiffly and she heard rustling leaves as he left.

She sat down on an old wooden bench in the dark shadows of one of the big scrub oak trees on the north side of the cemetery.

"Why did you keep watch on us, Ezra, if you didn't want to have us around?" she mumbled. "I can't figure it out."

She glanced at the tombstones closest to her. They were her grandparents somewhere back down the line. "Grandparents!" She slapped her knee. "That's it."

It had come to her in bits and pieces, but when she analyzed the whole thing, she'd figured it out. If any one of them had given birth to a son, that child would have inherited Malloy Ranch. He'd kept a watch on his three daughters to see who was the smartest, who worked the hardest, and who wound up with the best man.

The pieces fit together like a jigsaw puzzle.

If his daughters all had sons born the same month or the same year, he would have had to choose among them. What if the oldest son was a lazy shit who wouldn't work or the youngest one got picked up for selling drugs on the street corner? Or what if one son was illegitimate and the other two had fathers but one of the fathers was a rancher and the other one was an airplane pilot?

Ezra would have chosen the best one to inherit his ranch and money through what he'd learned about his daughters. Abby thought it sad that he'd missed so much with his own daughters, only to die knowing that he didn't have a grandson to leave his ranch to after all.

She didn't realize how long she'd sat there until the north wind had started to blow hard enough to push its way through the bare tree limbs. She shivered and pulled her hat a little tighter. Time to head back to the house.

Leaves crunched again to signal Cooper's approach. He sat down on the bench beside her.

"You are still here?" he asked.

"I didn't mean to be, but I figured out something important." She told him about the grandson idea.

"You could be right. Ezra was a cagey old fellow," Cooper said. "Now about what you said on the phone."

"I was drunk," she whispered.

"I know that, so let's delete it just like we do things on the computer," he said.

"Is that possible once it's been said?"

He slid over closer and put his arm around her, drawing her close to his side. "We did it with sex, didn't we?"

She laid her head on his shoulder and it wasn't awkward. "Okay, then, hit the 'Delete' button."

"I know you aren't growing roots, yet, Abby. But you will if you stay until spring. One day you will wake up and wonder where your wings went."

"I'm beginning to hope you are right, Cooper, but I'm not taking that to the bank. Not yet." She thought about leaving and suddenly there was a hole in her heart. In the next instant she let the idea of roots and staying take precedence and everything felt right in the world. But right then she was in Cooper's arms and that could influence her decision a lot.

"You don't have to. Just tell me when it happens."

She nodded. "I promise."

"That's good enough for this day," he said.

His black cowboy hat was pulled down low enough on his brow that she couldn't see his eyes, but she could feel him looking at her.

"Thanks, Cooper. I might not be the woman I am today if Ezra had accepted me as a daughter, so I'm trying to think about that and not hold on to the bitterness."

Cooper squeezed her hand. "Ezra wasn't all bad, Abby. His mother died when he was a little kid. I don't know if it was in childbirth or if it happened when he was a toddler, but he wasn't very old. His father raised him right here on the ranch without any women around, not even a cook or housekeeper. Your mother was the first woman in fifty years to live on this ranch."

"How did you know all that?"

"He told me bits and pieces through the years," Cooper answered.

"He got his comeuppance in the end, didn't he? All that work and money he had to have paid out and still no satisfaction. Now his three daughters are living together and we really don't hate each other, which is what he wanted us to do. I pity a man like Ezra who couldn't move past a woman who broke his heart and love one of the three women he married."

"Knowing Ezra, he would rather have your hate than pity."

"It is what it is. Today it's pity. I wonder what these other folks saw in this canyon. It doesn't have a lot to recommend it."

"It's home," he said.

"I guess it is at that."

He tucked a fist under her chin and lowered his face to hers. Their cold lips met in a kiss right there in the cemetery under a scrub oak tree that had shaded part of the cemetery for years.

Crazy, insane thoughts chased through her mind. No one should think about fertilizer when a handsome, sexy cowboy was kissing her. But that's exactly what came to Abby's mind. With each kiss, each touch, and every glance, it was as if she really was putting down roots in the canyon. Perhaps that meant everything he did was like the root stimulator her mother used on the petunias in the flower boxes at the café. If so, maybe growing roots wouldn't be such a bad idea after all.

Several long, lingering kisses later, he pulled away. They were both panting by now and she forgot about anything but the ache down deep that wanted so much more than kisses.

He gripped her hand in his and led her out of the cemetery. "I'm walking you home now, Abby."

"And then I'll drive you home," she said.

"I can hop the fence and be there in a few minutes. Besides, as hot as I am right now, I need the cooldown time," he said.

"I know," she whispered.

Had she really been making out like a teenager? And in the cemetery? A slow burn started at the base of her neck and crept around to her cheeks.

Keeping her hand tight in his, he walked her right up to the door, with Martha tagging along behind them. He kissed her and whispered, "Good night, Abby. Thank you for taking care of the cattle, the bull, and the fence. And please make Chinese food on one of your days to cook this week."

"It's a promise," she whispered.

He let go of her hand and she felt empty, as if someone had torn all her new little roots out of the ground. She wanted to reach out and tell him to come inside with her, even if only for a cup of coffee, so she could reclaim the feeling, but he was jogging toward the barn. She watched until he was completely out of sight before she went inside.

Martha rushed in ahead of her and curled up in front of the fireplace with Vivien and Polly.

"Where have you been?" Bonnie looked up from the sofa.

"The cemetery."

Shiloh picked up the remote and put the television on mute. "Was that Cooper on the porch with you?"

Abby dragged one of the wooden rocking chairs across the floor so it was close enough she could prop her boots on the coffee table and then sat down. But she was far too antsy to prop her feet. She set the chair into motion with her foot. The constant movement rested her frazzled nerves a little bit. "It was Cooper, and I figured out something about those boxes under our beds while I was at the cemetery."

"I'd rather hear about Cooper and if he kisses good. Cemeteries give me the creeps," Bonnie said.

"What'd you figure out?" Shiloh asked.

Abby told them her theory about why Ezra had kept such close tabs on them.

"Wow!" Shiloh whispered.

"The old shit! If it had been me who'd had a son, he wouldn't have even looked at my boy," Bonnie said.

"What makes you think that?" Abby asked.

"Because he would have liked me the least."

Shiloh shook her head. "I don't think so. He would have been proud of you, Bonnie. You know more about ranchin' than either of us and he would have respected that."

"And you are a lady, so he would have liked you," Abby told Shiloh.

"And you are so smart, Shiloh."

"But you, Abby, you are the one who showed him that a woman can be anything she wants, including a soldier. No, Bonnie, I think in his own way, he was probably proud of all of us. Not that he would ever admit it," Shiloh said.

"Maybe so, but it's damn sad that he gave up knowing us and waited for a grandson that never came along," Abby said.

# Chapter Fifteen

Cooper hadn't shown up for dinner either Monday or Tuesday. At first Abby was antsy, but by Wednesday she was bitchy. Just when she thought she was putting a couple of roots down, Madam Fate created a virtual tornado that tore everything up. She was glad she was cooking that day so she could be alone. Neither Shiloh or Bonnie needed to have to deal with her bad mood.

Damn that sheriff business that kept him at the courthouse both days and today he had a prisoner escort from Silverton to Lubbock. It was less than a hundred miles, but it would take all morning and part of the afternoon by the time the paperwork was done.

Abby and her sisters had set up a pattern that first week. The living room and dusting belonged to Shiloh on Monday. Cleaning the kitchen and utility room was Bonnie's job on Tuesday and the bathrooms were Abby's on Wednesday.

With all her jobs completed, and an hour left before the rest of the crew came home for dinner, she was bored. She'd called Haley earlier but she was in class all day. Both her sisters were repairing the corral so they could bring up the cattle next week to be vaccinated and tagged. After dinner she'd be out there with them, slinging a hammer and tearing away rotted boards, learning still another ranchin' job. She only hoped her mood softened by then.

She heard the crunch of tires coming up the lane and looked at the clock. No, it was still at least forty-five minutes until dinnertime. When Martha barked, Abby jumped. Usually all three dogs went with whoever was going out on the ranch. It didn't matter if they were fixing fence, plowing, drilling wheat, or feeding in the morning and the evening, the dogs were there.

Surely those Bible-toting folks didn't come all the way into the canyon looking for lost souls. She flung open the door just as Nona raised a hand to knock on it. Nona's bright smile put a little light in the dark mood she'd been toting around all morning.

"Hi, Abby. I hope you meant it when you invited me to drop by."

"Yes, of course we meant it. Please come in." Abby motioned her inside the house. "Would you like a glass of sweet tea or a beer?"

"Tea would be nice." Nona followed her into the kitchen. "Something smells good in here. Are you the cook?"

"Today I am. We take turns cooking. I'd rather be outside." She filled two glasses with ice and sweet tea. "It's chicken and rice. Can you stay for dinner? There's always plenty."

"I'd love to. What can I do to help?" Nona picked up the tea and downed a third of it before coming up for air. "Our cook is taking the morning off to go grocery shopping. Travis took a sandwich with him to the fields so he didn't have to stop plowing today. And I can't cook worth a damn, so I'd love to eat with y'all."

"Your mother mentioned that you just got married recently," Abby said.

"Only three weeks ago. I should have come over and welcomed all y'all to the canyon before now, but things have been crazy on Lonesome Canyon. Learning so much all at once sometimes overwhelms me."

"Yes, ma'am." Abby nodded. "I can understand that. I'm trying to learn how to be a rancher and it's not easy."

"Can I be of some use and set the table?"

Abby pointed. "Plates are there. Silverware is in the drawer beside the sink. Five today. Cooper's on his way to Lubbock with a prisoner transport, though he usually stops by. His bachelor cooking isn't as good as ours."

"Rumor has it that he's interested in you," Nona said.

Abby shrugged. "He hasn't been here for three days and I've got to admit it's made me pretty cranky."

"I hear you. When Travis and I had to be apart, I don't think Jesus could have lived with me."

Abby giggled. "That's where I was this morning. Angels would have given me a one-way ticket to Hades to get rid of me."

"Cooper is a good, decent man. I had a terrible crush on him when I was sixteen, but there was no way Daddy would allow me to date a man nine years older than me, even if Cooper had been interested. I threw a hissy worse than any Mama ever pitched because he wouldn't let me invite Cooper to the Fourth of July picnic as my date."

"My mama wouldn't have allowed it either." The way Nona made herself at home made Abby feel as if she'd known her for years rather than such a short while. While she didn't feel the same bond she had with her sisters, she could still see Nona being a good friend.

Nona peeled off five paper towels and folded them. "This okay for napkins?"

"Yes, that's fine," Abby said and then changed the subject. "Did you know Ezra well?"

"As much as you know any neighbor, I suppose. He was rough as sandpaper, and so was his voice. You could tell he was a heavy smoker. I liked him, but Mama says he lived by the old books. Women had their place and men had theirs, and the two didn't mix. He'd be turnin' over in his grave if he knew his daughters were out there plowin' and fixin' fence. And he'd come up out of the grave if he ever caught you castratin' bulls come springtime. Women were supposed to cook and clean and obey their husbands. But somehow, I still think he'd be proud of all y'all for your independence and your willingness to learn how to run a ranch. Truth is, though, I bet he didn't think any of you would stick around even this long."

"Do you do that same work on your ranch?" Abby asked.

"Hell, yes! I'm a rancher, not a prissy princess. I never was too good at that obeying shit."

Thinking of Ezra spinning around in his grave because she and her two sisters were working cattle put a smile on Abby's face. That would teach him to leave the ranch to his daughters.

"I'm an only child, too," Abby said.

"But you have two sisters."

Abby refilled Nona's tea glass. "I'll rephrase. I was raised as an only child. And so were Shiloh and Bonnie. We had no idea we had siblings until the lawyer called us about Ezra's death and told us about his will."

Nona finished setting the table and leaned on the bar. "Bet that was a shocker. It's not a whole lot of fun being the only child, is it? I wish Mama would have had twins when I was two years old instead of twenty-two. So where did you grow up?"

"In Galveston." Abby was amazed at how easy it was to talk to Nona. Maybe it was because she was so open and honest. Whatever she was thinking sure had a way of coming out of her mouth and showing on her face. She reminded Abby of Haley, with her soft southern twang and openness.

"What did your mama do there?"

"She owned a doughnut shop and café from the time I was born until about six months after I graduated from high school."

"Then she sold it?" Nona asked.

"No, then a robbery went bad and she was shot during it."

Nona's hand went over her mouth and her eyes misted. "I'm so, so sorry, Abby. I can't imagine life without my mama. And you were so young."

Abby nodded. "I was and it was very hard. Her lawyer gave me some good advice about the café, and one year faded into another. I reenlisted for another six years then with the intentions of making it a career, but after twelve I was burned out."

"What about Ezra's other two daughters? Where did they live before coming here? Their mamas are still living, aren't they? I don't want to bring up any more bad memories."

"I'll let them tell you at dinner. I hear truck doors slamming right now. And Nona, it's okay. It's been long enough now that I've only got good memories of my mama. I wish she was here, but I still hear her in my head when I need advice."

Nona cocked her head to one side and nodded. "My mama would be like that, but I don't want to even think about not having her here."

"The door is opening. Would you get the salad from the refrigerator? And there's a plate of cranberry sauce. I'll take the casserole from the oven," Abby said.

Nona opened the refrigerator and whistled through her teeth. "Is that chocolate silk pie?"

"Made from scratch. Even the pie shell," Abby said.

"I see why Cooper comes for dinner every chance he gets."

❁ ❁ ❁

The longer Abby wielded a hammer that afternoon, the more she had doubts about staying on the ranch. It wasn't the job or the fact that she'd hit her thumb twice, but Cooper. If she left right now, it would be over and she wouldn't have to make those difficult decisions later, like telling him good-bye and then having to see him in church or out on his morning run around the Lucky Seven.

When the day was done and Rusty drove them back to the house, she sat on the porch with Martha at her side for half an hour, trying to talk herself into staying, but it didn't work. She took a quick shower, packed a few things in a duffel, and tossed it in her truck.

She hated good-byes, so if she decided to stay gone, she wouldn't even have to come back. She had her mother's ashes and the most important things of her life in the duffel bag. The boxes under the bed could stay there, but everything else was going with her.

Driving down the pathway she'd seen Rusty take seemed to take hours, but in reality it was only about a five-minute drive. The little bunkhouse sat deep in the shadows of a pecan grove. When the leaves were on the trees, it would be completely hidden.

He opened the door with a worried expression when she knocked. "What's happened?"

"Nothing on the ranch. A lot inside of me."

"Humph!" He crossed his arms over his chest. "I figured you'd be the last one standing."

"I may be, but I need some time. What does the will say about taking a day off?"

"It says you can sit on the porch and drink sweet tea or beer or stay drunk on moonshine, or you can take your third of the money and go anytime you want. But if you leave for more than twenty-four hours, then you are declared officially out of the runnin' for the ranch. And you only get one twenty-four-hour leave."

"I'm taking mine now. If I'm not back at six tomorrow evening, I'll call you with a bank number where you can wire my money," she said.

"You'll be back," he said.

"What makes you so sure?"

"I just am, Abby. You are not a quitter; you are a fighter."

"We'll see," she said. She started to walk away and turned back. "One more thing, Rusty. In case I don't come back, why daisies?"

"Daisies?" he asked.

"At the funeral. Why did you give us daisies and why did you tell us to put them in the casket with him?"

"It was my idea. He said no flowers, but it didn't seem right. And I felt like he should take something from his daughters with him. I went to get roses since he cultivated beautiful roses all summer. Unfortunately, the florist didn't have any roses, so I bought three daisies," Rusty said.

"Thank you. I wondered why he'd want us to do that when he didn't give a shit about us while we were growing up," Abby said.

The knowledge of the daisies left her feeling flat. In the back of her mind, she'd thought maybe he knew that daisies were tough little flowers, and had been telling them that he appreciated their strength. But Ezra hadn't even known about them, so it hadn't been any seal of approval on the three girls he'd fathered.

She got back into her truck, turned off her phone, and shoved it into the glove compartment. She didn't even want to talk to Haley or her sisters and especially not Cooper until she had this figured out. It was dark when she parked her truck in a motel parking spot, picked up her duffel bag, and carried it into the lobby.

She paid for a room and told herself in the elevator on the way up that she could figure things out now. At the ranch house, a memory of Cooper popped up every which way she turned. At the dinner table, she could feel his presence even though the chair beside her was empty. Out in the pasture, she could visualize him hopping over the fence if she looked up. Even the cemetery contained memories of all those kisses they'd shared on the bench under the bare oak trees.

Here she wouldn't have a single distraction and she could make up her mind, once and for all, about her future.

✺ ✺ ✺

The sun was setting when Cooper finally finished his work in Lubbock and stopped in at Fuzzy's Tacos for a couple of fish tacos. It had taken a hell of a lot longer than he'd expected, but he'd gotten a late start and then there had been an accident that held up traffic for a solid hour. Then there was the transfer paperwork.

He'd tried to call Abby a couple of times but it went straight to voice mail. He figured she'd left her phone in the bedroom and couldn't hear it, so he sent a couple of text messages.

The waitress was a tall redhead with brilliant green eyes and the way she winked and smiled, he had no doubt that she would give him her phone number if he asked. The woman was exactly his type, including the green eyes and sassy attitude. Two weeks ago he would have flirted with the lady, but he missed Abby, plain and simple.

He inhaled deeply and let it out slowly. His vibrating phone said he had a text message. Hoping it was from Abby, he hurriedly unbuttoned his pocket to get at it, but the picture that came up was Rusty.

*Come by the bunkhouse when you get home.*

Cooper replied: *At Fuzzy's eating tacos. What's up?*

The reply: *We need to talk in person. See you in a couple of hours.*

# Chapter Sixteen

*A*bby opened the door with a key card, tossed it on the top of the television stand, dropped her duffel bag on a chair, and stretched out on the bed.

"Talk to me, Mama," she said, offering free access to her conscience.

*Not tonight. You don't believe in fate or omens. And you are not superstitious, remember?*

That was it. There were no more voices inside her head that cold, blustery evening. Nothing to help her decide if she should go back to Galveston, walk into the recruiting office, and reenlist. She had thirty days to put her name on the line and not lose any of her rank, and she could request a duty station. Hawaii might be nice after the past few days.

When her eyes grew heavy, she removed her boots and pulled the side of the duvet up over her body and went to sleep. It was a deep sleep that produced a dream that played like a miniseries, lasting all night. In the first part, they were young and he was chasing her through a field of wild daisies. She giggled like a little girl, her blonde hair flying behind her as she ran through the soft red dirt in her bare feet. In the second scene, they were at his house at the Lucky Seven, alone and working the ranch with him teaching her something new every day. In the third part, there were children, but were they her children? A little dark-haired girl watched her from a window in the house and a B-2 bomber plane flew overhead.

She awoke with a start and sat up in bed, trembling, sweating, and a lump in her throat that wouldn't go away no matter how hard she swallowed. She looked up into the pitch-black darkness.

"What are you telling me? That I'd be a horrible mother?"

She went to the bathroom, washed her face, removed all her clothing except for her underwear, and this time turned down the bed and slipped between the cool sheets. The dream picked up where it had left off. The little girl in the window waved and Abby waved back. In a minute she ran out the front door and into Abby's arms. In the fourth part of the dream, she and Cooper had gray in their hair. They were walking hand in hand across a plowed field.

She awoke at four thirty in the morning, made a pot of coffee, and paced back and forth while it dripped. The hotel cup was one of those paper kinds without a sleeve so she'd take a sip, set it down, make a trip from the door to the window and then take another sip on her way back across the floor.

"Why couldn't it be clear? All of it? I came for answers and all I get is more questions," she asked the blank screen on the television as she passed it.

She flung the curtains open and looked out at the darkness. "You are going to have to spell it out to me, Mama. I dreamed about Cooper. Does that mean I'm not supposed to reenlist?"

Nothing. Not a damn thing. No voices in her head. Not even a shooting star. She made another trip across the floor and drank some more coffee.

She shook her fist at the moon that time. "I hate for things to be unsettled."

Falling back into the chair beside the window, she threw her hand over her eyes and the pieces began to fall together. She was supposed to stay at the ranch until spring, when she would scatter her mother's ashes somewhere symbolic. She was not supposed to reenlist and the part about Cooper, well, that was always going to be a day at a time. Some things were hers to know and brought a modicum of peace. Others, evidently, were not—and Cooper fell into the latter part.

She dressed, picked up her duffel bag and room key, and checked out of the motel.

❋ ❋ ❋

Cooper tried to watch a movie on television, but he couldn't stay focused enough to keep up with the story line. He picked up a mystery book, but that couldn't keep his attention either. He made a trip to the refrigerator and stared at the contents for five minutes before he realized he couldn't eat if he wanted to. Finally, he poured a double shot of whiskey and carried it to the living room. He sipped it slowly and picked up his phone to call Abby to ask her to rethink leaving for good. But she needed to make the decision on her own. If anyone influenced her, she might have regrets later. Still, it was a long restless night of dozing a few minutes on the sofa and awakening to check the time. Then falling back asleep only to wake again in fifteen or twenty minutes.

At four thirty he gave up even trying and let Delores out, made a pot of coffee, let Delores back inside, and sat down on the sofa with her at his side. Two hours later he awoke to Delores whining and cold nosing his hand. Delores wagged her tail.

"Do you think she'll come home?"

Her tail wagged faster.

"I hope that is a yes."

❋ ❋ ❋

Abby parked her truck and walked into the house with Martha right on her heels. It felt different now, even with her two sisters staring at her like she had two heads or maybe three eyes.

"Where have you been all night?" Bonnie asked.

"Was it good?" Shiloh asked.

"What?" Abby's eyebrow shot up.

"The sex?"

"I didn't have sex," she said.

"Don't lie to us. You are coming in at daybreak with a duffel bag in your hands. Where were you?" Bonnie asked.

"At a hotel, alone," Abby said. "Y'all want to help me bring all my stuff back inside?"

"Why'd you take everything with you? Oh! Oh! You were leaving, weren't you?" Shiloh gasped.

"I didn't know, but I do hate good-byes, so if I had decided to leave, I might have called, but I wouldn't have told either of you good-bye," she said.

"I'll help you unload your things, but first I want to know why," Bonnie said.

"Everything. The ranch. The work. Having two sisters. Cooper. It all came crashing down on me yesterday and I needed to get out of the forest to see the trees."

"So did you get it settled?" Shiloh asked.

"Some of it. I've got my mind made up firmly not to reenlist and to stay here until spring. I have my mother's ashes and I intend to do something with them when spring comes and the flowers are blooming in the canyon. The thing with Cooper? I have no idea what is going on there."

"You aren't supposed to," Bonnie said.

"But why?"

"Where's the fun in knowing everything? Life has to have some surprises to make it interesting."

"I talked to Rusty. It was his idea to put the daisies in Ezra's casket," she said bluntly.

"I'm not surprised. Were you?" Shiloh asked.

"I think I wanted it to be in the will. I wanted him to think we were strong and that at the end he wanted a little of each of us to go with him into eternity." Abby sank down into the recliner and got a whiff of cigarette smoke. "Something, anything that would say we were something to him. I guess that's what I wanted."

"Let go of the past. Live today and look forward to the future," Bonnie said.

"Who said that?" Abby asked.

"I did. It's what I tell myself every morning. Now let's go unload your things and make breakfast. We've got a corral to finish today. I'll make sausage gravy and biscuits," she said. "And Abby, I'm glad you came home."

"Me, too," Shiloh said.

"Thank you both. It is home, isn't it."

"Oh, yeah. It's our home and it might take all three of us, but we'll make it work," Bonnie said.

꧁ ꧁ ꧁

Cooper alternated between whistling and worrying all day. Abby had sent him a text that morning just before daylight asking: *Ice cream at six tonight, or are you too busy?*

The answer he sent back was: *Never. I'll pick you up at six.*

Had she come back to stay or to pack the rest of her things, tell everyone good-bye, and leave for good? It was a good sign that she was back and wanted to go out for ice cream. But he hoped it wasn't only to explain to him her reasons or excuses for leaving.

"Got a date?" his deputy asked when Cooper looked at the clock again for the tenth time in less than five minutes.

Cooper nodded.

"I heard you were hot on the trail after Ezra Malloy's oldest daughter. That old man was a pistol. Be careful you don't get a feminine version of him." The deputy chuckled. "Maybe if you take her a rose, it'll help."

"Maybe so," Cooper said.

Abby was not a pink rose girl or even a red rose one. She struck him more as a wild daisy. With that in mind, he didn't go straight home when he left the office. He went to the tiny little flower shop in Silverton and barely made it inside before the lady flipped the open sign over to closed.

"Do you have daisies?" he asked.

"Yes, sir, we sure do. I'll get them out of the cooler. You almost didn't catch me this late in the day." She brought out a vase full of bright-colored flowers.

"I want a dozen of those right there." He pointed at the bright yellow ones with yellow centers. "And tie up some sky-blue paper around them with a blue ribbon."

"You sure about that? Yellow or white might make them more pleasant to the eye," she asked.

"I'm sure," he said.

"How long until you intend to give them to someone?"

He checked the time on his phone. "Less than an hour."

"They'll be fine for that long. I'll just put them in a box. Why blue ribbon?" she asked as she rang up the charge.

"She's a blonde with blue eyes." He smiled.

"Well, then, that does make sense. Birthday?"

"No, ma'am."

"Then pick out a blank card from the assortment there and sign it."

"Don't need a card. I'll be taking them to her directly."

He set the box in the backseat of the car and started the engine. Singing along with the radio, Cooper wondered what his grandpa would think of Abby.

*You could be falling in love.* The voice in his head sounded a lot like his grandfather's. *She could be your soul mate.*

"Whoa! Grandpa, I'm not sure I'm ready to admit that much." Cooper said.

He hurried through a shower and left his uniform in a pile on the bedroom floor. He jerked on jeans and a T-shirt and his boots and was out the door at ten minutes until six. When he rang the doorbell, he remembered that he'd left the daisies in the truck, so he jogged back out across the yard, jumped over the fence rather than opening the gate, and grabbed them. Abby was standing at the door with a smile on her face when he returned.

His mouth went dry at the sight before him. Her blonde hair hung in wavy curls to her shoulders and she wore a pair of jeans that hugged her curves, a cute little light blue sweater, and a denim jacket with shiny rhinestones scattered on it. When he talked his eyes into leaving her face and traveling down, he noticed the boots on her feet.

"Wow! You are gorgeous," he said hoarsely.

"Well, thank you, Cooper. When you took off toward your truck, I figured you didn't like what you saw," she said.

"I forgot something." He put the box of daisies in her hands.

"If this is flowers, you'd best come on in here so I can put them in water before we go," she said.

"Hello, Cooper," Shiloh said from the sofa.

"Evening, ladies." He tipped his hat at her and at Bonnie, who was sitting on the floor in front of the fireplace with the dogs.

"Oh, they are beautiful," Abby squealed from the kitchen. "I'm putting them in a quart jar in the middle of the table. Y'all can look at them, but if you steal one I will know."

"Roses?" Shiloh raised an eyebrow.

"Daisies," Abby answered. "Look."

She held up the jar with twelve daisies, some greenery, and a sprig of something the florist had said was baby's breath. The blue ribbon that had been around the box was now tied in a perfect bow around the top of the jar.

"One for each day you've been in the canyon," he said.

"How sweet," Bonnie said.

"I've changed my mind. I'm going to be selfish and put them in my bedroom," she said. "I'll just be a minute more. Thank you so much, Cooper. Daisies are my favorite flower."

Shiloh looked up from her book. "Better have her home by midnight. She turns into a mean soldier when the clock strikes twelve."

"I'll remember that," he said as he tucked her hand in his.

"So will I." Abby pointed at Shiloh.

"Looks like y'all are getting along better and better," Cooper said on the way outside.

"We're not doing too bad for three women who had to start from scratch."

"That's the way all relationships start," he said.

"Yes, but most siblings get to start from babies and grow," she said.

When they were in the truck and driving toward the road, he said, "You are right, but it's still from scratch and the first thing you have to do is build a foundation. Without that, nothing will withstand the storms of time. Silverton, Claude, or Amarillo?"

"Do you have ice cream in the freezer at your house?" she asked.

*Yep, I told you she could be the right woman for you. She reminds me of your grandma. That woman wasn't a bit bashful, either*, the voice in his head said.

With his heart racing like he'd just run five miles, Cooper agreed with his grandfather.

# Chapter Seventeen

The cleaning lady comes on Thursdays, so the place isn't as nice as it would be tomorrow," Cooper said as he flipped a switch and lit up the foyer.

"A cleaning lady, but not a cook?"

"Grandpa hated cleaning, but he didn't mind cooking. He always said that Granny was worth more to him on a tractor than she was scrubbing bathrooms. That was one area where he and Ezra disagreed. Granny and Grandpa shared the kitchen, so when she died Grandpa took comfort in making supper every night."

"Do I get the grand tour?" Abby let her eyes shift to the doors in the foyer when she really wanted to know what was up that long stairway.

"Sure. Let me take your coat first." He slid it off her shoulders slowly, taking time to kiss her on the neck along the way. The quick quiver in her heart and the delicious little shiver down her back created a quick intake of breath that she sincerely hoped he did not hear.

He hung it on an old-fashioned hall tree on a peg to the right of a long mirror. She hadn't seen one of those since when she and Haley were little girls. Haley's grandma had had one in her foyer before she sized down and moved into a retirement home.

He put his coat beside hers and draped an arm around her shoulders. "Through this door is the master bedroom. It sits empty these days, because I've always had a room upstairs and this belonged to Grandpa and Granny. Someday if I have a house full of kids, I might remodel it for a nanny."

"Why would you need a nanny?"

"Maybe my wife will mean more to me on a tractor than chasing down a dozen kids all day." He grinned.

"A dozen, huh?"

"Well, there are seven bedrooms upstairs. I figure if half share rooms with the other half, an even dozen would be nice," he answered.

"And if your wife would rather not hire a nanny, but take care of her children?"

"Then the wife and I could move into the master bedroom and give the kids the upstairs and we could have two more."

A smile tickled the corners of Abby's mouth. "You're thirty-one, right?" He nodded. "I reckon you'd best find a woman about eighteen if you want someone to produce a dozen or more kids before her biological clock flat-out shuts down."

He chuckled. "Way I see it is if I say a dozen kids or more, then when I tell her that what I really want is three or four, it'll be such a relief she won't argue with me."

He threw open the door into the room. It smelled like potpourri. She scanned the whole room before she saw the bowl of dried leaves and flowers filling a basket on the dresser. A white chenille spread covered the four-poster bed. Two overstuffed rockers shared a small round table with a lamp. An ashtray and a Bible were placed on the table.

"Your grandpa smoked?" she asked.

He shook his head. "Granny smoked cigars, but never outside the house. She was partial to the story of David in the books of Samuel, so she'd sit with a cigar while Grandpa read the Bible to her before they went to bed. These days she would have been diagnosed with dyslexia, but in her time they thought she was too dumb to learn to read."

"That is the sweetest thing I've heard in a long time," she whispered.

He kissed her softly on the forehead. "They had what it took to withstand a hell of a lot of disappointments and joys. I want what they had."

"But they only had one child?"

"Just my dad. They wanted more, but Granny said God gave her a perfect son and she guessed he just didn't intend to try to outdo himself with another one."

Abby could feel the memories in the room and she envied Cooper having them. She wished the housekeeper hadn't put the potpourri on the dresser and she could catch a faint whisper of cigar smoke still lingering in the chairs. She'd missed that since her mother had been gone—that little touch of smoke the ocean breezes couldn't quite remove from her shirt when she stepped outside in the alley for a cigarette.

"And over here"—he steered her to the other side of the foyer—"is the kitchen where the ice cream is kept."

It was one of those huge square country kitchens with cabinets on two sides, an enormous window that looked out into the backyard and a round dinner table that would easily seat ten people. She shut her eyes for a moment and imagined Cooper as a little boy, running in and out the back door, slamming the screen every time. She could feel the pain his grandmother had felt when she lost her only child and the bittersweet joy of raising her only grandchild because of that loss.

"And through that archway is the living room." He led her in that direction and flipped on another light. It was twice as big as the kitchen, with a fireplace on one end. Comfortable, buttery-soft leather furniture was arranged like a woman had had a hand in it, and beckoned to her to sit down.

"I love it," she whispered.

"Have a seat and I'll dip ice cream. You want rocky road or butter pecan?"

"Both." How sweet of him to remember her favorite was rocky road.

A big yellow dog peeked out from the shadows of a corner and wagged its tail. It was gray around the nose and it limped when it got up and came forward. Sitting down right in front of her, it lifted one paw and almost smiled.

She knelt before it and shook the paw. "I'm Abby Malloy. And you are?"

"That's Delores. I told you about her, remember?" Cooper said. "Named for a great-aunt that my granny hated. She didn't want Grandpa to bring that puppy into the house when he found it on the side of the road with a busted leg. He named it Delores just to needle Granny and it worked. She declared that she hated the dog but when no one was lookin', she'd talk to it like it was a baby. It was the last year she was alive, so that makes Delores seventeen this spring."

"Well, Delores, I'm glad to meet you." Abby scratched her ears and the dog flopped down flat on the floor.

Abby sat down and Delores scooted closer until her head was in Abby's lap. "Why did your granny hate her great-aunt?"

Cooper sat down beside her and said, "Because the great-aunt was a pistol. She didn't have children and she thought all kids should be seen and not heard. Granny was not a quiet person. If she had an opinion, the whole damn world knew what it was."

"That's not such a bad thing," Abby said.

"Abby, why did you want to come here rather than going for a long ride and then visiting an ice cream parlor?" he asked.

"I dreamed about this house last night. I wanted to see if it was like my dream," she said.

"And is it?"

She shook her head. "No, Cooper, it's better. I'd like to see all of it, if you don't mind." It was better because he was there in the flesh and the sensations she felt were so much deeper and more real than what she'd seen and felt in the dream.

"So ice cream now or after you see the upstairs?" he asked.

"Give me the tour and then we can come back down here for ice cream. I wish this house could talk. I bet it could tell me lots of tales," she said.

"Give me a minute to put this back in the freezer until we're ready for it. Abby, I'm glad the house can't talk. And I'm almighty glad it couldn't when Granny and Grandpa was still alive. I would have never been allowed out of my room." Cooper returned and extended a hand.

"Ah, a bad boy, were you?"

"Bad enough that I'm glad Granny didn't know everything," he answered.

She let him lead her up the stairs. Common sense told her that she had no business even looking into his bedroom. Her heart told her to push him backward on the bed and land on top of him while she had the chance.

"At the end of the landing you will see three doors. The one to the left is the linen closet. The other two are bathrooms—a ladies' and a gentlemen's. Granny liked her own bathroom. I'll show it to you first," Cooper said.

"Oh, my! This is one big bathroom," she said when he threw the door open. A big tub like the one at the Malloy Ranch didn't even put a dent in the room. It had one of those long chaise lounges beside a vanity with two separate sinks. A separate shower and potty was hidden by a half wall covered with pink rose wallpaper.

"Grandpa never said as much, but I had a feeling that the chaise lounge was for him so he could talk to her while she took a bath, or"—he wiggled his eyebrows—"maybe for something else when they were younger."

"You can think of your grandparents like that? I can't even imagine my mama kissing Ezra." She could feel her nose curling up at the thought.

"I wouldn't know about Ezra and your mom. But my grandparents were so much in love—way past Granny's dying day. He survived on her memories." Cooper tipped her chin up for a scorching kiss that made her knees turn to jelly.

Instinctively, her arms snaked up around his neck, one hand tangling itself into his thick blond hair. She tilted her head so she could see his face and their gazes locked in the moonlit room. He took her hand in his and led to another door across the landing.

"This is my bedroom," he said. "Don't leave. I'll be right back."

The room was empty without him. No, the universe was empty without him. The canyon had magical powers. It had drawn her mother to Ezra and now it was doing its damnedest to draw her to Cooper.

He carried a tray bearing a huge bowl of ice cream. Her heart fluttered and she wished she could trade the ice cream for a romp in that big four-poster bed. It would be a hell of a lot more satisfying, because ice cream wouldn't do a damn thing to cool what was hot inside her.

"One bowl? One spoon?" One of her eyebrows rose slightly.

"We only need one spoon if I feed you." Cooper sat down in a brown leather recliner beside the double doors leading out to the sun porch. He pulled her down on his lap and when she reached for the spoon he shook his head and said, "It ain't happenin', darlin'. I get to feed you."

She opened her mouth when the first spoonful came toward her. "We've got until midnight, so I intend to eat slowly."

"Yes, Cinderella."

She swallowed quickly and laughed. "That's the first time anyone ever called me Cinderella."

"Maybe no one saw the princess beneath the combat boots. Which reminds me, you are gorgeous tonight all dolled up like a cowgirl."

"I didn't buy many clothes in the military. Just a couple of things for nonmilitary weddings I attended. It seemed like a waste of money and I've only been out of the service a few weeks. If it was a military party, my dress uniform worked just fine. It's hard to explain," she explained.

"You don't have to explain, Abby."

"But I do, and it's hard to put into words. I wanted Ezra, even in death, to see that I'd done all a boy could do," she said. "But thank you for the compliment about the way I'm dressed tonight. I suppose when my camouflage is worn out, you'll be seeing more of me in jeans and maybe even flannel shirts."

"I like that idea of seeing more of you in anything you want to wear. But"—he grinned and his brown eyes twinkled—"I think I like you in nothing at all best."

Another bite went into her mouth and she had to swallow fast to keep from choking after that comment. She covered his hand with hers and before he could protest, she dipped deeply into the ice cream and slowly brought it to his lips. If he wanted to play that game, she was more than willing to join right in.

"Darlin', I like you naked best of all, too."

He bent slightly and kissed her. His tongue traced her lip line and sent shivers down her backbone.

"Cold?" he asked.

"Hot. Very, very hot," she murmured.

"Would it be another mistake?" he whispered softly, his breath caressing her ear.

"I hope not." Right, wrong, or somewhere in between, she wanted to feel Cooper's naked body next to hers.

His hands were rough against her face when he cupped her cheeks in his hands and kissed her eyelids shut, then moved to her lips. The first kiss was soft and tender. The second lingered but was still sweet. By the fourth they'd grown more passionate. One hand cupped her chin tenderly, his thumb making lazy circles on a sensitive part of her neck.

She shifted slightly so she could raise his shirt up over his head. The kissing stopped but only long enough to get the shirt out of the way. Then she splayed out her hands on his chest. The soft hair tickled her palms.

Getting down to nothing was a slow process that required so much making out that she was panting by the time he made it to a kneeling position in front of the chair to take off her boots and jeans.

She had one moment of panic when she realized her socks were mismatched but he rolled them off like they were pure silk stockings and tossed them over to the side. She quickly forgot about them when he kissed his way from her toes to her lips.

"God, Cooper, I can't wait much longer," she gasped.

"I want this to be perfect." He picked her up and carried her to the bed, where he gently laid her on the bedspread and put a knee on either side of her body. She wrapped her legs around him and arched upward.

She was so ready that when he filled her she began to match his rhythm, stroke for stroke. His lips lowered to hers again and she tangled her hands into his hair, holding his head steady.

This was not raw, passionate sex. Cooper was making love to her, and there was a major difference. It was deeper, more satisfying, crazy but almost peaceful, even though she could scarcely breathe for the emotions and desire shooting through her body.

"Abby, my God," he said just as he took her over the edge and into the most intense climax she'd ever known.

"Yes," she whispered as her legs relaxed and unwound from around his body.

He rolled to the side, keeping her in his arms, and for the first time Abby Malloy experienced that thing she'd read about in romance books called an afterglow. So it was real and not just a figment of an author's imagination—and it was beautiful and warm and made things right.

They slept.

Until midnight they slept in each other's arms. Happy, contented, and life was good. And then they awoke at the same time, laughed about her missing curfew as they got dressed, and Cooper took her home.

She was so glad that her sisters were asleep so she could keep that warm, sweet afterglow a little longer.

# Chapter Eighteen

Abby sat cross-legged in the middle of the bed, her mother's two-page letter in front of her. She'd made up her mind to stay in the canyon somewhere between the drive between the Lucky Seven and the Malloy Ranch at way past midnight. And that morning when she awoke, she thought about it but hadn't had time to read it. The day had passed and it had stayed on her mind until evening, when she'd taken it from the accordion file of her important papers and removed it from the envelope. The first time she read it had been the day after her mother's funeral, when the lawyer had given her the key to the safe-deposit box and told her that she was now the owner of a prime piece of property on the strip.

"I was eighteen, Mama, and in the army." Tears flowed down Abby's cheeks. "I was too young to be alone in the world."

She wiped the tears from her cheeks and reread the portion of the letter she'd never understood until that moment:

*My dearest daughter,*

*I'm writing this because it dawned on me when we said good-bye that if something happened to me . . . well, I don't want things to end without you knowing what I want you to do. Your kiss is still warm on my cheek and you are off to your military training. I'm so proud of you and what you are doing, Abby.*

*If you are reading this letter, then I'm gone. Don't throw my ashes out in the Gulf where we had so many good times. Don't let them sift through your fingers onto the sand where we built castles and watched the sunset. Those places should always come to your mind as good memories, not final ones. I want you to wait until the right moment and the right place. Don't fret about it, Abby. When the place and the time are right, you will know. It might be in ten years and it might be tomorrow, but you won't have a single doubt in your mind.*

*As I write this letter, I'm thinking of the day you were born. When they put you in my arms, I lost my heart to you that very moment. I loved Ezra Malloy that year we were together, but I truly believe now that he was only put into my life so that I would have you. So there's no hatred or bitterness in my heart for him or the decisions that he made. There is a degree of pity, though, because he never knew the lovely daughter who would have brought him so much joy. Death is final, but it's not the end. My love and memories will go with you throughout your entire life.*

There was more, but Abby stopped there and hugged the paper to her chest. Martha raised her head from the rocking chair and growled down deep in her throat. She cocked her head to one side as if listening and then she jumped down and started toward the living room.

Abby didn't care if there was another stampede or two old tomcats fighting out in the yard. She wanted to sit on the bed with memories of her mother flooding through her mind and remember the good times.

Martha barked once and then there were the sounds of boots on wood before a gentle knock. The front door opened. Martha nosed her way out of Abby's bedroom, her body pushing the door all the way open, and disappeared up the hallway toward the living room.

Abby swiped at her eyes with her shirtsleeve and laid the letter down on her pillow. She could hear Shiloh whistling in the bathroom where the shower had been running moments before. Soft laughter came from Bonnie's room, which meant she was talking to her Kentucky friends on the phone.

"Rusty? Is that you?" she called out.

She slung her legs off the bed and Cooper's shadow filled the doorway to her bedroom. Her breath caught in her chest, still tight from crying so hard.

"I missed you today," he said softly.

She put her hands over her face and sobbed so hard that there was a whooshing sound in her ears. Suddenly his strong arms slipped under her knees and around her back. He lifted her from the bed and carried her to the rocking chair. He sat down with her in his lap and she sobbed until only sniffles were left.

"What brought this on?" Cooper asked.

"Mama's letter," she whispered.

"Is that it on the bed?"

She nodded.

"And you've never read it before now?"

She shook her head. "One time before, but I was eighteen and still in shock and it didn't make as much sense then as it does now. After last night, I was drawn to get it out again. Now I understand it better."

"Abby, about last night," he said.

She put a finger on his lips. "Don't say it."

"Why?"

"I can't bear to hear that it was another mistake," she whispered.

"I wasn't going to tell you that, Abby. Last night was amazing. I was going to call you, but I wanted to hold you and kiss you tonight, not just hear your voice." He traced her jawline with his forefinger and tilted her chin up.

His brown eyes fluttered shut and then his mouth was on hers, sweet at first and then deepening into something that chased all the sadness from her body and soul. She leaned into the kiss, wanting it to last forever, wanting him to simply hold her.

Martha cold nosed her bare foot and she jumped. Abby dropped her hand to pet the dog at the same time Cooper did. He wrapped his big hand around hers and brought her knuckles to his lips. Slowly, he kissed each one before he laced his fingers through hers and held her hand against his chest.

"I didn't want last night to be a mistake," she said.

"Neither did I, and I was so afraid you'd tell me that it was. Guess we both have to learn to trust a little more and worry a lot less. I'll see you or call tomorrow. Good night, darlin'." He carried her back to the bed and set her down where he'd found her. After a kiss on the forehead he was gone.

"Good night, Cooper."

※ ※ ※

The next morning she awoke on her bed, the quilt from the living room thrown over her. Her mother's letter rested on the pillow beside her. For the first time Martha had left the rocking chair and was sound asleep on the foot of the bed, her chin lying on Abby's knees. She sat up, pulling her legs away from the dog, who gave her the old stink eye for waking her up.

"Good morning to you, too." Abby laughed, her spirits as high as the clouds she'd dreamed about the night before. "Look at that gorgeous sunrise. It's going to be a nice day."

Martha wagged her tail and did a belly crawl up closer to the pillows.

"Lord, girl, you smell like a dog. I'll have to give you a regular bath if you're going to get on the bed," Abby said.

"You let that mutt sleep with you?" Shiloh said from the open door.

"You don't let Polly sleep in your bed?" Abby threw back at her.

"Not in a million years. She can have the rug beside the bed but she's not getting up on my bedspread after she's wallowed in the dirt and walked through pig shit." Shiloh shivered. "You slept in your clothes?"

"I guess I did," Abby said. "One fewer thing I have to do before chores this morning. Is Bonnie up yet?"

"In the bathroom. Shall we start breakfast?" Shiloh asked.

Abby bounded out of bed. "You make the biscuits and I'll do sausage gravy."

"You sure are happy this morning, and you haven't even had coffee yet."

"I figured out that I'm supposed to live in this canyon, maybe even longer than spring," Abby said.

"Well, good for you. I figured that out the first time I drove down that windy road into it."

Bonnie joined them in the hallway. Her face was scrubbed clean. She was dressed in work jeans for the day and her blonde hair hung in two ropy braids down her back.

"Good for her for what?" she asked.

"Deciding that she belongs in the canyon," Shiloh answered.

"I never had a doubt that I belonged here. You must be slow," Bonnie teased.

"Cooper have anything to do with that decision?" Shiloh grinned.

"Hell if I know anything where Cooper is concerned. Like you said, Bonnie, life is full of surprises. I just now figured out that I'm not leaving."

"That's a damn fine start," Bonnie said.

❊ ❊ ❊

Friday started out as a Murphy's Law type of day. If it could go wrong it did; if there was no way for it to go wrong, it found one. Abby was reminded of Haley's grandmother's saying: *What will be, will be; what won't be, might be anyway.*

The first thing that happened was the coyote in the henhouse.

Abby had just finished feeding the hogs when she saw Shiloh tearing off toward the house at a dead run. Abby went from a walk to a run to see what had happened, hoping the whole time that Shiloh hadn't cut herself on a piece of the rusty sheet iron covering the chicken coop.

"Are you all right?" Abby yelled when she was in the house.

"A damned rotten old coyote," Shiloh shouted.

"Where?" Bonnie had just set the bucket of milk on the cabinet and reached for the straining cloth.

"In my henhouse," Shiloh hollered.

"Want me to kill it?" Abby asked.

"It's my henhouse. I'll take care of it."

Abby didn't know just how Shiloh intended to kill the coyote. Maybe she was going to asphyxiate him with nail polish remover. But her doubts in Shiloh's ability to take care of matters disappeared completely when she came back through the kitchen holding a purple Ruger pistol.

"This I've got to see," Abby mumbled.

"Me, too," Bonnie said.

They followed Shiloh out of the house, across the yard, and through the gate. When he saw people, the coyote dropped a dead chicken and started pacing around the pen, trying to find his way back out. Feathers floated on the morning breeze and chickens huddled together in the corners. The rooster, minus most of his tail feathers, was on top of the henhouse, but he wasn't crowing about anything that morning. He looked downright pitiful sitting up there with fear written all over his cocky little face.

"Rotten coyotes. Noah should have forgotten to take the miserable things on that big gopher-wood boat, if you ask me," Shiloh fussed.

"Where'd you get that gun?" Abby asked.

"I bought it, along with a pump shotgun, a twenty-two rifle for hunting squirrel, and several others I left in my gun safe in Arkansas."

"Ownin' firepower doesn't mean much if you can't shoot straight," Bonnie told her.

Shiloh muttered something, popped a hand on her hip, brought the gun up from hip level, and fired. The coyote dropped on the spot and the rooster let out a squawk that was louder than the blast.

"Mama doesn't like it when I waste ammo," Shiloh said. "Hold this for me." She handed the gun to Abby.

"Sweet little gun," Abby said.

"It caught my eye at a gun show. I wanted it so I bought it. It doesn't have as much recoil as some of the other nine mils and I liked the color," Shiloh threw over her shoulder on the way to the henhouse.

She picked up the coyote by the tail, dragged him outside the pen, and the three dogs circled the carcass, growling and biting at it as if they'd killed the critter. "Okay, ladies, that's enough. The whole bunch of you shouldn't be sleeping inside the house. If you'd been out here doing your job, you could have run him off and I wouldn't have lost two of my best layin' hens and the rest of my chickens wouldn't be scared out of their minds. I bet we don't get an egg for a week."

"What are you going to do with him?" Bonnie asked.

"Take him to the back of the ranch and hang him on a fence as a warning to the rest of the coyotes," Shiloh said. "When we go to feed this morning, I'll toss him in the back of the truck."

"That's what we'd do with him in Kentucky." Bonnie's head bobbed up and down.

"If they had coyotes in Kuwait, we probably would have eaten it," Abby said.

"Yuck!" Shiloh's nose snarled. "I don't mind squirrel, especially made with dumplings, or venison or elk, but I'm not eating coyote or possum."

"Rabbit?" Bonnie asked as they started back toward the house.

The dogs wouldn't leave the coyote alone, so Shiloh picked it up by the tail and dragged it along behind her. "Fried rabbit with sawmill gravy is almost as good as frog legs," she answered.

Shiloh threw the carcass into the back of the work truck just as Rusty's truck came to a stop outside the yard fence. He bailed out and yelled, "What is that and why are you putting it in the truck?"

"It's a dead coyote. The dogs won't leave it alone and we're taking it out to the back of the property for the buzzards," Shiloh said.

"It wreaked havoc in the henhouse," Bonnie told him.

Rusty stopped and ran his fingers through his hair. "Abby kill it?"

"She did not! I did. It's my chickens and my gun," Shiloh told him.

Rusty's eyes widened when he glanced over into the bed of the truck. "Right between the eyes."

"With one shot," Bonnie said proudly.

"Remind me not to ever mess with her chickens." Rusty laughed.

※ ※ ※

Abby filled two buckets with hog pellets and started toward the pens when she noticed the hole in the fence and three of the biggest hogs rooting around outside their pen. This was a day for disaster for sure.

The hogs recognized the feed buckets and ambled toward her, grunting and squealing the whole way. She felt like the Pied Piper as she led them into the pen without a problem and watched them belly up to the feed trough like cowboys up to a bar.

"Thank God Bonnie programmed her number into my phone," she said as she hit the button to call her.

"What?" Bonnie answered.

"Are you finished milking?"

"Yes, and I'm in the kitchen. It's my day to make dinner."

"I need help." Abby told her about the pigs.

"Be right there. I swear this is the day for it," Bonnie said.

Abby followed Bonnie's orders as they fixed the fence so the pigs couldn't get out again. Then the two of them carried a couple of cement blocks from the hog shed feed room and secured the area.

"One of them bastards probably dug his way under the fence and the others tore it when they were too big to get through the hole," Bonnie said. "But this will fix it so they can't do it again."

"Thanks," Abby said. "You said this was the day for it. What else happened?"

"I had finished milking the cow and be damned if a honeybee didn't spook her and she kicked the milk bucket over. Lost every drop of the milk. I hope you weren't planning on using the cream for something tomorrow," Bonnie said.

"I wasn't." This must be the big test to see if she would really stay when the going got tough. Well, she'd made up her mind and she wasn't going anywhere.

"Good. Shiloh is already on a tractor. You're supposed to call Rusty when you get back to the house. He said that he's sending you to the feed store in Silverton for a load of pig and chicken feed," Bonnie said.

The gears in Abby's head started turning so fast it made her dizzy. She'd be in Silverton. Maybe Cooper would have time for a coffee break. She'd wanted tell him how much it meant to her to see him last night. She called Rusty as she walked toward the house and told him she'd take her own truck so he didn't have to bring the work truck in from the field. She was downright giddy until Bonnie sniffed the air.

"What? Don't tell me the house is burning down," Abby said.

"No, but you smell like hog shit. I'd take a quick shower if I was you, and put on them jeans with the fancy stitchin' on the butt. And it wouldn't hurt to spray a little perfume on your hair," Bonnie said.

"I'm going to the feed store," Abby protested.

"I'm not stupid. You're picking up pig and chicken pellets at the feed store. You're going to see Cooper in his place of work for the first time. You want everyone in the courthouse to smell you like this?" Bonnie asked.

"How did you know that?" Abby asked.

"You had the Cooper look on your face."

"You are full of shit."

Bonnie pointed right at her. "You are fighting an attraction, which is worse than bein' full of shit."

It was the fastest shower Abby had ever taken in her life. She dried her hair in record time and followed Bonnie's advice about the perfume. She applied a touch of makeup and hit her hair with a curling iron, all in thirty minutes.

It was eleven o'clock when she reached the feed store. The guys there couldn't have been prodded into action by a stun gun. They moved so slow that she wished she'd offered to load the feed herself. Finally, a baldheaded fellow in bibbed overalls handed her a bill fastened to a clipboard. She signed it and headed straight for the courthouse.

She parked the truck, checked her reflection in the mirror, and suddenly had second thoughts about even going inside. He'd never invited her to stop by, and it was his place of work. Maybe she should call first. Surprises weren't always welcome.

She opened the truck door, but couldn't make herself get out, not without calling first. Even that would put him in an awkward situation. She reversed the situation and thought about how she'd feel if he suddenly showed up at her office in the army unexpectedly.

"Complicated deluxe," she mumbled.

"Good mornin'. Could I help you? You look a little bit lost. Hey, didn't I see you at Ezra Malloy's funeral? You are the oldest daughter, right?" An elderly man extended his hand. "I'm Everett Talley. Knew Ezra his whole life."

"I'm Abby and yes, I'm the oldest," she said.

"Well, I'm right pleased to meet you." He dropped her hand after a firm shake. "Hope y'all are gettin' along all right on the ranch. You here to see Coop? I heard y'all had been steppin' out some. If you are, you done missed him. He pulled out in the sheriff car 'bout the time I drove up. See, his space is empty." Everett pointed toward the reserved spot a couple of parking spaces down from her. "Got to get on down the road. The wife has already called three times. She's ready to go to Amarillo to do some shoppin' and I don't want to be in no more trouble than I already am."

"Thank you. Nice meeting you," she said.

She shut the truck door and started the engine. "What now?"

That's when her phone rang. She fished the phone from her purse and Bonnie's name came up on the front. "Hello."

"Where are you?"

"On my way home. You need something before I leave town?"

"How did it go at the courthouse?"

"Do you believe in fate?" Abby asked. "Cooper isn't here."

"Yes, I do. My grandparents were very superstitious. There's a reason you weren't supposed to see him today. You might never know what it is, but it's there, so don't doubt it."

"Thank you, sis," Abby said.

"Imagine that."

"What?" Abby asked.

"You called me sis."

"I guess I did," Abby said.

☀ ☀ ☀

Cooper didn't get home until almost dark, and then he had to take care of the ranching part of his life. When he finally called Abby, it was near ten o'clock. He'd wanted to talk to her all day, but his deputy had been with him from near noon until quittin' time, and by then his phone battery was dead.

But finally the stars lined up—the phone was charged and work was done. He sat down on the porch steps and called her.

"Hello, Cooper. How was your day?" she asked.

"Gettin' better now that I can hear your voice." He grinned. "How was yours?"

"Shiloh killed a coyote. The cow kicked over Bonnie's milk bucket. My hogs got out of the pen and it had to be fixed. I came to see you and you were gone," she answered.

"At the office?"

"Yes. A sweet little feller named Everett said you'd just left."

"I'd love to see you right now, but it's late."

"Got any rocky road left?"

His heart threw in an extra beat. "Yes, ma'am. You hungry for rocky road?"

"Have been all day."

"The door is open."

"See you in a few minutes," she said.

※ ※ ※

Holy shit! She had lost her mind. She had just agreed to a booty call. Her actions since she'd gotten to the canyon had been pretty sketchy, but she wasn't that kind of woman.

*What kind is that?* her conscience decided to pipe up as she tied her combat boots.

"The kind that stalks a man," Abby answered in a whisper.

*Looks like it to me.*

"Go away. I just want to talk to him. No sex tonight. Ice cream with him, a little conversation, and then I will leave. Plain and simple."

She drove down the lane, past the cemetery, onto the paved road, and to the Lucky Seven, arguing with the voice in her head the whole time. If he hadn't been standing on the porch when she drove into the yard, she might have turned the truck around and never gotten out.

He waved and opened his arms. She got out of the truck and walked into them.

"I thought about you all day," he said.

"Cooper, we should talk."

"I don't like that line. It usually means that things are over."

She sat down on the porch steps and he sat down beside her, his arm around her shoulders. His thumb made lazy little circles on her bare skin, causing her pulse to race and her resolve to just talk to fade away into the darkness.

"This is not a booty call," she said bluntly.

"You think I'm that kind of man?" The thumb stopped moving and his whole body stiffened. "I can get sex anytime or anywhere. I thought we had more than that."

"I'm scared," she said.

He moved his arm from around her. "Of me?"

"Of us."

"Me, too. This is all overwhelming."

"What do we do?"

He wrapped his big hand around hers. "Trust."

"That's all. Just trust."

He gave her hand a gentle squeeze. "It covers a lot of territory."

"What if . . ." she started.

He put a finger over her lips. "Trust doesn't have doubts. *What ifs* are doubts."

"Why doesn't life let us see just a little into the future?"

He kissed her on the forehead. "Where's the fun in that?"

"Bonnie said that when we were talking. I could stand a little less fun and a lot more settled."

"Couldn't we all. Still want that ice cream?" She nodded. "You sit right here and I'll bring it out."

She pulled her coat tighter across her chest and waited. Two words kept circling through her mind: *trust* and *overwhelmed*.

"Cold?" He startled her when he sat back down beside her.

"A little, but a little cold clears the mind."

"We talkin' literally?"

"Maybe both literally and figuratively, Cooper. We need to go slow."

He shook his head. "I'm afraid to go slow for fear you'll leave again."

"How'd you know about that?"

"Rusty is my friend."

"I needed to get out of the forest for a little while so I could see the trees."

He laid a hand on hers. "What happens next time the trees start to smother you? Will you leave without even talking to me?"

She shook her head. "No, I won't. It's not fair to you or to my sisters."

He handed her one of the two spoons he'd stuck into the ice cream. One bowl. Two spoons. Was it symbolic? Dammit! She wanted answers, not more questions.

"I don't think you've completely gotten rid of those wings yet," he said.

"Maybe not." She dug deep into the ice cream. "But I know I belong in the canyon. That much I did get settled."

"That's a start." He smiled.

"And everything has to start somewhere, right?"

He leaned across the distance separating them and brushed a kiss across her lips. "You got that right, ma'am."

They finished the ice cream and she shivered. "Cold now, and it's literal. I should be going home. It's late."

"Thanks for coming over, Abby. I'll walk you out to the truck." He set the empty bowl on the porch and dusted off the seat of his jeans when he stood up.

She put her hand in his when he held it out and wasn't a bit surprised at the reaction in her body when his skin touched hers— or that she liked it.

He kissed her on the forehead when they reached the truck. "Abby, I would never hurt you. Trust me."

"It's not you I have to trust, Cooper. It's me, but I'll figure it all out eventually."

"I know you will," he said and waved from the porch as she drove away.

At midnight she was in her own bed. She'd beat the pillow into submission half a dozen times. She'd rolled from one side to the other, disturbing Martha so many times that finally the dog relocated to the chair. When sleep finally came, it was riddled with dreams of little girls, of Cooper walking away from her, of Malloy Ranch burning to the ground. The alarm woke her at the same time it did every morning, but she was more tired than when she went to bed.

# Chapter Nineteen

*M*artha wiggled around in the big velvet rocking chair to catch more of the fading sunlight on her face. Bonnie sat cross-legged on the floor on one side of the chair with Shiloh on the other side.

"There's a bed right there. Y'all don't have to sit on the floor," Abby said.

"I've only conquered sitting in Ezra's chair in the past few days. I'm not ready to sit on his bed," Bonnie said.

"Your superstition is showing." Abby leaned closer to the mirror above the chest of drawers and applied mascara.

"I was raised up in the hollers of Kentucky. Superstition is part of our culture. It will surface real often, so get used to it," Bonnie answered.

"I thought that belonged to folks in Louisiana," Abby said.

"They don't get to claim all the rights. Neither does Kentucky. In my family, it's put into our DNA long before we're born," Shiloh said. "How about you, Abby? You superstitious?"

She shook her head. "I'm not so sure I know what I am anymore."

"Wonder if Ezra was superstitious?" Bonnie asked. "My mama is, so if he was, I got a double dose."

"So is my mama. She'll drive around four city blocks to keep from crossing the same road that a black cat has," Shiloh said.

"So was my mama. She had lucky numbers and she always read her horoscope, but I've slept in that bed every night since we arrived on this ranch and lightning hasn't struck me. I haven't even dreamed about Ezra. He hasn't appeared like a hologram in the corner at night, either. If he had, I wouldn't be here." Abby laughed.

Bonnie chuckled. "Changing the subject here. How are things with Cooper?"

"Remember that conversation we had about commitment? I'm scared out of my mind at this point when it comes to Cooper."

"Cooper is a good man," Bonnie said.

"I know that. My heart knows that, but there's a little part of me afraid of getting hurt if . . ." Abby left the sentence hanging.

"Ever hear that song, 'The Dance,' that Garth Brooks sang years ago? One of the lines says something about 'you could have missed the pain, but you'd have had to miss the dance,'" Bonnie said.

"That makes sense. Life don't come with promises of rainbows without the rain first. You and Cooper belong together. Don't be afraid," Shiloh said.

"Coming from the person who has the same issues I do?" Abby asked.

"Yes, I do and when I find someone, I'm going to come whining to you about it being complicated. Don't you just love that word? It covers a multitude of stuff. What happened between you and Cooper that you haven't told us?" Shiloh asked.

"Not the sex part." Bonnie laughed. "You can keep that part secret, but tell us what happened afterward."

Abby hesitated as she tried to put into words the feelings she'd had the night before.

"Either get out of the water or dive in. You can't stand on the shore with your toes in the surf," Shiloh said.

"My advice is to dive, because if you don't, you will be miserable your whole life. And," Bonnie said, "you'll have to go to church tomorrow and pray for a crop failure with all those seeds, won't you? I do hope you used protection of some kind."

Abby's chest tightened up and she had trouble catching her next breath. She hadn't even thought of protection. The prescription for her birth control had run out several months ago and since she wasn't seeing anyone, she hadn't bothered to see a doctor to get a new one. Shutting her eyes so she could think better, she replayed both times she'd had sex with Cooper.

God Almighty, had the canyon wiped out her ability to think straight or did Cooper get that credit? Not once in all her life had she fallen into bed with someone as quickly as she had with Cooper—or been as irresponsible, either.

Before she could form words to answer Bonnie, someone rapped on the front door. Abby checked the clock beside her bed and saw that Cooper was right on time for their date to go to the Sugar Shack.

"Don't just sit there. Go let him in," Bonnie said.

"And have fun," Shiloh said.

"Why don't y'all go have some fun tonight, too? You don't have to have a date to get in the doors at the Sugar Shack." She fished in her purse for her keys and tossed them at Bonnie. "Take my truck. They might not even let you park a van in the lot at a honky-tonk."

"Why not?" Shiloh asked.

Bonnie caught them midair. "Because it's a cowboy place and they might only allow trucks. Don't argue. She's offering to loan us her royal chariot tonight."

"Hey, is there a gorgeous woman in this house who's promised to dance with this rusty old cowboy tonight?" Cooper's voice floated down the hall.

"It's not a royal chariot," Abby said.

"You are the queen, the firstborn, which gives you the crown until you jump the barbed-wire fence over onto the Lucky Seven. Right, Bonnie?" Shiloh grinned.

Bonnie dangled the keys in the air. "Yes, ma'am, she does."

She rolled her eyes at her sisters and made her way to the living room, where Cooper waited with another bouquet of gorgeous daisies. This time they were all yellow with brown centers and arranged in a quart-sized fruit jar with a big blue ribbon tied around the top.

He held them out to her. "For the lovely blonde lady with the blue eyes."

She took them in one hand and rolled up on her toes to kiss him. "They are beautiful."

"But you are gorgeous this evening," he whispered.

"Thank you," she smiled up at him. It would be easy to fall in love with him, just like she'd said when she was drunk off her ass.

"More flowers. I'm jealous," Shiloh said as she made her way down the hall.

Bonnie was right behind her and held out a hand. "Give them to me and I'll put them in your room."

"Thank you," Abby said.

Cooper laced his fingers in hers. "We're off to the Sugar Shack to do some serious dancing."

"We might see you there in a little while. If you'd give us directions, we would appreciate it," Bonnie said.

Cooper quickly told them how to get there and then he led Abby outside. The sunset had finished its show for the evening and the stars had popped out. A big lover's moon rested on top of the chimney-shaped formation as if it were a gazing ball. Too damn bad it couldn't show her a glimpse of the future.

With his hand holding hers on the console, she should be giddy with excitement at going on the first real date in months, but instead she was thinking of that fear-of-commitment thing.

✻ ✻ ✻

"You have got to be kidding me. This is the Sugar Shack?" Abby asked when Cooper parked the truck in the lot of the ugliest building she'd ever seen.

"No, ma'am. Up until a couple of years ago it looked like a shack. And then Tiny Lee—that would be the owner of the place— had a customer who couldn't pay his bill."

"And he spray-painted the thing with Pepto-Bismol?"

"That's not paint, darlin'. It's vinyl siding. The feller who couldn't pay hung siding for a living. He'd ordered too much for a job, so he was stuck with it. Tiny Lee said he could work off his bill by using it on the Sugar Shack."

"That is some seriously ugly stuff," Abby said. "You should have loaned him your pistol so he could shoot the fellow rather than let him put up pink siding on a honky-tonk."

Cooper chuckled. "He has a pump shotgun up under the bar and he's not a bit afraid to get it out. Are we ready to let me show you how I can waltz a lovely lady around the dance floor?"

"No, if I've got to sit on the sidelines while you dance with a lovely lady, then you can take me back home," she said.

He leaned across the console, turned her to face him, and kissed her. "There won't be another lady in that joint who will be able to get me to take my eyes off you, darlin'."

"Then let's go dance."

Dance. Drink a little beer. It was a date, for God's sake, not a damn proposal. She should enjoy the flirting and the evening, not be wound up tighter than a hooker in the front row of a tent revival. She determined that she would loosen up and enjoy the time with Cooper and most importantly, push all the heavy thoughts out of her mind.

Lord, nothing could go wrong anyway in an ugly pink building called the Sugar Shack. In that she could trust.

Cooper opened the truck door for her and she put her hand in his. "Have I told you that you are one sexy cowboy tonight? I'm sorry that I forgot my pistol."

"What on earth would you need a pistol for?"

"To shoot all the wild women who try to worm their way between me and you." She smiled up at him.

"Maybe you could borrow Tiny Lee's shotgun," he flirted right back. "I was just thinking that I might need to use it to keep the cowboys away from you."

He looked like sex on a stick that evening in his tight jeans, polished boots, brown-and-yellow plaid pearl-snap shirt, and the faded denim jacket. She couldn't wait to get inside to dance with him.

Country music echoed out across the canyon long before they made it to the door. Folks must have been line dancing because Abby could hear "Yee-haw" periodically as Travis sang "T.R.O.U.B.L.E."

"That's an old one," she said. "The way the women are turning around to look at you, I think you might be the trouble who just walked in the door."

Cooper grabbed her hand and twirled her around right there on the porch. "Tiny Lee keeps a few current ones, but he likes the old stuff best and no one argues with him."

"Hey, Coop, that don't look a thing like the redhead you brought in here last night," the enormous man behind the bar yelled.

"Who was the redhead?" she asked.

"Tiny's teasing. I was with you eating ice cream on my front porch, remember," Cooper said.

Tiny Lee motioned them toward the bar. "You bring her on over here and introduce her proper, or else I'll get the gun out and chase your sorry ass out of my honky-tonk."

Cooper draped his arm around Abby's shoulder and led her to the bar. "Tiny Lee, this is Abby Malloy. Abby, meet Tiny Lee, the owner of this fine establishment."

Tiny Lee extended a hand as big as a ham with fingers like sausages across the bar and shook hands with Abby. "Truth is, Miz Abby, that I'm glad to see Coop with a woman. He's been runnin' single too long. And any kid of Ezra's is welcome in my bar. He was a salty old bastard, but he was honest and paid his bills. He could dance the boot leather off half the women in the canyon without breakin' a sweat."

"Thank you," Abby said.

"First drink is on the house. What will it be? You have to belong to Martha, the first wife, because you look just like her. What's the other two girls look like?"

"Coors, longneck in the bottle," she said. "Shiloh and Bonnie seem to look like their mamas, but I understand we all got Ezra's blue eyes and stubborn streak."

"God save the canyon." Tiny Lee rolled his eyes as he wiped the chilly water from a beer and set it on the counter. "And what are you drinkin', Coop?"

"The same," he said.

Tiny Lee leaned over the bar and whispered. "He's a good man, but if you want a man with a steady income who'll appreciate you, then you need to flirt with me."

"I'll remember that." Abby grinned.

"I see an empty table. Let's go claim it and then hit the dance floor. And Tiny Lee, you stop trying to beat my time or I'll take your sorry old ass into the county jail for serving beer to minors," Cooper said.

Tiny Lee threw back his head and laughed. A man that size should have laughed like a biker or a trucker, but his laughter was as high-pitched as a little girl's.

Cooper took Abby's hand and wove his way through the people until they were at an empty table for four. Before they could set their beers down, Nona, Travis, and Waylon joined them. Nona counted chairs and sat down in Travis's lap.

"Abby, it's good to see you again. Where's the other two sisters?"

"Shiloh and Bonnie might be along in a little while. Nice to see you all again," Abby said. "This cowboy right here has promised me a bunch of dances. Miz Nona, you are welcome to my chair."

"I kind of like the one I have right here. A cowboy that promises a woman a bunch of dances means he's gettin' the brand heated up," Nona said.

"I hope not," Abby said.

Luke Bryan's voice singing "Drunk on You" came through the jukebox and Cooper had not been lying when he said he could dance. But something was wrong. He was executing a fine fast two-step, but he wouldn't look at her.

"We need to talk," she said.

"Yes, we do. You go first," he said.

"We need to talk about protection," she said.

"I can't hear you over the music. Did you say election?"

She raised her voice. "Protection."

"As in a bodyguard or as in mosquito spray or . . ."

The song ended at the same time she blurted out in a loud voice, "As in sex."

The whole bar went quiet and she could hear Tiny Lee's girly giggles in the background. Thank goodness no one made a comment, and the next song on the jukebox brought the people onto the floor for a noisy line dance. Her face turned scarlet and she threw her hand up to her mouth.

"Shit!" she muttered.

Cooper picked up her hand and led to the far end of the bar. He twirled the stools around so that they were facing each other, dropped her hand, and stared at her without looking into her eyes. She'd seen amusement, laughter, and a multitude of other emotions in Cooper's dark brown eyes, but never the anger that flashed right then. With only a little imagination she could see steam coming out his ears.

"I assumed you were on the pill," he said.

She shook her head. "Prescription ran out a couple of months ago. I knew I was getting out of the service, so I didn't get another one."

"Then you could possibly be . . ." The sentence trailed off.

She nodded. "But not likely. I should have been . . ."

He put a finger over her lips. "I would marry you, Abby."

She didn't want a man to marry her because she was pregnant and she damn sure didn't want to marry one who was so mad he couldn't even look at her. Her mother had raised a child alone and she could do it, too. Today's world didn't tar and feather a woman for getting pregnant before she was married.

"You look like you are about to explode," Cooper said.

"What if I don't want to marry you?"

"You made that clear already. But a child needs two parents."

"Why? Your grandpa was your only parent and I never had a father."

"But it wasn't a perfect situation, was it?" he argued.

"Life isn't perfect."

"If I father a child, I will be part of his or her life, Abby."

"I would not marry you, Cooper. Not for that reason."

"I'm not surprised one bit."

"Why?"

"You just told Nona you hoped I didn't have a branding iron. Where are we headed with this thing, Abby?"

"Don't. Just don't." She put up her hand.

"I need some air and I see your sisters coming in the door. I'll be back in five minutes." He left her sitting on the stool and didn't even speak to Shiloh and Bonnie as he went outside.

"Where's Cooper going? Did he get a call to go back to the sheriff's office tonight?" Bonnie hiked a hip on the stool he'd left behind.

"Look. There's Rusty over there dancing with a woman," Shiloh said.

"And there's your cowboy sitting at the table with Nona and Travis." Bonnie smiled.

"Waylon is not my cowboy." Shiloh blushed.

Abby had to swallow the lump in her throat before she could speak. "I need my truck keys. I'm leaving right after I make sure Rusty can give y'all a ride home."

"Fight?" Shiloh asked.

"Big one."

Bonnie leaned in closer so she could be heard above the noise of the jukebox. "I'm going home with you, then. You don't need to be alone. Come on. Shiloh, you can stay and flirt with your cowboy."

Shiloh's mouth clamped together in the same firm line that it had the morning the coyote got into her henhouse. "I'm going with you."

Cooper was standing with a group of cowboys beside a black pickup truck. His back was to the Sugar Shack, but his stance told Abby that he was still angry. Shoulders thrown back, legs slightly apart, arms folded over his broad chest. She didn't need to see his face to know that a mad spell was sitting firmly on his shoulders. A woman with flaming-red hair pushed her way out of the crowd and plastered herself to his side. In the moonlight, Abby could see one of her hands teasing its way up his inner thigh as she gazed up into his face.

Abby made it to the backseat of the truck before she gave way to the tears.

"Start talkin'," Bonnie said.

"She can't talk. She's cryin' too hard. They had a fight and now there's a redhead trying to get his zipper down and she saw it," Shiloh said.

They were home before Abby's sobs turned into sniffles. With Bonnie on one side of her patting her shoulder and Shiloh on the other, keeping her supplied with fresh tissues, she was finally able to tell them about the argument.

"Neither one of you is settled in a commitment like you should be. Everything has happened right on the heels of a funeral that unnerved us all," Shiloh said. "It's like you got the foundation put up for a house and an earthquake has come and shook it real good. Now what do you do? Shore it up and keep building or stick some dynamite under it and blow it all to smithereens?"

"She don't need a bunch of mumbo-jumbo therapy shit," Bonnie said. "She just needs us to be here for her so she can vent. She'll figure out what she wants to do after the fire dies down from the argument."

"What I need is a shot of whiskey," Abby said.

"What you need is moonshine. That would knock you on your ass and tomorrow things will look better, but we don't have any more," Shiloh said.

"Whiskey will have to do." Bonnie started for the kitchen. "Want a beer, Shiloh?"

"I'd love one."

"I'm so sorry I ruined your night," Abby said.

"You didn't ruin anything. Having a sister is more important than dancing in a butt-ugly pink honky-tonk," Shiloh answered.

"That place was one ugly son of a bitch." Bonnie put a double shot of whiskey in Abby's hand and gave Shiloh an open bottle of beer.

Abby took a sip and a weak giggle escaped from her chest. "Anything that damned ugly is sure to stir up trouble. Blame the whole mess tonight on the color pink. I vow to never even eat strawberry ice cream again."

"That's the spirit." Shiloh touched her beer bottle to Abby's glass. "We shall all three boycott pink from this day forth."

"Never liked it anyway. It reminds me of Pepto-Bismol and puke," Bonnie agreed.

# Chapter Twenty

*A*bby's mama always said things looked much better in daylight than they did in the dark. She was right again. Sunday morning was one of those beautiful days that promises winter won't last forever and spring is on the way.

The argument was the last thing she'd thought about as the whiskey and tears dulled her senses so she could sleep the night before. It was the first thing she thought about when she awoke that morning. It had been as much her fault as Cooper's, because she'd run from the problem rather than showing him that she was willing to fight for what they'd built. Now she just had to figure out how to make it right.

She stumbled from bedroom to kitchen to find Shiloh cooking and Rusty with a cup of coffee in one hand and a stolen piece of bacon from the platter where Shiloh stacked it up next to the scrambled eggs.

"Where'd you go last night? One minute you and Cooper were all hugged up and the next you were gone. He was an old bear all evening. I finally told him to go home because he was putting a damper on the whole place with his pouting," Rusty asked.

"He deserved to be in a bad mood." Bonnie rubbed sleep out of her eyes and went straight for the coffeepot.

"What did he do?"

"Ask him," Shiloh answered.

"He was a jackass," Bonnie said.

"Never saw him act like that and I've known him since we were kids. What did *you* do, Abby?" Rusty eyed her carefully.

Rusty turned his gaze on Abby and she felt like those big green eyes of his behind the thick glasses could see straight into her soul. "It's a long story and I'll take partial blame for the argument. Neither of us handled it right."

"She's fighting a commitment war," Bonnie said.

Rusty shivered. "That word scares the bejesus out of me."

"It does most men and women, too, if they are honest," Shiloh said. "Let's eat before this gets cold. We've got chores to do and church and then we're all expected at Nona's for dinner today."

"Damn! I forgot about that. Maybe Cooper won't go," Abby groaned.

Rusty picked up a plate and started loading it up with breakfast food. "Cooper does not turn down home-cooked meals, and you should know that."

Abby sat down to breakfast and suddenly her mother's voice was in her head. She shoved crisp bacon in her mouth, but not even the crunch of chewing could make Martha Malloy hush.

*You are acting like a child. So you and Cooper had a fight and you are miserable. You think he's not in the same fix as you? Adults talk things out, girl. They don't run away from their problems. And remember, you could be pregnant, so you need to talk about that rationally, too.*

Bonnie kicked Abby under the table. "You are doing that again."

"What?" Abby asked.

"Fighting with yourself. You have this look on your face. I reckon we all do when we're trying to figure out something and our heart tells us one thing and our head is saying something else," Bonnie answered.

"Do you ever get someone's voice in your head and you couldn't knock it out if you hit yourself between the eyes with a sledgehammer?" Abby asked.

"Oh, yeah. It's called your conscience and mine usually has my mama's voice," Shiloh said.

"And mine has my dad's." Rusty nodded.

"Granny's." Bonnie shrugged and looked at Abby. "So who are you fighting with this morning?"

"That would be my mother," Abby answered.

Her mama could give her a sign or maybe talk to God about sending one. She'd appreciate anything at all that would ease the turmoil in her soul.

"And what is she telling you?" Bonnie asked.

"To be honest with myself," Abby said. That was all she was going to admit until she figured things out. A sign would still be nice.

Rusty changed the subject. "Tomorrow we've got more plowing to get done. Right across the field from where Cooper is about to tear up a field and put another crop of winter wheat. Y'all enjoy the day off, because it's about to get really busy and believe me, come spring, it will be hectic even with all of us working."

*There's your sign.* Martha's voice came through loud and clear.

Signs should fall from the clouds with a full set of directions, objectives, and side effects. They should definitely not come in vague terms about plowing a field the next day, but that's all Abby had, so she'd have to figure it out on her own.

*Plowing, fence, busy:* those three words stuck in her head as she ate breakfast and did her part of the morning work. She'd finished feeding the hogs when it dawned on her. If she didn't go to church and instead plowed that field for Cooper, maybe it would be an olive branch and then they could sit down and talk rationally about that *commitment* word.

She left a note on the table telling her sisters that she wouldn't join them at church that morning and to give her regrets to Loretta and the folks over on Lonesome Canyon. She drove over to the Lucky Seven, picked the keys to the tractor off a nail in the barn, and settled in for half a day's work.

☀ ☀ ☀

Cooper looked in the rearview mirror as he drove away from the ranch that morning and noticed a truck that looked a lot like Abby's pull out onto the road and head toward Claude. But then she'd been on his mind nonstop, in both waking and sleeping time, since the argument at the Sugar Shack. Granted, the whole thing was partially his fault. He'd hoped that she felt the same way about him as he did her, but she'd shot that down with her comment about being branded. Then there was the possible pregnancy and the fact that she might be leaving the canyon for good.

*Or maybe it's not even her truck. How many in this canyon look just like hers?*

His fingers tightened around the steering wheel until his knuckles turned white. He should have taken care of protection or at least asked her if she was on the pill. That part was his fault. He'd behaved like a jackass or worse, like an immature teenager, leaving her sitting on a bar stool like that. He'd caught a glimpse of her leaving and he knew she'd seen the drunk redhead trying to put the make on him. He should have run after her or at least called her the night before.

*Don't use that damned cell phone. Go see her face-to-face and have a long talk. I bet she's as miserable as you are.* His grandfather's voice was plain and clear in his head.

He nodded in agreement. As soon as he finished taking care of the situation at the jail this morning, he would do just that. He'd show up with his hat in his hand and hopefully she wouldn't slam the door in his face.

It was well past noon when he finally got away from the courthouse and drove back to the Lucky Seven. A dozen scenarios played through his head as he rehearsed what he'd say to her, and what she might say back to him.

"What the hell?" he mumbled when he saw her truck out in front of the barn. He wasn't ready to face her, not yet. He still didn't have the words all down just right to let her know exactly what was in his heart. He parked and his heart thumped around in his chest as he entered the barn.

"Abby," he called out, but got no answer. "Abby," he yelled louder.

Then he realized that one of the tractors was missing. He could hear the tractor engine running to the west and remembered telling Rusty that he had one more pasture to plow before spring. Trouble was the field that needed to be plowed under was to the south of the ranch house, not to the west.

"Dammit!" he muttered as he ran to his truck and left in a cloud of dust.

He could see the tractor before he got to the field where he'd just sown seed for a stand of grass a few days before. That seed had cost a fortune and little green shoots would be coming up any day. Yet there was Abby turning it all under. Was this his punishment?

*She's trying to help. Which is more important? A few dollars or her gift of labor?*

He parked the truck and leaned against the fender as he waited for her to finish the very last round. The rows were straight, and not once when she turned the tractor did she grind the gears. And the pasture was all ready to be replanted. The Lord or fate or whoever it was had a damn strange sense of humor.

❊ ❊ ❊

Cooper was supposed to be at church and then at dinner with Loretta and Jackson. But there he was waving at her and there was no way to get home without talking to him. Her hands went clammy and her eyes misted. She'd thought about him the whole time she was driving but hadn't come up with a single way to approach the problem. Now she had to wing it and Abby hated not being prepared.

*Life doesn't come with a manual. You have to listen to your heart, Abby.*

"You've been busy," Cooper said when she stepped down to the running board and then to the ground.

She nodded. "It's been a profitable morning."

"I don't like this feeling," Cooper said.

"Me, either," she said honestly.

"Can we talk?"

"Right now?"

She nodded, the lump in her throat getting bigger by the second. Abby covered the distance between the tractor and the truck and leaned on the rear fender, leaving a couple of feet between her and Cooper. Those old familiar sparks flitted around like butterflies in the spring. And that equally familiar ache in the pit of her stomach started the moment he gazed into her eyes. Then he moved around her and put down the tailgate. His hands went around her waist and he picked her up. He set her on the tailgate and sat down beside her, close enough she could smell his aftershave.

Desire twisted her insides into a pretzel and the temperature went from a chilly forty-something degrees to something so warm that she removed her stocking hat.

Cooper reached up and smoothed down her blonde hair.

"Static," he said.

"Everywhere," she answered.

"In the air. With us. I don't like it," he whispered.

*That which does not kill you will make you stronger,* the voice in her head said clearly.

*Then I should be able to bench-press a damn Cadillac,* she argued.

His hand covered hers and he squeezed as if he understood her thoughts. Five minutes passed before he said anything.

"You going first, or am I?" he finally asked.

"If you're going to tell me this is over, then don't. Just get in your truck and leave and I'll take the tractor back to the barn and we'll pretend what we had never happened," she said.

"And if I'm not going to tell you that?" he asked.

"Then you can go first."

"I sat in Grandpa's bedroom all night and thought about how to say this. I thought if I was in his room, maybe he would give me some advice. He didn't, so I'm having to wing it on my own. It was the most miserable night I ever spent in my life. So here goes, and I hope it don't send you running like a jackrabbit with a coyote right on its heels. I'm going to marry you. It might not be this year or even next year, but eventually you will figure out that I'm in love with you and that you love me, too."

"If I run?" she asked.

"Then I'll chase you to the ends of the earth. That's how much I believe in us. I realize it's only been about a month since the funeral, but looking back, I knew then that you were the woman for me."

She scooted across the bench until their sides were touching. "How?"

"I felt it in my heart, but I didn't want to admit it. After all, I like red-haired women, not brunettes or blondes."

"Like that one trying to undo your pants last night?"

"Yep, that's the kind I've always liked, but I sent her packing because now I can't get you out of my mind and I'm afraid that what you told Nona meant you don't want to be branded."

"I guess she meant that you were going to put the Lucky Seven brand on me, right?"

He nodded. "It's an expression."

"I'm not property and I'm not a cow."

He grinned. "No, you are not."

"What's funny?"

"Your temper."

"Are you a bull?" she asked.

"I will be if you decide to be a cow."

"This conversation is crazy. I was joking last night. My first thought at being branded was that I'm afraid of needles, so I don't have pierced ears or tattoos. I can't imagine being branded. If she'd said that you might want to call me yours instead of branding me, I would have probably answered her differently."

"Okay, now what about the baby?" he asked.

"I'm not pregnant. Before I started plowing I drove up to Claude and bought a test. I should have waited to be sure before I said anything to you," she said.

He let go of her hand and dropped down on one knee in front of her. "Abby Malloy, I love you. I'm sorry that I made such a mess of last night, but I want you to be the mother of my children. It can be in nine months. In nine years. That part doesn't matter right now. I want to wake up every morning with you in my arms and to go to sleep at night in the middle of a sweet afterglow. I want to grow old with you on the Lucky Seven and if you die before I do, I want you to walk up the steps to the pearly gates real slow. I'll be behind you real quick, because I can't live without you."

"That is the sweetest thing I've ever heard, but are you absolutely sure that this isn't just the moment talking?" she asked.

"I'm more sure of this than I've ever been about anything in my life, but if you aren't, then I'll wait until you are just as doubt-free as I am."

She leaned forward and looked past his sexy brown eyes into his soul, and there were no fears.

Not a single one.

"I don't have a ring today, but by damn, I'll get one tomorrow soon as the stores open, if you'll say yes. You can choose the date, the time, and the place. Just don't ever leave me, Abby," he said.

She cupped his cheeks in her hands and kissed him. "Yes, I will marry you. And Cooper, I love you."

There, she'd said the words. She was ready for commitment, ready to start a life in the canyon with Cooper and it was right—that much she could feel in her bones, as Haley always said.

"You've made me the happiest man on earth," he whispered.

"And the happiest woman is right here beside you. Can we go home to Lucky Seven now, Cooper? I want you to hold me for the rest of my life."

# Chapter Twenty-One

*Six weeks later.*

The wild daisies were in bloom, giving the canyon a splash of yellow that day. Haley and her husband had driven up from Galveston for the wedding so that she could be one of the bridesmaids with Shiloh and Bonnie.

"I'm so happy for you." Haley hugged Abby.

"You being here makes my day extra special. This couldn't be any more perfect," Abby said.

"You are in love—everything is rosy to you." Haley smiled.

Ezra's lawyer had handed her the check that morning. Seeing that many zeroes boggled her brain and the worst part of the whole thing was there was a disclosure paragraph that said she couldn't tell her sisters how much they'd inherit if she accepted it.

"Hey, it just dawned on me," Shiloh said. "You left. That means you've forfeited your share of the ranch and took your inheritance. Was it worth it?"

"It would have been worth it if it had been zero dollars. I hope that y'all are as happy someday as I am right now." Abby handed Shiloh the coronet of white daisies laced with ribbons and pearls. She set it on top of Abby's blonde hair, securing it with the combs attached to the sides.

"Look, Bonnie, now she's really got a crown."

"That doesn't make me the queen." Abby smiled. "It makes me a bride." She went to the window and blew a kiss down at the small tombstone in the tiny fenced area under a big oak tree. "Mama likes it here."

"I like that you buried her ashes like that and put up a stone. It brings peace to you, I can tell. And I'm really, really glad that you are having this wedding. She would have liked that," Haley said.

"She always talked about the big dress and the fancy wedding I'd have," Abby said. "I would have been happy going to the courthouse, but not in camo. I left that at the house. Y'all can have it or throw it away. I did keep my boots, though. And Haley, thank you for loaning me your dress. Mama loved this thing."

Abby adjusted the sleeves of the white satin-and-lace ball gown. It was definitely not what she would have chosen, but when Haley had reminded her of the fun they'd had the day they'd picked it out, she couldn't refuse. Martha had clapped her hands and said, "When Abby gets married, I want her to have a dress just like that one. I want to see her waltzing down the aisle carrying a bouquet of daisies."

"You look like you are about to cry, and if you do and mess up your makeup that I just spent more than an hour getting perfect, I'll shoot you like I did the coyote," Shiloh said.

Abby forced a smile. "I'm just thinking of Mama. I'm not going to cry, I promise."

"Well, changing the subject here, but I don't like it that you took Martha away from Vivien and Polly. They're lost without her," Bonnie said.

"I would be, too," Abby said. "Are we ready? I hear the first strands of the music and the guys will be waiting for us at the bottom of the steps."

"Are you sad that our father won't be giving you away?" Shiloh asked.

"No, I'm not sad. Today I'm marrying Cooper. There is nothing to be sad about. The future is beautiful. The past is gone," Abby said.

Cooper waited at the bottom of the steps with Waylon, Travis, and his deputy. Jackson was supposed to be the fourth groomsman, but Loretta had gone into labor on the way to the wedding.

Bonnie came down the steps first and Waylon escorted her out to the yard. Thank God, it was one of those lovely spring days that don't come along real often. A nice morning breeze moved the cool morning air and big white puffy clouds dotted the sky. Abby had sent Cooper a text that morning saying that the clouds were providing a chair for her mother so she could see the ceremony.

Shiloh was next and Travis took her arm. Then Haley started down and stopped at the bottom of the stairs to hug Cooper. "Be good to her. She's tough as nails on the outside, but she's fragile as glass on the inside. I'd hate to have to shoot you if you break her."

"Never happen," Cooper said. "I love her so much I'll carry her around on a satin pillow."

"Make it velvet and you might live a long life." Haley winked.

Haley was outside when Abby appeared at the top of the stairs. Cooper's breath caught in his chest. Her hair had been pulled up and she looked like an angel with that halo of daisies on her head. She carried a bouquet of daisies tied with blue ribbons and he could already envision all of it on the floor of their bedroom as soon as the reception was over.

Then she pulled up the front of her dress so she wouldn't trip over it and his eyes widened out as big as saucers. Underneath all that angelic beauty, she wore her camouflage combat boots.

"Like it?" she asked.

"Love it." He grinned. "That's my Abby. Tough as nails, but soft at the same time."

She looped her arm in his and rolled up on her toes to kiss him, but he shook his head.

"Not until the preacher gives me permission." He grinned. "You wouldn't let me see you until now, so we're not taking any changes with jinxing the marriage. And before this all starts, Abby, you should know you're stunning today."

"You look pretty damn handsome yourself. Now let's go outside and get this marriage started," she said.

He escorted her out to the porch, down the stairs, and to the aisle they'd made by setting up folding chairs facing an arch entwined with greenery and daisies. Martha ambled along beside them with her head held high.

"I don't think I could be any happier than I am right now," Cooper whispered when the pianist hit the beginning chord and the friends and neighbors stood up.

"Oh, I think you could be," Abby said softly. "Remember that fight in the Sugar Shack?"

"How could I forget it? That was the most miserable night I ever spent," he said.

"Remember what started it," she asked.

"Yes, I do. Are you . . ." He paused and looked at her.

"Not right now, but if we got pregnant on our honeymoon, which starts tonight right here on the Lucky Seven, by the end of the year we could have a family started."

Cooper stopped in the middle of the aisle, right in front of the pianist playing the old-fashioned upright under the shade tree, in front of all the people attending the wedding and even in front of the Almighty. He picked her up and swung her around in a circle, showing off her combat boots to the whole crowd before he set her down and hugged her tightly.

"I love you," he said loudly.

"I love you, Cooper," she whispered in his ear. "But remember, no kissin' until the preacher says it is okay."

# Acknowledgments

Dear Reader,

Thank you for coming back to visit the canyon again. As I finish this book, it's springtime in southern Oklahoma and the Arbuckle Mountains are yellow with coreopsis. Last week I noticed the wild daisies blooming along with the red clover and buttercups. The whole area is full of beautiful color. Winter, with all its bitter winds and chilly weather, is finally gone.

Writing this book has been cathartic to me in many ways. I never knew my father very well and didn't see him for many years before he died. As I looked into his casket, I grieved for the father I'd never known. I could feel Abby's pain and knew all about her commitment issues and I truly hope that I've told her story well.

*Thank you* seems like such a small thing, but I do thank many people for taking this book from an idea to the finished product. First of all, thanks to my husband, for all the takeout food he's eaten while I wrote *Daisies in the Canyon*. It takes a special person to be married to a writer and he's the best. A huge thank-you to Krista Stroever, my absolutely fabulous editor, who pushed me to write a stronger book. To the entire Montlake staff, from my editors to the folks who create and design covers—y'all are the best and you have my undying gratitude for believing in me! And finally to my sister, whose spirit talks to me like Abby's mama did to her, and continues to tell me to keep writing.

I'd also like to thank all of you readers for continuing to support me, for talking about my books, telling other folks about them, sending me encouraging notes about them, and everything you do! You are all awesome. Keep your boots on! There are more cowboys on the way.

All my best,
*Carolyn Brown*

# About the Author

Photo: © Charles Brown, 2014

Carolyn Brown is a *New York Times* and *USA Today* bestselling author and a RITA finalist. Her books include historical, contemporary, cowboy, and country music mass-market paperbacks. She and her husband live in Davis, Oklahoma. They have three grown children and enough grandchildren to keep them young.